VIOLET SEABORN'S
unfinished soul

V KNOX

'VIOLET SEABORN'S
UNFINISHED SOUL' **ISBN 978-1-7750471-8-6**

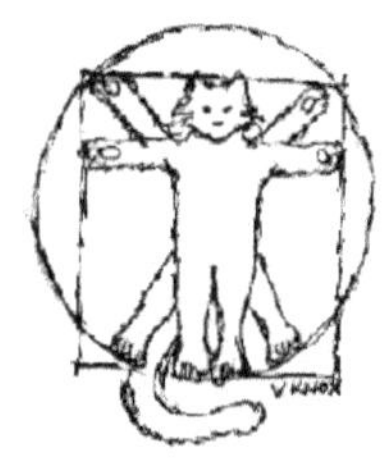

SILENT K PUBLISHING
Vancouver Island, British Columbia, Canada

https://veronicaknox.com

for Sarah & David

TABLE OF CONTENTS

THE MOURNING AFTER
THE BOOK OF EVIE

GOOD GRACES
THE BOOK OF SURRENDER

A MILLION HOURS
THE BOOK OF THE GOOD FAIRY

THE HIGH COURT SUPREME
THE BOOK OF DIVINE LAW

A MILLION GAMES
THE BOOK OF LILA

THE DEEP END
THE BOOK OF EPONA

- AQUA EQUA PRINCEPS -

BIRDS OF A FEATHER
the book of Violet & Sam

LILA
(pronounced LEELA)

*LILA accurately describes the notion
within yogic philosophy that the whole world is the
spontaneous creation of BRAHMAN. It is sportive and playful,
as opposed to self-conscious or volitional in intention.
Lila emphasizes the fact that the world is born in freedom
and playful creativity, rather than necessity.
In this way, the whole world can be seen
as a stage for LILA - the DIVINE PLAY.
It is an illusion to see the actions on the stage as real,
and those who see them in this way are said to be under
the spell of MAYA. In other yogic schools and teachings,
Lila is used to denote the divine interaction
between male and female.*

FLYING SOULO

"I can't go back to yesterday
Because I was a different person then."
LEWIS CARROLL

1901

- VIOLET -

It was on board a sinking ship in the North Sea off the eastern coast of Scotland that I gasped my first breath, bleating softly under a bloodied sheet, and promptly fell asleep, exhausted, chilled to the bone, and utterly soulless.

In hindsight it was several months after my traumatic birth that my true soul came into being. Slowly my image developed as a thought of life exposed on light sensitive paper – a formless haze and then, as a ghost surely accumulates color and substance, it formed a complete portrait of a child with silver hair and violet eyes.

Watching my past as an objective spectator, I sense a slight thinning of the air around me from time to time, where my soul generates enough electrons to manifest like a shimmering heat wave. It was like having an invisible friend moving closer, whispering in my ear that all was well.

There was a divine reason why Lila's dream of the elysian fields decreed I could only meet my mother a thousand years after her untimely death. But then, no death was ever ill-timed in those enchanted goddess-spun days when Epona's clan of wisewomen served her in peace.

We were going home, my mother and me. And since there was a likelihood that I could be born enroute, every contingency was considered.

All but one.

In hindsight, Mother's astrologer could have read the stars one last time, but later, as I came to fully appreciate the perverse intelligence of the universe, that ship had sailed.

But just then, I felt Mother's happiness as my own. Dorota was always happy. I like to think she had an amazing smile.

Our last morning broke under a blood red sky.

Mother went into labour just after dawn.

At midday, our ship grazed a submerged mountaintop with a sickening jolt. It convulsed like a wounded animal, let out a howl of pain and kept moving to outrun its surprise attacker.

The first signs something was amiss in my little world was the sound of frantic drumbeats pounding in my ears and being squeezed awake. I experienced an involuntary quickening of panic as the calm warmth of my internal sea swirled red and I tasted bitterness, both physical and emotional.

I had nowhere to hide, so I flailed for an eternity in the clutches of an invisible snake intent on choking me. After the relentless bully proved impossible to evade, I gave up and let it coil about my neck.

As the creature claimed me, my fears floated away on a wave of surrender. But no sooner had I entered a peaceful dream, than a new assault from aggressive contractions pitched me senseless, headfirst towards the world.

I strained to hear Dorota's soothing words of comfort but a terrified voice I didn't recognize called out for a lady I know now as the Green Goddess, Lady Flora.

The worst of it was my head being gripped by an icy hand that pulled me towards the light against my will. It retreated only to return with more force. But although I fought valiantly to escape, the hand eventually won, and I was born drained of willpower into the sharp lingering scent of antiseptic and carbolic soap.

My initial expectations of maternal tenderness were replaced by a foreign presence of deep loathing and a haunting echo of spiteful laughter followed by terrifying silence.

And as Dorota succumbed to our enemies, I swooned lifeless into the fusty stink of mildew that has never entirely left me.

In some ways, I'm always there on the ship, newborn and helpless.

As always, an eerie silence evokes the aftermath of a deserted battlefield. Ghosts tickle my skin, and the supernatural stench of fetid air brings back my fight for a place on earth.

I am compelled to remember and so I continually return, and search, and leave exhausted.

The hastily abandoned sick bay glows sickly green from a suspended oil lamp swaying above a sink of soiled towels, evil sponges, and miles of sodden bandages.

A terrifying bowl holds the silenced body of a grey snake weighted down by an instrument of torture covered in gore that I recognize at once as the disembodied hand that had attacked me.

With every heave of the dying ship, the burning oil sputters erratically, and the ship lists. I watch the birthing room fall apart, strangely removed from the horror of it, floating with my back against the ceiling. I look like a cherub from an old master's painting.

A white enamel operating table displaying the corpse of a

woman loosely wrapped in gauze, careens across the undulating floor, and slams into the opposite wall.

The impact exposes the patient's foot from under its makeshift shroud. Its toe points accusingly at my basket in the shadows.

Each spasm of light reveals a new detail.

Finally, the moment I'm here to discover is at hand. The stink of charred flesh and woodsmoke herald the arrival of the stillborn child's attending soul. It emerges as a swirl of soot, accompanied by the heat and crackle of flames.

It approaches the infant, surveys it dismissively, and takes a turn about the room to hover over the dead mother.

The weak light emanating from the woman's corpse flares into white fire at the entity's approach and flickers out.

Finally, the hostile entity turns away and slowly melts through the ship's hull, without looking back. The layer of grey ash that settled on the infant's winding sheet blows into an opaque cloud that obscures my view. For years the nightmare stench of betrayal haunts me.

It's not lost on me that both Mother and child, officially beyond saving, will be consigned to the scrap heap we souls call the 'Void of No Return' behind the universe's back.

The saving grace for such an indisputable act of malice is that babies without souls tend to look identical to ones who do… slightly distant and disoriented… bored and sleepy. But I was no ordinary child; destiny had a mission planned for me, so secret the universe had yet to be informed.

The child's dispirited nemesis may have failed to complete its mission, but it left me 'unfinished' with an extraordinary mystery to resolve.

A kidney dish vibrates across a steel countertop sloshing a trail of red water towards the edge of the world. The metallic crash as it hits the floor revives the woman's spirit. She leaves her body to shiver helplessly beside her lifeless infant.

Without hesitation, she touches its foot poking from a bloodied sheet in the basket, and for a heartbeat her spirit burns aflame once more.

The woman is Dorota, my mother. The child is me. My skin is translucent, bloodless as white paper tinged blue, but still warm.

Fate, in a morbidly theatrical mood, has duplicated Mother's exposed foot precisely in the same position as mine, except hers features a gold anklet against bronze skin, and an exotic purple silk hem embroidered with green dragons that reveal the red pedicured toenails she adored. I am heartbroken. I will never see my mother's smile.

A sudden lurch of the ship quickens a spark in the dead child. I inhale my first breath. My foot twitches. I am alive and very much alone.

On the table's last foray, it smashes the lock on a warped door that bursts open revealing a corridor of rushing water.

The walls of the room buckle. But before its contents are crushed to atoms, the rising floodwater gently lifts my basket and carries it downstream on a raging river winding through the ship.

It's deposited in one seamless motion on the open sea.

Mother's vigil continues to hover over me until the disembodied voice of a boy calls out: *"Row harder. There's a good lass. I'm here, waiting."*

"I'm pushing the basket towards the sound of your voice," Mother calls out. *"Do you have her?"*

"She's almost here," the boy replies. *"I can feel her, My Lady. Everything is ready. I'll take good care of her."*

My wicker cradle rocks madly on a froth of whitecaps until a memory in the water bumps hard against the bottom of the basket. Its spirit comforts me.

I fall asleep, safe at last. All smiles.

Seagulls cry *"there's land and love ahead."* The boy will find me. The loving presence releases my 'boat' and dives deep. My basket floats free, and I dream I'm a bobbing champagne cork from my seventieth birthday party.

Mother called to me from far away as I slept: *"If at first you don't succeed just breathe little one. Just breathe."* And so, I did.

LIFE IN THE SLIPSTREAM

"And would it have been worth it, after all?
After the cups, the marmalade, the tea,
Among the porcelain,
Among some talk of you and me,
Would it have been worthwhile,
To have bitten off the matter with a smile,
To have squeezed the universe into a ball?"

T.S. ELIOT

- VIOLET -

Moving from life-to-life is not always smooth sailing. I struggled to breathe. But such was my ardent desire to reunite with an old friend I loved more than life itself, I rallied to his strong presence calling me from the shore: *Row harder, my angel. I'm here waiting.*

By the end of the day, three beautiful souls had joined hearts to save me from being recycled into the universal void of unconsciousness. I learned a powerful life lesson: human love works miracles when you let go of struggling to live.

Later, by all accounts, my violet eyes engaged onlookers with unblinking wisdom although most backed away from first contact, distinctly unsettled.

The sisters of the Scottish convent that took me in crossed themselves, hastily went about their prayers with increased concentration, and avoided future eye contact with me by pretending I didn't exist.

Evie Watts, the sisterhood's hired cook and washerwoman, took one look at me and burst into rapturous smiles, embracing me as the daughter she'd always wanted after giving birth to six fine sons. "At last," she said. "I thought you'd never come."

I grabbed Evie's finger for dear life the way a barnacle latches onto a rock.

We smiled a lot that first day. She named me Violet, and ever afterwards we were mother and child, a constant force of survival against a harsh climate of wild weather and treacherous religious fervor.

Sam, Evie's two-year-old son, the child of her old age, was the special friend I'd come to meet. Naturally we were inseparable from the start… and so began my best life, equally adored and dismissed, visible and invisible, blessed and cursed, known to the village as Violet Seaborn, a child to be reckoned with.

It is said that life begins with our first breath. Oh, my soul! Tis' not so. The truth is infinitely more creative. Life begins the moment we're claimed by the universe – the precise instant a divine spark of consciousness enters our body.

That said, spiritual intakes of cosmic energy are bestowed via an often-overburdened college of master souls charged with vital missions of life and death. But due to the high volumes of supply and demand during population explosions and depletions (especially pandemics), overextended souls sometimes miss transcendental appointments with destiny. In fact, *'spiritus interrupit'* occurs more often than one might expect.

Souls may appear to be somewhat thoughtless when they fail to manifest 'on time' which is unfair considering the extreme pressures they face. Double-booked transitions can be tricky at the best of times.

Every immortal spirit is programmed to make on the spot decisions that, above all, best serve the universe. Essentially, the highest destiny always takes precedence. Strangely, despite each soul having a mind of its own, the universe records no mistakes and unfolds seamlessly according to constantly revised plans. Follow up appointments are rescheduled; life and death go on.

I present my experience as a case in point, entering the world-stage earlier than expected. My designated soul-to-be had abandoned me as I clung tenaciously to a shadow life.

Months went by. Evie was singing me an old bittersweet love song of heartbreak and lost love when my true soul showed up.

Without warning I had suddenly emitted a most unbabylike shriek of laughter and clapped my hands. My eyes grew brighter still as I continued to giggle uncontrollably. And so, whenever I was restless or sad, Evie sang me the verse that had so engaged me:

"There is a ship that sails the sea
She's loaded deep as deep can be
But not as deep as the love I make
I know not how I'll sink or swim."

ANY PORT IN A STORM

Fragile dreams
teased from the swaddling blankets
of newborn children
break like soap bubbles
on a new shore

AUGUST - 1917

Portmatilloch, Scotland

Our village of Portmatilloch lay exposed on all sides, assaulted by wind and rain, and in distant times, Viking raids, situated as it was on a finger of land pointing accusingly to the marauder's homeland across the North Sea.

But the most extraordinary feature in our landscape, awe-inspiring up close and breath-taking from afar, was the white prehistoric figure of a 360-foot-long tribal horse carved deep into a hillside that waxes visible on solstices for goddess followers and wanes invisible for non-believers the rest of the year.

A matrix of twelve separate trenches form its body, legs, and head, each deftly packed with lumps of chalk from the nearby cliffs, pulverized into sticky white dust on site, and regularly refreshed by the clanswomen of the Sacred Horse.

It had been created eons before to celebrate a white horse that, as legend has it, led the sun across the sky, glowing brightly on the green turf of Horse Hill for 3,000 years so the goddess could find her way home.

A contemplative religious order purposely chose Portmatilloch for its isolation and gruelling climate and founded the convent that eventually housed me there.

The first abbess claimed the abandoned shell of a burned-out church and hired laborers from a nearby town to painstakingly rebuild it incorporating a discarded mountain of charred stones.

By the time I arrived, five centuries later, the convent had sprawled into several outbuildings including an extended facility for a public laundry and a small farm managed by Evie's two eldest sons who ran a successful business supplying the local villagers with turnips, milk, and bacon. Her youngest, my beloved Sam, was born to save me. We were born to save each other.

Portmatilloch's unforgiving environment bestowed a harsh existence open to the unforgiving storms of man and nature. Even so, the goddess took pity on me.

Since my presence played havoc with the sisters' vows of silence, none of them were officially assigned to raise me. They generally assumed I was under the protection of sea fairies due to my miraculous survival. For hadn't I washed ashore from a sunken ship, in a basket, as dry and snug as you please – a strangely silent infant with silver hair and violet eyes.

SPLITTING HAIRS

*"There will be time, there will be time
To prepare a face to meet the faces that you meet;
There will be time to murder and create,
And time for all the works and days of hands
That lift and drop a question on your plate;"*

T.S. ELIOT

- VIOLET -

Apart from the poverty, a frightful climate, and a silent killer wending its way towards us, Portmatilloch promised a long happy life for Sam and me.

I was never one to split hairs over friendship, courtship, or hardships. I mention this because differences in appearance, temperament, agility, and brute strength made for a diverse population.

Portmatilloch girls were prized for their silence, ample breasts, stout ankles and strong arms. Wide hips were the purview of childbearing females, schoolmarms, and (ironically should they be so inclined) nuns.

I stood piggy in the middle as Violet Seaborn, a dreamy girl who could read a person's fortune in teacups, palms, or the stars; also hailed as the unrivalled healer for any obnoxious ghosts that persisted in haunting, spreading malicious gossip, or dabbling in crop failure.

My silver hair was almost white. I stood out like a swan in a flock of religious crows with my porcelain-doll skin shining to the point of transparency. Evie said my cherry lips looked like a rosebud, and so her pet name for me was Petal.

Portmatilloch boys were evenly split into two main body types: Nordic broad-chested muscular bodies of boy warriors proclaiming the ancestry of their Viking fathers with blue-eyes, tanned skin, and hair the color and texture of straw.

By contrast, lean wiry Scots with hazel eyes, ruddy complexion, ginger-haired or every shade of brown from ash to auburn, like my Sam, were adept at climbing and running, and came by their natural savvy and cunning early.

I favoured Sam's auburn hair, soft and curly tied at the nape of his neck with a black ribbon.

Then there was me, a feisty outspoken small-boned fairy child with nerves of steel who exhibited the unusual bearing of a wise old woman in a child's body. Violet was my name and violet were my eyes – catlike in shape, piercing in nature, penetrating to a fault, and deep as the North Sea. Superstitious folk avoided falling in at their peril. Staring contests were my forte and everyone wisely left me to it.

Although she hid it from the nuns, Evie had the 'sight'. She discreetly warned allcomers, even Sam, that her daughter was not to be trifled with. I came with a secret, she said. I was a sky puzzle never meant to be solved.

Beyond my strange features, Evie saw ancient sailing ships. She heard the clashing of swords while I slept and smelled the exotic spices of pepper and cinnamon on my ivory skin. To Evie, my face was an unfurled map plotting the constellations of faraway stars.

Sam was fearless. We lived soul-to-soul. We were each other's life preserver. And after a plow revealed Sam's first Roman coin, I was delighted to be his partner in a fever for buried treasure.

I held every brooch, coin, and pottery shard we found as if they were holy relics and spoke the owner's name out loud. I knew the history of each treasure because the apparitions of their long since deceased guardians appeared before me and told me.

THE 'OLD ONE'

"There is no religion without love,
And people may talk
As much as they like about their religion,
But if it doesn't teach them to be good
And kind to man and beast,
It is a sham."
'BLACK BEAUTY' BY ANNA SEWELL

- VIOLET -

Evie hinted at my mysterious heritage so often I cornered her one day in the kitchen with a saucy question. "What *precisely* is having the sight *for* if not to answer your beloved Petal's questions?"

Evie sighed, peered at me over her glasses and gave me the same answer she always did. "Someday, Petal, when you're old enough".

She waved a paring knife at a mountain of apples. "One thing I *can* foresee is a market stall with no pies if I don't peel this lot. Be off now, young lady and start the ironing for me. I have pastries to make."

I wasn't gone an hour before Evie's voice filled my head summoning me from the kitchen with some urgency.

I had been playing a mind game of pin the tail on my life, as I so often did during idle moments of repetitious tasks. Evie's tone was commanding. "No dawdling, Petal. I need you here. Look sharpish, now." I hastily unplugged the iron, happy to be liberated from the laundry, thinking whatever my past, apples were my future.

The kitchen was suffused with dreamy light from white flames crackling in the grate. Evie waited for me on the settle, nursing a cup of tea.

Even though an impossible row of a dozen perfectly baked apple pies cooled on the table, the notion that I might still be asleep in the laundry never occurred to me.

I should have known I was out of body because I didn't have to walk towards Evie; I was already sitting beside her as if I'd been there for hours.

"What's troubling you lass?" she said. "Have out with it afore ye burst, child."

It was a rare invitation to fill a blank page of my history book so, I got right to it. "If it pleases you to look, I don't remember my mother or where our ship was bound or our place of departure," I began. "And when I revisit the ship in dreams, why am I not permitted to see the face of the soul who left me for dead? I felt a great power in the water, too, but then I go blank until I see your smile. More importantly, I've never heard a word about my father. And why *precisely*, am I a *sky* puzzle?"

Evie chuckled. "I was making a wee joke, lass. You're a water puzzle more like."

I crossed my arms and sent her a look of do NOT humor me.

I needn't have bothered, Mother Evie always read me loud and clear. "Dear girl, there's no need to look at me like that. You're not meant to know anything too soon or too late. But I've had a think and tis true you're a young lady for sure and certain. I'll give ye that."

She patted my knee as if I was one of her cats. "Listen Petal, there are things you *never* need know. Knowing why something didn't happen or believing it shouldn't have happened or how it could have played differently, is unwise. So, considering that, how would knowing what you presently seek help achieve what you need to do next, *hmmn*?"

I opened my mouth with a snappy comeback but never got the chance. Evie was testing me.

She held a finger over her lips for silence. "All in good time, Petal, otherwise you might misthink an event is ill-timed, or worse, a mistake."

"I'm ready, Evie. I don't know what for, but I've had this feeling for days. I'm seventeen on the outside but inside I'm as old as time. I need your help. *Please*."

Evie grew in size until the walls crumbled to dust and we stood atop Horse Hill. Her voice rang strong in the wind. "Be slow to anger, surrender to what comes, and give thanks," she shouted. "There are no mistakes."

That said, her voice returned kitchen-sized.

I startled from the rattle of a coal skuttle. "There now, that's *four* truths for ye," Evie said feeding the dying fire. "But I see you're still not happy."

Evie's reply blew cold inside my head. The flames in the grate released a cloud of red sparks as she poked the coals. They collapsed into a tumble of white ash, and I watched hypnotized as Evie stirred them back into a roaring fire.

I heard the distant thunder of hoofbeats and took a deep breath, squeezing my eyes shut, all the better to demand a desperate wish. "WHO AM I! *please, Evie*."

I came to, holding a warm iron in midair.

Evie stood, hands on hips, studying me. "I thought you'd never ask," she said. "Best leave that ironing aside, Petal, and we'll take a wee stroll to the spring. We don't have much time."

The thought 'never look a gift horse in the mouth' flashed across my mind as Evie filled a small pack with five apples, a fresh Bannock, and two clay cups. Next, she stuffed a pair of scouring mallets wrapped in a horse blanket into a large bucket.

She winked and handed me the pack. "I believe this is yours," she said. "The fairies can finish the pies."

"Wait, we need one more apple," I said, choosing a good one. We set off with me shouldering the pack and Evie carrying the bucket.

The weather was fine, a perfect day for a picnic. Evie took my hand, which was unusual. I had the feeling I was being led somewhere only Evie knew and yet I'd walked the forest path a hundred times to gather water from the sylph's spring.

Evie was the *real* puzzle. Something had to be up for her to take a day off. I wondered what it could be all the way to the spring but said nothing. What did she mean we hadn't much time.

Evie winked. "Patience, Violet. I'm about to gift you a horse."

Her words shocked me. "Evie, I never said anything out loud about a gift horse. What's going on?"

"Aacht! Didn't ye? I thought I heard ye. I must be getting old."

When we reached the spring, Evie invoked the sylph known to guard it. We formally greeted her presence and knelt respectfully in silence until it was time for the marking ritual. We each dipped a finger in the spring and made the sign of a watery star on our foreheads.

I spread the blanket, and we basked in the sun to dry our stars. When our skin tingled with power we broke bread, toasted the day with sacred water, and savoured every bite of two luscious red apples. "Let's sit here all day," I said forgetting we were somehow racing a clock.

After expressing our gratitude, Evie filled the bucket with water, and I left one of our apples as an offering in pride of place on a flat altar stone.

I bundled the blanket and mallets under my arm. We carried the bucket between us and proceeded to Horse Hill where we set to work refreshing the chalk outline.

Grooming the white horse is a sacred duty. Not the place for small talk. Chalk meditation we called it. Evie and I slipped into our rhythmic three count/pause pattern, pounding chalk in time with each other. And as it invariably did with repetitive chores, the melodic communion of twin mallets striking chalk acted like an incantation that induced a natural trance within us.

So, it startled me when Evie absentmindedly announced the words 'divine timing' out loud without missing a beat.

I kept pounding, waiting for the other shoe to drop. It came a half an hour later. "The reason I'm taking a day off," Evie said.

The hours passed like minutes as we tended the horse in silence, devotedly mashing the exposed chalk until she glowed.

We tidied up, drank a cup of water, wetted the horse's mouth, and descended the hill to the sea.

I wiped my brow, exhausted, "Thank you for the gift horse," I said sarcastically.

Evie seemed amused. "You're most welcome," she said chuckling.

We sat cross-legged on the beach mesmerized by the tide until the moon rose, full and white. Evie rose, standing tall with her bare toes in the water and embraced the sea. "Mother Epona, your beloved daughter awaits you. She's ready to take her vows ahead of her appointed time."

The reflection of the moon in the water swirled anticlockwise into concentric ripples. Evie took both my hands and positioned them outstretched towards the water.

A small black shape emerged from the sea. It grew larger into the head, neck, and shoulders of a black horse that swam to shore. My invisible 'power in the water' friend.

Epona greeted us with a loud neigh, tossed the water from her mane, and pawed the sand. I stood in awe suppressing an urge to curtsy as Epona eyed me. She gently nuzzled my hands and Evie handed me an apple. Epona's breath blew warm on my palm as she daintily accepted the offering.

"Behold the old one," Evie intoned, combing seaweed from the goddess's mane with her fingers. "She's been pining for you for a thousand years, so don't keep her waiting, child."

I opened my mouth to speak but no words came.

"Epona will hear your thoughts," Evie whispered. "Don't be afraid. She's not the dangerous Kelpie monster of old wives' tales. Those stories were used to control mischievous children, but they backfired and scared the bejeezus out of their brainless mothers. Fathers too, as it happens. As you see, Epona is a true horse."

Fear was the furthest emotion from my mind. Love consumed me, surrounded me, filled me. I felt I could fly.

"I'm not Pegasus," Epona said playfully in my head. "Pegasus and I are distant cousins."

I put my arms around Epona's neck and rested my forehead against her. The present world vanished into a lush paradise of vast primeval forests covering Britannia before it had a name.

I witnessed a race of gentler humans living in harmony with the nature spirits, carving mighty stone circles in accord with the solstices.

I looked to Evie for help. "How do I prove my worthiness?"

Evie covered Epona with the blanket and waved me forward. "Just tell her what's in your heart, child."

Absurd thoughts rivalled each other for words that would best confirm my devotion. But as I dithered, Epona spoke.

"Are there any more apples?" she said, nosing my pack.

I checked. "There are two," I answered, feeling awkward holding one in each hand.

Epona snorted softly and tossed her head spraying me with water, and as the droplets splashed my face, a powerful energy awakened within me. I knew what to say. I took a deep breath and looked directly into her eyes. "My Lady, Mother. Today as I refreshed the chalk of your hill shrine, I beheld a vision of a wild horse towing the sun across the sky, and when I thought of the three apples I carried in my pack, I heard a voice say *bring them to me if your heart is true*. And here I am after presenting you with one and now two more. It seems you have accepted my heart is true, and so all that remains for me to do is agree with your wisdom." I took a bite from each apple and extended my arms again, an apple in each hand. Epona ate them.

She paraded around us three times leaving us inside a circle of protection before cantering the length of the beach. Her joy was catching. Evie and I cheered as Epona broke into a full gallop, racing past us nostrils flaring, in a storm of sand. She stopped on her second pass to drink from our bucket, kicked out her back legs, and galloped off again. I caught the blanket on her third pass. And then the performance was over.

I knew it was time for Epona to go when she nibbled my sleeve. *"I shall come to you tomorrow night little goddess,"* she said. *"Only a true heart could have heard me call. Only a true heart would understand my request. A true heart stands before me, now. You have done well my ancient child. I thought this day would never come."*

I watched in awe as Epona the water horse splashed through the surf and disappeared underwater. The moon's reflection rose from the water like a ghost, spun into a star and completed the constellation of a maiden carrying water in the sky.

"Observe," Evie said pointing up. "The sky puzzle that always reminds me of you – Aquarius, the water bearer." "Now pay attention for I'll only say this once. Your father is Lord Pan, the Green Man. Your human mother, Dorota, was possessed by his consort the Goddess Flora when you were conceived. You are twice royal, and then some, Violet.

Think well on this, little goddess. Your legacy is an infinite source of power beyond human understanding. And as befits your station, it is your duty to serve the old one unto and beyond death!"

That night, I slept under Epona's blanket that smelled of stars. And true to her word, the following night I rode Epona overland from Portmatilloch to Inverness. We swam through the loch that made her kind an infamous household legend in a shape that never was serpentine and never would be. She was Epona, the water horse, the black beauty of ages gone by, celebrated in a children's book about a devoted mother horse.

Her hooves thundered over the hills, fairly flying but never leaving the ground. I never felt so awake. That night, I was formally initiated into the Clan of the Horse… as an elder.

The incident hadn't surprised me so much as it reminded me, I was profoundly ancient. Epona filled my soul and opened my heart to the alchemy I was born to serve. I had been awarded responsibilities beyond my earth years that harkened to the ancient times of past lives. Evie told me I had to grow up fast.

My childhood effectively ended and silenced me for the first time in my hitherto chatty life. And if I'd learned nothing else, it was that humanity was running out of time…

And that Sam had finished making the pies.

- 6 -

SAINT 'M'

Merrily, merrily
merrily, Mary Lee,
life is but a dream.

- VIOLET -

Evie straightened her back with a painful sigh, having bent overlong on the ironing board. "Fetch me some water, there's a good lass," she said. "I need a bit of a sit down."

Her sit downs were rare, but they promised a reasonable length of time where I might ask a question, and Evie's answers were always fascinating because I asked beguiling questions.

Evie looked drained, but she tended to ignore her discomfort to humor me, which I admit I used to my advantage. She wiped her brow with her apron, massaged her old stiff fingers, and took the cup of water.

"Now then," she said. "What do ye want to know, Petal?" She winked. "Go on then. Surprise me."

I opted for one of my favorite stories because Evie had once mothered another soul under her charge who had mystical powers. "Please tell me more about Saint 'M'," I begged.

Evie smiled and engaged her storytelling voice. It invariably began the same way. "Sister Mary Lee had been dead eighteen years by the time you arrived in your wee basket."

I waited while she drained the cup, delaying for effect.

Evie kept Sister Mary Lee's soul alive by telling me stories of the miraculous years when, through no fault of her own, little Mary held Portmatilloch spellbound as a powerful oracle.

"Before you were born," I prompted Evie, settling down for a listen, arms wrapped around my knees.

"Aye. Sister Mary arrived shortly afore I was born. My mother…"

"Angela," I shouted out.

"Aye, will ye no let *me* tell it, childy." She waited until I had my excitement under control and resumed her performance. She folded her hands and turned her eyes piously towards the ceiling. "My mother looked after her first, ye ken. I was only a bairn and Mary was no more than sixteen, so she was. And when my dear mother died, I was pressed into Mary's service. It was as if my mother had bequeathed me Mary Lee in her will.

Well, from the start, Mary's presence caused an uproar because it was soon discovered the poor wee soul had fainting spells and the foaming fits, unkindly diagnosed by…"

I interrupted Evie with an exaggerated hissing sound which made her raise her eyebrows and shake her head. "Her fate sealed as you well know, by yer wee *friend*, the abbess, as fits of demonic possession. That auld bissom was a good deal more than unkind. She took keen pleasure from humiliating our Mary, so she did.

Sister Mary Lee was shunned and placed under lock and key to shield the sensitive holy sisters from contamination, and there she stayed for two years until auld Father Dominic became aware he had a money-spinning miracle under his wing.

In short order, Sister Mary's standing changed. And when it was plain her babblings held true, ah well, auld Father Dominic's nose for sniffing out a pretty penny, sure enough twitched with fever. He put it about that our Mary…"

Evie pursed her lips as if she were sucking a lemon and raised her voice an octave for effect. "And here I have to quote the pompous auld bugger for his powerful words: *"exuded an aura of divinity. Several folks have seen a halo waxing and waning over her head like a hallowed moon."*

She snickered and patted her knees as if to rise but slumped back down in pain. "Aye, he were a shameless schemer – a right auld scold if ever there was.

But as ye may ken, a divine gift such as Sister Mary's required a grand title."

Evie's eyes glazed fixedly on a horizon I couldn't see. "Miracle worker, the father called her. Well, the higher ups put their oar in and let it slip that a kindly nun with the holy sight was available to give private *consultations* for a wee fee. In my opinion it was a fancified version of the regular *pardons* sold under the table to addle-brained sheep for imagined sins."

She sniffed. "*Indulgencies*, they called em. All nicely hidden and paid for proper like.

And when the high and mighty got wind of a powerful profit to be had, the title of saint lifted poor Mary Lee from a wee nun to an oracle of God, so powerful a common soul could ne'r look upon the lass wi'out a blindfold."

Evie cleared her throat with an angry *Aacht!* Her voice lowered so I could barely hear her, but I knew what was coming. An opinion best kept from idle busybodies and eavesdroppers.

"T'was nay time a'tall afore a few well-placed rumors raised up Portmatilloch to a pilgrimage site. The beginning of the end, it was. All hellfire was lowered upon us. I was proper feared for the goddess. The church had already swept aside the old religion, ages back, to purge the land of demons and fairies."

She snorted and raised her eyes staring hard into mine. "At least it *thought* it had!"

The story, while charming me, always put Evie in a fitful temper. She rose suddenly and waved her arms as if banishing a demon. "Off wi ye. Away ye go now. There's work to be done."

I knew the rest by heart. The village women loved a tale wagged freely on their silly tongues. Old Sister Lee, the anchorite, had been sealed into a cell attached to the exterior north wall of the main church since she'd arrived as a teenage novice in 1850.

Such was the mercurial nature of Sister Mary's many *appointments*, each customer felt specially 'selected' and could be easily recognized for their fixed dreamy expressions, entranced for days.

Evie brought the old days to mind at least once a day, ever mindful to cross her fingers behind her back for the benefit of spying eyes. The church believed a dreamy-eyed state was a sure sign of demonic possession. Mary was lucky *not* to be accused of witchcraft. The fate of many a poor woman was so sealed within living memory.

The needy and the wonderstruck travelled to us as desperate pilgrims. Local boys charged a penny to shepherd them about, pointing out the locations where our miraculous Mary had appeared.

Much to the church's horror, their last stop, a rowan tree within a stone's throw from the locked anchorage door, soon had its branches tied with small offerings of food, jewelry, and clothing to grease the palms of local fairies for more auspicious results.

People clamoured for audiences. Visitors made long excursions to gaze upon Sister Lee's cell door, in the hopes of experiencing a vision of the Virgin Mary who was said to companion her.

Locals and strangers alike, gathered in candlelit vigils at nightfall for a glimpse of holy light said to render the solid brick walls of the anchorage clear as glass.

One enterprising woman in the village did a brisk trade in blindfolds embroidered with the letter M. Another sold crucifixes made of twigs from the Rowan tree overlooking Mary's cell.

Saint 'M' as she became known, was all the more dangerous, perched between the slippery slopes of Scottish folklore, divine intervention, and being in league with the devil.

But as Evie was wont to publicly declare at every opportunity, the universe had room for us all. And so, two sisterhoods worshipped side-by-each with the church never the wiser.

The goddess Epona had prevailed since time immemorial. Her roots thrived patiently underground presided over by the Green Gods who bide their mysteries in silence as they still do, and the Goddess gathered her faithful followers together in the 'Clan of the Horse' to keep the 'old one' safe.

Every month on the full moon, the old one, refreshed her symbol in the wild grasses on the flank of Horse Hill. A svelte horse the length and breadth of a hectare, stretched across the grass at full gallop that only clan members could see.

But since I was privy to it day or night, I was able to take ailing creatures and lay them inside the horse's belly to be healed. As such, Horse Hill became a covert hospice for rebirths of all kinds, including some of my half-baked ideas.

Evie knew of my compassionate acts, and worried for me that my 'miracles' may come to the attention of the sisters. She needn't spell out the violent consequences of church fathers, but she hinted as much. History can repeat itself, she reminded me, so, mind how ye go.

But even so, I preferred to live under the protection of the goddess that easily overpowered anything the church could throw at me.

Sadly, this hadn't always been the case. Barely three hundred years back, a fair few gentle women of Portmatilloch were burned as witches. We still lay flowers for them inside the white horse on the solstices.

Evie and Sister Mary Lee were close as mother and child could be without sharing blood. They were family. And as it happened, I was too, although just how close I had yet to learn.

Evie's unwed mother, Angela, had been one of the first to kneel before Saint 'M' to bless her infant daughter. But Mary Lee had done much more; she'd secretly agreed to be Evie's godmother.

Evie was never one for mincing words. She used her inherited aura of superstitious divinity as Saint 'M's confidante to her advantage. It wasn't many who crossed her, and if they did, they soon regretted their folly.

Evie came by her reputation honestly, as an unflinching authority, never flaunting her opinion nor shirking from it.

On the surface, she earned the respect of the village as a steadfast woman who despite her outward status as a common servant, was a compassionate and generous neighbor.

Goddess knows what they said behind her back, but I'll warrant it came with a crucifix hidden in their pocket.

I have Evie to thank for the reluctant deference villagers acknowledged to my face as Miss Violet Seaborn, but Evie was mysterious enough in her own right to command fearful respect.

The gossips outside the Horse Clan lowered their eyes in her presence to avoid receiving one of her tirades saved for any who cast doubts on my birth.

Except for Evie's and Sam's protection I may have suffered the fate as an abomination to be locked away in Saint 'M's old quarters as a curse. But ignorant superstition has its advantages.

In due course, Saint 'M' received Lady Flora's blessing and Epona infused Evie's soul with the alchemy of limitless power. I never guessed just how far Evie's powers had escalated.

Saints preserve us! One day soon, it will be my turn, high time for me to break the Old One's silence.

7

TREASURES PAST

"I have been here before,
But when or how I cannot tell.
I know the grass beyond the door,
The sweet keen smell, the sighing sound,
The lights around the shore."
DANTE GABRIEL ROSSETTI

1918

- VIOLET -

When the scent of wet earth woke me, moonlight still hung over the world. Evie had been gone an entire day after leading the clan, to Horse Hill for a Moondark ceremony under the stars.

Each young woman carried their sacred bundles: Linens stained with menses, bedsheets bloodied from childbirth, discarded umbilical cords, and occasionally, the lifeless body of an infant daughter who failed to thrive. Each old mother crone carried spring water and candles.

All manner of 'moonblood' was buried atop Horse Hill overlooking the sea in a sacrificial graveyard. The consecrated ground suffused with an aura of feminine power honored Our Lady Flora of the Greenwoods ward of the High Goddess, Epona.

Evie sacrificed in other ways. Her menses had stopped, and she'd already offered up the bloodied sheet from my cradle the first full moon after my arrival.

Even though I had been formally presented to Epona, I had yet to see the Lady Flora, being under the age of requirement.

I walked north toward the rumble of thunder gathering over Horse Hill and waited for the sign of the horse to brighten on the grass. Once the elegant outline of the horse glowed white under the stars I resumed at a faster pace.

Moments later, I took my appointed place in the center of Sam's potato field. I knelt in a fresh furrow ploughed the day before, scooped two handfuls of earth, silently invoking Epona.

The rumbling of thunder drew closer. A lightning bolt seared the sky. A twig snapped simultaneously with a crack of thunder. I crouched low to the ground waiting for Epona's shiver of power to quicken my spine. I repeated the words in my head that Evie taught me as soon as I could walk. "My Lady Epona, I am ready to receive thee," and settled deeper into the furrow, eyes closed, until the base of my spine melted into the warmth of new earth.

A blackbird serenaded me and abruptly ceased. And in the ensuing silence I heard Evie chanting from the Hilltop above and a distant thud of hooves approaching at a gallop.

The arrival of Epona, the hooved sylph of the local springs and streams, and the open waters of the sea was imminent. I scrunched my eyelids tight and held my breath.

My Lady Epona drew nearer until the ground beneath me trembled. She circled me several times. A delightful sea breeze cooled my skin each time she passed. Her hooves pawed the ground when she stopped in front of me sending electric shocks through the earth into my spine. And when she paused to sniff my hair, her mane brushed my face.

She neighed softly. I tingled from the power of her love that filled my head. *"Dearest child, it always pleases me that you do not fear the sight of me. Do you remember when we first met?"*

"I do your grace. You befriended me in the water, the day you guided my cradle to safety, although I was newly born and too young to see you. And last year when we met formally when I was seventeen."

"That is our secret, little one. I will stand perfectly still before I depart, and you must behold a vision of me and hold the memory within you. For we will meet again albeit not as soon as I wish. So, I greet you now to sustain you until the time allotted to us draws nigh."

I looked into Epona's gentle sea green eye and spied a hide of burnished navy blue, slick with seawater, and a mane tangled with seaweed silhouetted against the moon.

"We are blood kin, you and I," Epona said tossing her head, showering me with droplets of energized water.

The air stilled before I could reply. I never saw her go, only the watery stream she left in her wake.

I swooned deep into a riot of color, dreaming of a land where trees ripe with fruit bent low to the earth and hosts of wee flying folk tended roots and blossoms in flowering meadows. Glorious birdsong filled the air, and best of all, Epona's hooves rang out as the natural heartbeat of the greenwoods.

Sam arrived to wake me at the appointed time of the sun's zenith with a thermos of sweetened tea. He offered me his hand.

"Are ye ready? Can ye walk? Are there lights? Will ye show me."

I took his hand, and he pulled me from the soil like a human plant. The earth released me joyfully, the same way I release baby birds to the sky with open arms. "It's lucky you came," I said. "I was about to grow roots."

Sam sent me an uncertain smile knowing it might be true. "Let's get started, then. I've been ready for days."

Sam's beautiful face was bathed in the green energy that streamed from my hands. The same colour now emanating from patches of soil pulsating with light.

The purified land primed by Epona was ready to give up its treasures risen to the surface during the night.

Unlike me, Sam was unable to see each artefact glowing through the transparent mounds, but he came prepared for harvesting, ready with a hand trowel, an armful of hazel switches, and a picnic in the old basket that had been my cradle.

Sam followed close behind me, breathing excitedly, planting a twitch wherever I pointed.

"I wish you could see what I see," I said.

He hugged me close and whispered in my ear. "Describe it to me again, Violet, I never tire of seeing it in my mind. You are my eyes."

I engaged my storyteller voice. "The entire field is navy blue with a pattern of tiny, raised mounds shining green like enchanted mole holes. It's like looking at the night sky peppered with green stars."

"Well, I see a wondrous crop of ghostly saplings at first light," Sam said. "Knowing their roots now reveal a precious relic."

I squeezed his hand. "Then you see rightly."

He bowed graciously and kissed my hand. "Let's get to digging my fair maid."

We watched the twitches crumble to dust. And in each empty place, I saw a spirit arrive to stand guard. "Are they here?" Sam asked. "Can we begin?"

I giggled. "Sam Watts, you're twitchier than a whole forest of birch trees. Yes. They're here."

I thanked each spirit individually and asked permission before we broke ground. Beneath an inch of topsoil lay a cherished possession lost and mourned for years with a story to tell.

I sipped tea while Sam dug. The hilt of a sword, a golden torc, a garnet brooch, and an ivory comb, soon filled the basket that had served as my lifeboat.

One-by-one the spirits filed by the basket and lovingly touched their possessions one last time before rising into the sky as shapes filled with light.

Sam pointed to the white scar on my left big toe. "You're going to carry that to your grave, does it hurt?"

"No, it's a foreshadow of things to come that reminds me to look before I leap, so it's rather handy."

When the last shape disappeared, the land was healed, its energies restored after the troubled spirits were freed to take their places as true souls. Sam's future career was born, and I was happy, content to be his dowsing rod.

8

FOR HEAVEN'S SAKE!

"Do not feign affection.
Neither be cynical about love;
for in the face of all aridity and disenchantment,
it is as perennial as the grass."
MAX EHRMANN

1901 -1918

The sisters glide from prayer-to-prayer through the convent grounds like a single-minded sailing ship without a compass, seemingly weightless, levitating a few inches above the ground, their billowing black skirts and veils filled with salty wind.

The similarities between my story and the sisterhood were not lost on me. The image of an adrift sistership floundering on demon rocks overlapped a vivid memory of my basket floating on the sea in a field of debris. As I conjured it, the water parted and a shape backlit by the sun filled my sky. The words "sleep my child," set me dreaming, safe in the protection of my water horse.

And when the vision cleared, I suddenly knew the sisters perfectly, without a wit of sympathy for what they truly were. Weak-willed women who had deliberately chosen to separate themselves from the goddess. Fools!

The nature of blessings and curses is often an uneasy balance. I never flaunted my special abilities. Prophecies served the population best when Evie downplayed them as a series of lucky coincidences.

Evie was rarely subtle in her dealings but somehow, I was eventually considered a lucky charm in homage to Saint 'M' who was still revered. The fact that Sister Lee was ignored by the church as an incident best forgotten gave me a degree of protection.

The sisters invented what they assumed was a seamless way of crossing themselves in my presence. I smiled innocently pretending to defer to their high ground of false morality, and by acting simple-minded I ceased to be a threat. And once immune from their suffocating neediness I gained the blessed relief of a vast stillness, open to the presence of Epona, with my thoughts to myself.

Being alone, I listened to Epona, at peace in her presence. And if I needed to think, I had my thoughts to myself.

I was able to spontaneously mindread, but I was never an eavesdropper. I blocked out the whinging sisters as a waste of time. There was no need for us to interact. But then, one day as I meditated in the sun, I let them in, or perhaps they lowered their guard.

For a moment I was involuntarily privy to their general misgivings as well as a few singularly intimate thoughts. One novice lusted hungrily after a robust village lad. Another swooned over a comely lass half her age. Yet another was in search of a surrogate role model missing the birth father she'd never met. Several sisters dreamed carnal dreams of our menfolk day and night.

Whatever their sins, the sisters turned their back on the goddess and united in blind faith to a Father/God whose lackeys claimed to know the way to heaven.

Collectively, they were troubled souls drained of feminine power. A sorry guilt-ridden excuse for the female sex: downcast maidens and crones plagued by fear, regret, denial, and ashamed of longings intensified by supressed sexual desires.

Surprisingly, the abbess was the most conflicted of all. Her heart was still set on the handsome priest she'd lost to the church, twenty years back, constantly reawakened with every new arrival of a priest with bedroom eyes. She caught me gawping at her and sent me a conspiratorial smile as if she heard my thoughts.

And then a shy voice rose above the others. Sister Veritas's frail thoughts were growing stronger – a budding flower in a bed of choking weeds choosing to blossom with feminine power rather than die on sterile soil.

Quite unexpectedly, the word plague roared in my ears so loud I lost my balance. Thundering hooves pounded inside my chest and left me gasping for air.

I ceased to be. My body was no more. My feet were hooves pawing the ground running red with blood. The scream of a terrified horse issued from my throat and died away.

A barren landscape replaced the village. I saw clear across the hills to the sea, and just as suddenly, life reappeared as the noisy bustle of market day.

I came to, grovelling on all fours, retching in the street. The black hems of the nuns, rancid with woodsmoke brushed against my face. I heard my voice calling for help, but no one came until the face of Sister Veritas wavering in my mind's eye gave me enough strength to compose myself and run to the laundry.

Evie was ironing. She took one look at my face and returned to her ironing. "So, it's upon us, then," she said under her breath.

In accordance with Christianity's teachings of love and compassion, the sisters were obliged to keep me, but it was clear to me they only did so to comply with the church's male pecking order that overruled them with an iron fist.

In time, I learned that women robbed of their feminine power can be especially vindictive. Left to their mercies I doubt I would have survived. But then, human jealousy had long since decreed them resentful of any girlish happiness.

It is therefore in hindsight, that I can appreciate how the sisters' submissive routine of never *'rocking the boat'* worked miraculously in my favor.

The novices whispered within my hearing, that I was a witch's brat and remained in fear of my calm unblinking stare and the manner of my deliverance.

The sisters, intently focused on their prayers, imagined I was guarded by demons and were happy to give me a wide berth.

It had been left to Sam, as young as he was, to steer me away from the open fires of the kitchen, bubbling vats of boiling water in the laundry, and the hooves of the workhorses.

The sisters of questionable mercy were, pardon the expression, so 'hell bent' on suffering, so severely lacking the humane virtue of empathy, and so deeply gratified that their sacrifices would be rewarded by an ill-tempered man in the sky, they positively glowed with pride.

Deferring to their 'betters' as subservient females, effectively guaranteed them a place in heaven and simultaneously rendered me invisible by refusing to acknowledge my presence.

Without meaning to, their pushing me out of sight inadvertently spoiled me.

Unlike the shivering chilblained sisters, I thrived in comfort in the only two warm rooms of a stone church that was freezing twelve months of the year.

Evie worked in the kitchen and laundry from dawn to vespers. My days were happily spent there prattling to her and Sam, the church cats, and myself, after it was made apparent by the cold shoulders and grim looks from the abbess that a chatterbox underfoot was an unholy distraction of the worst kind.

I was accordingly released to roam free when the weather was fine, out of sight, out of mind, and more importantly, out of hearing.

On those sweet days I shadowed Sam working in the fields and together we sang his mother's plaintive folk songs of love grown cold.

For seventeen years I blossomed under the tender ministrations of Evie Watts who sang while she scrubbed and stirred and ironed. I thrived innocently on bittersweet folk songs of love and heartache and lived in a succession of laundry baskets that grew bigger with time.

Once I learned to walk, I slept in a cozy corner on a pile of laundered linen sprinkled with fresh lavender, drowsy and warm from the steamy smell of soap and calming lullabies of sailing the seven seas to find the lost silk road to Timbuktu.

By the time San was nineteen, he had proved himself an invaluable farm hand and I had been sufficiently tamed into learning my letters to read passages aloud from the bible to anyone who cared to listen. The sisters did not.

I didn't care. Sam, in awe of my ability to read and write, was enchanted by my stories. Had we survived the Spanish Flu I would have told him my secret that I was not as gifted as he thought because I only *pretended* to read the stories. In truth I had created every one of them my head and recited them by heart, holding the bible upside down which amused Evie no end.

Luckily for my imperilled soul, the sisters never noticed. And since the prioress and sisters were also deaf to my constant blather about talking animals and unrequited love they were never inspired by "the gospel according to Violet".

But Sam was.

The ancient church was easily the healthiest place to live considering the surrounding lowlands were often flooded with brackish standing water. But the rainfall was that heavy on the wild east coast that even in the adjoining hills of drained farmland, wooden buildings were subject to the holy terrors of damp and mould which is why Sam suffered coughing fits weeks before I did.

The spring of 1918 was uncommonly wet immediately before it became uncommonly dry. Waves of sickly heat rose from the parched soil and poisonous vapors wafted over the landscape like lost ghosts. The windswept fields disintegrated into toxic dustbowls void of soul and Epona's Spring drained into a shallow slurry of green slime reeking of rotting frogs.

Deep within a fever dream, the goddess Epona showed herself to me as a pale shadow covered in decaying seaweed, her eyes blood-red from thirst. But her voice rang true as ever. *"My child, the season of blight is upon us. And so, I must leave you for a short while. Do not be aggrieved. I have chosen you. Be brave and know that I will return to you in good time."* I watched in horror as her chalk shrine turned red like a fresh wound cut into the hillside and shrivelled to a brown scar.

Minor illnesses were to be expected but they lingered into listless fevers. And when the rains stopped, summer arrived as a blistering drought. The cows stopped giving milk and died, vegetables failed to thrive, and cruel heat baked our souls into an unforeseen plague of killing fevers. Looking back, it was Sam who unwittingly passed the sickness on to me.

Such was the religious ascetic lifestyle, the wasting sickness crept into the convent so stealthily we barely noticed.

Evie had sensed an invisible predator. She understood that the body's natural humours of blood, yellow bile, black bile, and phlegm carried cunning demons – servants to death himself.

The villagers had no reason to suspect an invisible enemy lurked on our skin or in the breath we exhaled. But Evie did.

9

TRUE BELIEVER

*"If you want to confirm your personal power...
tell a lie and watch it come true."*
EVIE WATTS

- VIOLET -

Evie was semi-awake with our kitten, Summer, on her lap when the sound of pounding rain pulled her into a trance. She sensed the approach of a kindred spirit and positioned herself by the door in readiness.

I watched her take a deep breath and count to three before answering the faint tap on the door to the wan face of Sister Veritas.

"How much does your horse potion cost?" the girl asked without saying hello or offering her name. She was apologetic. "For a week now," she stuttered. "I've been having dreams about a black horse and I …"

"I know you," Evie said. "Sister Veritas, isn't it?"

The girl nodded and stared at her shoes.

"Excellent, I've had my eye on you. Do please come in. But please leave your fear outside if you don't mind. You're quite safe from church gossip here."

Sister Veritas kicked off her soaked shoes.

"That's it. Come along in and sit by the fire, my girl. You can move Summer off the armchair. I'll just be a tick and put the kettle on. By your cloak I see it's still raining. Now then, get yourself nice and dry."

Sister Veritas shuffled barefoot towards the fire and stopped to pet Summer who had understood Evie's words well enough to have already vacated her spot. She nodded to me cleaning the kitchen.

Evie stirred the fire into a blaze. "I'm surprised you can see Summer," she said, her eyes twinkling. "You were quite right to come to me but who told you about the horse potion? It's a secret."

Sister Veritas squirmed in her chair. "You're going to think I'm crazy," she said. "But I think I may have dreamed that, too."

GOING NOVA
the book of Violet

10

HIC INCIPIT PESTUS
here plague begins

The water is wide,
I can't cross o'er
And neither do I have wings to fly
Give me a boat that can carry two
And both shall row
My love and I
SCOTTISH FOLK SONG

1919

- VIOLET -

The Spanish Flu epidemic of 1918 took me in its second year during the relentless winter of 1919 as the epidemic grew wings.

I remember the freezing December rains came and buffeted the stained-glass windows of the chapel where I died. The colors of the window bled together hemorrhaging down the glass in rivulets of tears and simply washed me away.

But even to the end, Sam and I conversed silently in thought and renewed our pact to die together if we had to.

I lifted from my body, tiptoed past Sam's cot, and blew him a kiss. "I guess I'm first. Don't be long," I whispered.

My transparent fingers brushed his hand lightly as a butterfly's wing. He smiled weakly struggling for breath. *"No worries,"* he rasped. *"I will never leave you. Wait for me."*

Evie dozed in a chair beside him. She stirred when I kissed her cheek and called out in her sleep. *"Petal? Are ye away, child? Aaaacht! Can ye no stay? Can ye no just breathe."*

I answered her gently. "I've already gone, Mam. Sam is with me. No worries. We will look after each other. May the goddess protect you."

But I'd spoken too soon. Had I looked back, I would have seen Evie's soul leave her body to follow me with Sister Veritas, and the ghost of old Saint 'M' restraining her, waving me goodbye.

I rose into a clear blue sky to wait for Sam to catch up.

He was two years older than me, world-wise beyond my seventeen cloistered years so I had no reason to doubt him. But he never came, and as my form dissipated into the morning mist his voice sounded all around and through me. *"I will find you,"* he called out. *"Never fear."* And so, I didn't.

11

SCOTLAND THE BRAVE

"Do your best,
And leave the rest,
'Twill all come right
Some day or night."
'BLACK BEAUTY' BY ANNA SEWELL

DECEMBER – **1919**

- VIOLET -

For the longest time, I dreamed I was floating on the salty updrafts of Portmatilloch with the seagulls. Exhilarated, I followed the roar of wild waves breaking on the rocks until I wore myself out.

Thus spent, calmed by the sighs of the tide lapping my adopted shoreline, I hovered high above Sea-Glass Beach where Sam and I collected precious ruby and ultramarine shards of broken glass polished smooth by sand and saltwater.

I felt gloriously free until I heard Epona scream in pain from a whirlpool of blood in the water.

I watched in horror as the vortex roiled into the eye of an underwater storm that churned the North Sea into a vicious swirl of malignant colours. The brewing storm spewed violently from the sea as a waterspout of blood, heaved itself into a mountainous red tidal wave, and hit the beach in a roar.

I was overcome with a wave of dizziness and wondered if I might still be suffering on my deathbed, but I was already dead.

The Lady Flora wept for her chosen one and a chorus of wailing erupted from the departed clan as they joined her in mourning.

A lightning bolt seared our white horse image deeper into the brow of Horse Hill and flickered red, and just as suddenly, the sea stilled, and silence covered the land. I was emptied of joy.

My soul bled for Epona. I had failed her. Portmatilloch was dying and I was powerless to stop it.

Home lay far below – a cluster of slate roofs huddled together on a green hill with the mist closing in. *"I'll follow you,"* a gull shrieked in Sam's voice. *"Despite appearances all is well. Now go or you'll be too late. Trust me. Do not look back!"*

I woke with a familiar fever, lying trapped inside a stranger fighting for breath in a white room where a wall alive with colored blinking lights, ticked softly like a clock underwater.

A masked nurse stood over me holding my hand. "It's time to let go my dear," she whispered.

But she wasn't addressing me; she was persuading an old lady, who seemed to have swallowed me whole, to give up the book clutched to her chest.

I reacted instantly. I sat up, swung my legs over the side of the bed and hightailed it to the corner.

Behind me, a mechanical cylinder sloshed up and down issuing sinister hissing and sucking noises that duplicated the laboured breathing I felt it in my chest.

From where I stood, the body on the bed was tethered to a bag of water by strings sprouting from the back of her hand. Other strings snaked from her nose and fingers, and she seemed to be swallowing a large snake.

She lay as if dead, laid out for burial like the bodies I'd seen many times in the convent's mortuary waiting to be embalmed.

Her shrivelled arms had been crossed over her chest like a pharaoh – a grotesque marionette being prepared for mummification like the ancient Egyptians, known to me from my previous incarnations in the land of Khem. But *their* souls had always been in evidence, hovering about their bodies, busily counting their possessions, and sorting them into boxes.

I expressly recall their vigilance, listening for the correct incantations necessary to deliver them safely to the underworld while searching the shadows for ever present thieves.

And then it came to me with a sickening jolt that I might be this woman's soul! Was I hovering or as I first assumed and still hoped, simply a lost soul making a wrong turn on my way to finding Sam?

It appalled me that I had been inside such an ugly withered body for even a second, so the ghastly prospect of entering it again or that I may not have a say in the matter was unthinkable.

On closer inspection I read the title of her book. Someone with a cruel sense of irony had tucked a copy of *"Sleeping Beauty"* under the woman's arthritic hands.

But the old woman refused to let go of it, so I sat in the chair beside her bed in a quandary, a fragile maid of seventeen, hoping someone would take pity on me and tell me where I was and how to leave as soon as humanly possible.

I called out for one of my mothers to come, but I remained alone. No Evie, no Lady Flora, no Epona… and no Sam.

I tried to dismiss everything as a bad dream but slumped into tears and fell into an uneasy sleep where Evie reminded me that I was a much beloved, exceptionally brave girl, on a mission. "Do your best and leave the rest," she said, "it all comes right some day or night."

I knew it as a haunting line from a book Evie kept at her bedside but couldn't recall the title.

12

SHOOTING THE RAPIDS

Give me a boat,
that will carry two
And both shall row
My love and I

- VIOLET -

I closed my eyes on the last days of 1919. It was still raining when I opened them one hundred years later, pitching on the swell of the open sea in a rowboat taking on water.

I was lightheaded but oddly untroubled, taking comfort from the circling gulls being close enough to smell land.

At long last, a hazy shape manifested on the horizon like a bank of low-lying cloud. As I got closer vague outlines of cliffs appeared through patches of dense fog, until an island materialised from the sea and a distinct treeline emerged behind a brilliant stretch of white sand.

Sam shouted, *"Welcome home, my love,"* inside my head.

But in place of Sam, a four-poster bed awaited me on the beach. Exhaustion overcame me. I questioned nothing. I needed to clear my head.

I crawled into the bed and called out to let Sam know I'd arrived. *"Sam, I know you're here. It feels as if I've been waiting forever. I'm so tired."*

Sam whispered inside my head. *"Close your eyes lassie. I will be along presently."*

And so, I slept.

A soft female voice answered from across the emptiness of sleep. "Don't you fret, sweetheart. Sam's on his way. You sleep, now. Everything's all right."

I fretted in the moonlight, anyway. *"Please Sam. Answer me. I don't have all day. I miss you."*

Then I heard him. *"Silly goose. I'm always with you,"* he said. *"Don't be frightened. Didn't I promise to find you."*

The woman's disembodied whisper rose and fell from the foot of my bed. "She's been calling someone named Sam. But there's no Sam on her chart."

Papers shuffled gently.

"She'll be in twilight sleep for a few hours," a man said. "Keep her sedated and call me if there's any change. She's reached the crisis point. It's up to her, now. She'll sink or swim. Let's not upset her. She needs all her strength now."

"Tell Evie something dire is amiss," I called out. *"Epona needs help. Hello! Sam, can you see me waving?"*

Sam waved back from his island lookout in a tall tree. *"Don't trouble yourself, lass. Evie knows. I keep my promises, Goosey. I'm always with you. I have your back."*

Relieved, I took a deep breath. *"There you are,"* I answered. *"I never doubted you."*

Sam's voice grew serious. *"Violet. Listen carefully, dearest. We'll be together soon. No worries. It's time to rest now."*

And so, determined to trust Sam, I set aside my disgust of being old, settled under the covers once more and slept like a wanted child.

HELLO DARK STRANGER
the book of Celeste

- 13 -

THE HOMECOMING

"There's no place like home
For the holidays
Cause no matter how far away you roam.
If you want to be happy in a million ways
For the holidays, you can't beat home sweet home."

JANUARY – **2020**

- VIOLET -

My new body had a name. Daisy – a body and soul connection I desperately hoped to nip in the bud.

She and I should have passed like ships in the night because I was program-bound for Sam's coordinates. Daisy, on the other hand, had no destination at all.

Daisy was an unknown quantity free floating on serendipity, decidedly out of her depth, out of her body, and quite possibly out of her mind.

And not to put too fine a point on it, old enough to be my grandmother. And while that can often be advantageous for meaningful reincarnation, I was on a specific mission, predestined to reunite with the love of my life.

Daisy Sinclair dashed my joyous expectations of life as a newborn. A sixty-eight-year-old crone on life support, yearning for death who exuded an aura of intense depression, was hardly a cheery substitute for a romantic reunion.

I thought of Daisy as a thief – a ravenous old leech involuntarily eating me alive. I was being cruelly depleted, consumed as empty calories by a spiritually starved bloodsucker.

Daisy as a host was no match for the real me of me, but she instinctively absorbed my lifeforce at an alarming rate. The few occasions I experimented residing within her gave me the impression of being a bar of soap that grows smaller every day.

I mused that Daisy, flying out of body on auto pilot, had bumped into me by chance in the ether and somehow random physics had turned metaphysical and locked onto my energy like a desperate tractor beam from the good ship Titanic.

At that moment, a malevolent presence hissed by me taunting derisive comments. "Look at you, a wilted violet. Who wants to be fresh as a daisy, then?" it jeered. "Think girl. Treading water is a waste of energy. A short-term solution at best."

I looked over at Daisy. Her thoughts were comatose in Lalaland. The murky voice came from a firebrand under the bed. It scuttled to the far side of the room leaving a trail of soot in the outline of a horse behind it.

The familiar design of the horse made my heart leap. I was almost home. "What… *who* are you?"

"I'm the friend of an old friend of an old enemy," it replied. "Someone who wishes to be remembered for old time's sake."

I refocused at once, concentrating my dwindling energy into a killing projectile but it dispersed short of its target and sank to the floor as an impotent mist.

The creature slipped under the door. "Keep watch," it cackled from the hallway. "The remains of a big bad day are heading your way. Remember, a withered old crone who can't swim is no fit companion for a strapping girl shipwrecked in the North Sea!"

The firebrand's words rang true. Daisy *was* all at sea, deciding whether to desert her aged body. I was a stowaway defending my presence at her deathbed with the lame apology of being a lost soul passing through on my way to my next life. The best life Sam and I had been promised. But a loving voice I assumed was Sam's entreated me to be calm.

"I am not Sam, little one," the voice continued now distinctly female. *"You and I are connected beyond heart and soul."*

I caught a vision of an infant floating in a basket and persuaded myself to stay in case the child was my next incarnation.

"That's my girl. Delays are not mistakes; they're challenges. You chose a selfless path of accountability before you were born. However, the highest roads are blessed with sacrifices. If you remain mindful, your twin destiny is secure. What faces you now is a test of love. For a time, you will fail to accept who you are. You will dismiss who I am. But you are a perfect soul, perfectly placed. Your energy will enable your ancestors to thrive despite the river of forgetfulness."

"Why am I here?" I asked. "I'm forgetting my old life as we speak. It saddens me that I don't remember who *you* are. I don't like feeling homeless."

"You and Sam accepted a complex mission of mercy. Personal objections are to be expected and tolerated to navigate the afterlife by acknowledging a universal consciousness greater than your own."

Daisy was, I blush to say it, literally 'beside herself' sobbing with despair, standing over her lifeless form that looked like an unwrapped mummy on the bed.

I tried to explain my appearance in her room was a mistake. And like a pair of spoiled children, we stamped our feet at the universe that from my point of view, seemed to be flirting with making its first mistake. Whatever was going on, it wasn't behaving as Evie had drummed into me that the universe was flawless, truer than true, and beyond criticism.

Daisy didn't want my soul; I didn't want her body, but I was, as Evie liked to pun, no shrinking violet. Suffice to say, we drew psychic lines in the sand, hoping like Siamese twins joined at the forehead, only one of us would survive separation.

I loomed over Daisy's bed like the angel of death in a foul temper. "I know you can hear me," I said. "The way I see it, if worse comes to worst, we may have to compromise for a while. But be absolutely clear of *one* thing. You are NOT my home!

I have no intentions of becoming a common homebody with bunions, who is terrified of the world. I will *not* answer to you. I am *not* some passive extension of life support while you waste away into senility. And the first chance I get, be assured, I will pull your plug! As far as I'm concerned, there's been a monumental mistake and I'm being tested. YOU are a TEST! The powers that be haven't heard the last of me. But, IF the universe is seriously out of order, you are on your own. Abandoned. Shipwrecked in a void! Welcome to *my* world."

I needed to take a breath. Strangely, that thought made me laugh. A warm feeling of love engulfed me. The benign voice of the Lady Flora resonated inside me. *"Goodness, Violet, calm yourself, child. Just breathe."*

I responded with relief. "My lady. This is so unfair. I was promised a life with Sam. What has happened? I need help."

"Have you considered that all three of you are being tested? Is it not possible that Daisy might have something to teach you? A loving future requires a karma-free past. Have you examined yours? You are the Old One's special daughter. Conduct yourself accordingly with compassion. And in your darkest hour remember Epona has your back. Trust her with all your heart."

"Why won't the Old One speak to me herself?"

"She is. I am here at Epona's pleasure. I often serve as her voice just as Epona serves Leela. If you cannot muster compassion for Daisy, then have some empathy for Sam. You are his sole lifeline."

"Who is Leela? Why have I not heard this name?!"

"Sweet girl. You've heard it many times, but you always refused to remember it. As an invincible royal child, you assumed the universe was a function specially created to serve you alone. This was not arrogance. I do not fault you. You were predestined to live a long time as Mistress of the Horse, but your death came early for a reason. As such, there wasn't enough time to complete your formal training. All-powerful truths must be revealed slowly. A word is not a name. Power without heart is not true power. Heartless power has no soul. Lila is the name of the universe. She/He represents the game of life. In your case, Lila is female. Her male counterpart is Sol. Do not rage so, child. Listen to the silence of your breath. Just breathe, Violet!"

Ironically, at this point, my dormant ego took offense on my behalf, and rose from the dead to fight the battle I'd been in the process of surrendering.

My wisdom rallied in silence, but my ego's unfiltered commentary drowned it out, and like all self-destructive thoughts it crushed any trace of omnipotence within me and re-emerged as an almighty test. So, in addition to fighting Daisy I had to fight myself.

Divine mission or not, I am in truth, deeply ashamed of my physical aversion to Daisy's body. Even so, I will fight her to the death from the *inside* out if it means finding my beloved Sam.

14

SOUL MATTERS 101

"In death's despite,
And day and night
Yield one delight once more?"
DANTE GABRIEL ROSSETTI

- VIOLET -

For a while Daisy and I were like befuddled sisters – rival siblings wondering what the hell was going on. For two months we held surreal conversations in a hospital room discussing our limited options.

Daisy was usually on the fence about sticking around but, sadly for me, other days she gravitated, albeit never robustly, towards having another go at living which unfortunately, thanks to Lila, involved my participation.

My opinion never varied. I wanted Daisy to die so I could 'move on to that 'better place' where mourners envision their loved ones have gone. My place was with Sam.

The prospect of becoming Daisy's permanent roommate was immoral. Moreover, I was deeply offended by being karmically matched with a passionless lifeform who could only survive as a parasite. My initially fleeting compassion wore paper thin. I clung to self preservation by indulging in an unsettling attitude, becoming more hostile by the moment.

Daisy's newly acquired wise-woman persona (that I hasten to say was once mine), struggled to dominate but initially I deferred to Daisy because Evie had taught me to mind my elders.

Essentially, the greater part of me was still seventeen years old, albeit an extremely advanced teenager. I had remained a mystical dynamo with a short fuse. I was feisty, but I missed Evie, and a woman of Daisy's mature years looked too much like a surrogate grandmother to be completely disrespected.

I comforted myself that Daisy's final death rattle would serve as a beacon for Sam to find me.

For ages, Daisy continued to sleep soundly with the help of a machine, childishly clutching her ancient dogeared copy of 'Sleeping Beauty' that had seen better days.

There were moments when our combined waning energies suggested the end of our struggles were at hand and we should both give up our ghosts.

But then we rallied again out of spite. We kept pace on separate spiritual paths headed into the horizon until our parallel arguments eventually converged into a single lane highway. We travelled forward lickety-split down what seemed to be a vast rolled-up tube of the night sky – a tunnel that amplified the sounds of sea birds screeching at the finish line.

There were days I felt sleepy and straggled behind. Truth be told, I was bored, too angry to function.

Daisy eventually flew so far ahead of me she looked like a lone star twinkling in a sea of black. That should have been my cue to surrender gracefully but I had other plans and Daisy needed a new soul. I was obligated to stay and see it through.

Daisy called out a farewell speech in her shiny new attitude that was meant to be profound. After addressing me as the *gracefully departed one*, she played her strong suit (also stolen from me) "I'll be better off on my own," she said. "I release you. Find yourself a new home." She waved me away like a mosquito, "You may go now. No doubt there's a baby waiting for you who needs a soul."

"I'll depart when I'm ready, sleeping beauty," I sniped back. "Maybe you should just swan into that white star at the end of the sky calling your name, or can't you hear it?"

Daisy blanched. "I have a dream to catch. Maybe that star is for *you*."

"Maybe that star IS me!" I crossed my arms determined to stare her down, but the thought struck me I may be looking into the face of karmic retribution. Surely, I had never been that snotty!

I took a cleansing breath intending to stand my full teenage height and hit her with my best Violet Seaborn impersonation, but it was then I noticed my shrivelled old-lady-hands speckled with brown spots.

The words *absolutely not* died in my throat.

15

AGE BEFORE BEAUTY

"But do not distress yourself with dark imaginings.
Many fears are born of fatigue and loneliness."
MAX EHRMANN

- VIOLET -

I did the math and surrendered to the path of least resistance. I had died in late December 1919 and Daisy lay dying in the last days of 2019, one hundred years from the frying pan into the fire. Very tidy. I understood the concept of a straight line being the shortest distance between two flu epidemics but not *why* I was there, caught in poetic deadlock.

As a slave to tidiness, I wrongly jumped at the perfect symmetry of our deaths and took the liberty of whitewashing the true date of Daisy's death. Because when Daisy succumbed to chronic depression in 2016, she'd effectively sealed her fate by formally declaring her death wish in a solemn ritual with an entity named Celeste. At which point, universal law pronounced her dead three years before the Covid 19 pandemic claimed her life-force.

Clearly from her periodic lack of *fight*, and my constant intension of *flight*, our affiliation seemed to have run its course. Daisy wanted to die. I had no argument with that, but I was mightily offended being paired with a spineless old bat who had settled for dying from whatever showed up.

Two synchronistic flu epidemics so evenly spaced seemed a convenient escape requiring neither ingenuity nor effort – a coward's way out. I envisaged her epitaph: Here lies Daisy Sinclair who died from a coincidence.

Daisy heard me and groaned in her sleep.

I was momentarily pleased with my success. I had set out to wear Daisy down so she might give up her ghost early and set us both free. Wishful thinking, perhaps, but at least I *had* worn her out.

For several days she lay like a statue, her thoughts twitching beneath marble eyelids. Victory! I had clearly breached her comatose hideaway. I would accept my crown of laurels with posthumous humility.

Surprisingly, Daisy ignored the open doorway to dreams that she so regularly visited. I seized the advantage and entered in her place to take refuge.

I found myself standing on a blank page where a diagonal set of hoofprints tracked from right to left on a stark field of snow. I listened intently for the sounds of galloping, but all was silent.

Winds scoured the Horse Hill of my childhood as best they could, but the grass lacked the vibrancy I once knew. Instead, the hill looked lost in a dull grey landscape. I failed to detect even the feeblest trace of power emanating from the white horse's tail, the last remaining trench.

I experienced a bleak landscape in shadow. I spontaneously called out "My Lady" into the surrounding desolation but the cold wind swallowed my words and whistled harder.

An exposed seabed loomed eerily in the distance – a vast stagnant field of salty slush where the horse tracks still showed stark and terrifying. They had moved from left to right.

I backed away slowly, slammed the night terrors behind the door, and wandered the hospital halls to settle down.

The cries of newborns issuing from the maternity ward's nursery touched a bittersweet memory that drew me to the beach where I'd arrived in a basket so long ago. How long I couldn't say but the cries I mistook for my own, merged into a chorus of welcoming seagulls.

For the first time in a century, I missed Evie. My mother who declared all manners of stress to be necessary wee storms to clear the air before true love could begin.

67

HEART & SOUL
the book of Sam

16

THE LATE SAM WATTS

"Though lovers be lost
love shall not
And death
shall have no dominion."
DYLAN THOMAS

DECEMBER – **1919**

- SAM -
Portmatilloch, Scotland

A fragrant breeze rippled the sheets strung between the convent's sickbeds like ghostly sentinels. The nearest *'ghost'* resumed its shape of Sister Cecilia waving a crucifix over me bidding me *"kiss it for goodness' sake, Sam. There isn't much time."* I turned my head towards the approach of Violet's footsteps. "Is that you, sweeting?"

But just then a frail voice from across the room called for water and my sentinel became a white shape retreating on a mission of mercy.

"Tis' me, Samuel Watts," Violet's voice teased. *"Am I still your sweeting, then?"*

"You never have to ask."

"But I like your answers."

The walls were raining when Violet slipped past me shushing me with a finger pressed to her lips. Her eyes were especially bright but no longer from fever even though she was in a fever to be away.

The returning Sister heard me babbling in delirium.

"Sam. Whatever you see, let it go," she said. There was fear in

her words. She crossed herself. *"Is it still here?"* She waved her crucifix to send the invisible demon packing and mumbled a prayer of protection. *"Save his soul, Lord. There are demons about us."*

I followed Violet with my eyes, too weak to leave the bed. The hanging sheets parted, and I was overcome with loneliness. *"It's not quite your time,"* Violet said. *"Close your eyes, count to ten, and follow me, ready or not."*

Violet dodged under Sister Cecilia's crucifix. Her violet eyes never left mine as she transformed into candle smoke and wafted to the ceiling.

I called out into the church rafters. "I WILL FIND YOU. NO WORRIES," and dived underwater into a dream where I sat on a low branch of a grandaddy oak growing on Sea Glass Beach as smug as you please.

Violet stood waiting behind a gate, tapping her foot. The waves crashed. Her eyes told me she was in distress. I saw her lips move. "SAM HELP ME!"

I cupped my mouth and gave what I thought was an almighty bellow. "I CAN'T HEAR YOU!"

I died the next day.

The breeze smelled of violets. It was then I had an epiphany. I had been and still was, revisiting the old days when Violet and I played hide and seek. I counted to ten, uncovered my eyes, and shouted, *"ready or not you're mine to catch."*

That was a hundred years ago, and I've been looking for Violet ever since.

17

BIRTH PANGS

"Keep peace in your soul."
MAX EHRMANN

1953

- SAM -
Canada

I was immediately drawn to a freezing room in the house where, moments before, James Eriksen, of Scandinavian descent, entered the world.

Our life together as body and soul began in the winter of 1953 on a prairie homestead where James was doted on by a weary geriatric mother, mothered by eight dutiful sisters, and spoiled by an astonished father, who was more like a grandfather at age seventy-two.

In the main, his three grown brothers spent a great deal of their time avoiding the perils of tripping over a small child underfoot, left alone to entertain himself, especially during critical times of planting, harvest, and heavy chores.

By the time James was old enough for big school the farm had been sold, his parents were retired to a nursing home, and he found himself hanging on to the apron strings of a forty-year-old married sister. Not James's finest hours, nor mine.

I disappeared into my thoughts of Violet far too often and left him to grow up unchaperoned any chance I could.

Even so, I managed to navigate James through his biggest challenge, transported to an unfamiliar city environment to attend high school that took up an entire building rather than a one-room country schoolhouse.

James retreated from his shy prairie roots into subjects ideally suited to his naturally inquisitive mind. The Sciences claimed him early.

He and I became closer as chemistry, physics, and history led him seamlessly into 'classical studies' – the enticing siren call that introduced both of us to the Roman world of lost coins and the irresistible romance of ancient Egypt.

Inadvertently, as a sensitive introvert, James picked up on my love of digging for treasure in Portmatilloch. He progressed in a straight line towards the love of his academic life, archaeology, where I became the delighted recipient of his glory years exploring Egypt, known to me as the ancient land of Khem.

Despite the loving rowdiness of a large working family, James endured a lonely childhood. I remember, most fondly: huge meals and warm fires and fiddle music and brother-talk, and women bustling in domestic servitude, while we lay on the floor out of the high traffic zones monopolized by the womenfolk.

James always clung frantically to his sheepdog, hoping no one would remember, as the hour grew late, that Buster was an outside dog rain or shine.

My human host was a born worrier. His fretting kept planes in the air and later, as an Egyptologist, tomb shafts from collapsing. Contrary to the spiritual norms of my experience, James's practice of meditation in later years only intensified his determination to believe the worst.

In retrospect, I was as much James's student as his guiding light. And as such, I can state unequivocally, that only an extremely focused man can live sixty-four years as an iconic heartthrob and remain single.

James's career-driven lifestyle was increasingly the perfect foil for wriggling out of the few close encounters he had with women who stalked him through the halls of academia as devoted secretaries and starry-eyed grad students.

The species I dubbed 'matrimonium succubae' pursued PhD's of any description, but when it came to James, a dead ringer for the tall softspoken movie hero, Gregory Peck, hunting took on the focused pursuit of a hungry predator.

Owing to the awe in which they held him, secretaries stayed late, and his female students arrived early, openly competing for attention showing more enthusiasm than lectures about musty plundered tombs could reasonably inspire.

James worked through countless traditional holidays, not significantly lonelier than the rest of the year.

Regular loneliness awarded him solitude. Surrounding himself with fine books and bachelor gourmet take-out that distanced him from the obligatory awkwardness of small talk and social etiquette. I was in complete agreement. It gave me more time to search the ether for Violet.

James loved his siblings' offspring when they were young and was grateful for the open invitation to join family celebrations. But it was obvious to me that without these forced cheery events, he may never have had any interaction with children at all.

Although my man James was always included in his extended family's plans, I was privy to his overwhelming feelings of melancholy afterwards, keenly aware of his suppressed need for emotional connection.

James few encounters with women hinted at closeness, promised sunny futures, but led to crushed expectations.

He occasionally dated the 'lookers' that cornered him, until they got hooked with a distant look in their eyes shopping for white dresses. He was indifferent; they left, shattered in emotional shock. If that was love, he wanted no part of it.

I had no argument with such a conclusion and stayed silent, happily indulging in my ongoing fantasies of reuniting with Violet. In my heart, the two of us wandered in a happy place in a dream of Portmatilloch, in denial of the real world.

Unexpectedly, James's early retirement intensified his longing for an intimate relationship.

And then, in 1984, when James turned thirty-one, the BBC television documentary 'Ancient Lives' confirmed a calling I knew all too well.

18

TEACHER'S PET

"Beyond a wholesome discipline,
be gentle with yourself."
MAX EHRMANN

- SAM -
(a soul-searching end-of-term report card)

As James's assigned soul I was also his 'home room teacher'.

And during his euphemistically called 'salad years', I set him many tasks including several examination papers. Academically James was an honor student but when I graded his social skills on a curve, he never scored above B-minus.

The plain truth was that James was a natural blue-eyed charmer, so he never had to *try* being charming. The lanky boy-James grew into the appearance of a sophisticated man, but it was all genes. His lean muscular body toned from prolonged tangos with nature, made him distinguished rather than aged.

He resembled a store mannequin with ideal proportions. His clothes draped seductively without effort.

Surprisingly, he was indifferent regarding his masculine powers of attraction. And whenever he caught the whiff of his desirability, he was embarrassed enough to slip away to the shadows and hide in a textbook.

He deliberately ignored liaisons with puzzling charmers, vaguely aware of their biological ticking clocks and parallel dreams that he could never meet, but sadly, equally ignorant of his devastating effect on their psyches.

Farm girls had been less stressful to hang out with as chums, but his head was turned by popular prom queens. His awkwardness from unfamiliar city ways meant he was out of their league. And by the time he realized his mistake, that he was a highly coveted target for their flirtations, he'd succumbed to a chronic shyness from which he never fully recovered.

Precocious women cornered him so often, blatantly asking him out, that he formed the notion that all female participants in the mating game were cunning predators forming three categories: shallow cheerleaders, greedy Golddiggers, or potential earthmothers, all of whom sacrificed their self-respect by catering to his every whim, wanting something he didn't have to give.

James was born a sensitive *Old*-Age guy. His brief collision with New-Age psychobabble claiming soul mates were destined to reincarnate forever, mocked science and his intelligence.

He compressed his lacklustre mating instincts into regular intervals between work permits. He remained aloof, never flattering the opposite sex with more than gratuitous courtesy, which looked an awful lot like romantic advances and was invariably mistaken for adoration.

No wonder I'd been assigned to James. Polishing a rough diamond into a dazzling jewel of a husband required divine intervention.

Consequently, as a B-minus dropout, James wisely tuned out, and redoubled his focus on anthropology, the positive study of human evolution.

Even so, a gentle spiritual flirtation with Buddhism settled in his subconscious as the faint memory of a program he'd once heard after falling asleep in front of the T.V.

19

HOME JAMES

"Strive to be happy"
MAX EHRMANN

- SAM -

No one knew better than I, that James's body was programmed to sleep on borrowed time. For years his schedule of field archaeology had been travel-jammed with workdays aligned to the Egyptian sun, where time was measured in optimum periods of seasonal weather for tomb digging. James used every second of official permit-time forfeiting sleep for the possibility of discovery.

Tonight, the television lay silent behind the doors of an imposing armoire whimsically decorated with papyrus flowers and Egyptian hieroglyphs reflecting the latest French fad – a breathless romance with the Sphinx, the Great Pyramid, and fabulous buried treasure.

A glint of gold winked from the eye of one of its brass lions-head handles. Next to it, a large conference table with carved lion legs served as a desk and dominated the large room stealing the corner that regularly caught the four o'clock sunbeams lingering over precarious stacks of paper and oversized books.

Atop each pile was a paperweight of singular beauty: a carved obsidian scarab that I purposely moved like a gaming piece while James slept to train him to pay more attention to his surroundings, a silver statue of the winged lion of Venice, a bronze sphinx, a brass lion doorknocker, and several sculptured fragments of ancient columns.

Lions protected James's domain. A pair of Florentine

'Marzocco' lions each resting a raised paw on a globe, stood sentry either side of the terrace doors.

A white statue of the 'Nike of Samothrace' placed on the mantelpiece overlooking the scene would have approved if she had a head, but she was an exact replica of the original which had been sabotaged in antiquity. Her broken form had become a symbol for Hellenistic art, so much so, that should her head be found, scholars would likely hide it away in deference to her modern state. Her wings were poised for flight as James had always been. A forever 'coming or going suitcase' lay pushed into the shadows, packed and ready beside a Marzocco lion.

It was a timeless honey-amber room, and apart from the accumulated paraphernalia of scholarship, the room displayed an exquisite suite of aged chocolate leather mellowed to perfection.

Just now it was painted with copper highlights by the setting sun's last glorious rays spilling through the French doors to reach James's second floor apartment. He had deliberately chosen to live in a renovated mansion over a minimalist glass and steel building. He resonated with the past enough to relish polished wood and ambiance of creaking stairs.

A PLAGUE ON OUR HOUSE
the book of Suffering

20

BREAKING NEWS

*"Nurture strength of spirit
to shield you in sudden misfortune."*
MAX EHRMANN

- VIOLET -

Despite our difficulties, I reluctantly admired Daisy Sinclair from afar. Like me she had no humble opinions. At first, we hadn't fought so much as bickered.

But before her fever broke, there was much work to do. Some days we were almost civil. It was a revelation to me that Daisy was more surprised at our meeting than I was.

Invisible hands pushed us in the name of transcendental evolution. And after a few false tugs-of-war starts, Daisy nearly surrendered. I rallied sensing victory; she dallied sensing defeat, until eventually, our game of three-dimensional chess stalemated with extended winter closing in for the long haul.

Daisy's game of life continued to play out as an endless obstacle course of snakes and ladders that stretched to infinity.

I had the advantage that her 'Boomerang Love' phase a.k.a. serial fictional monogamy, incidentally, the perfect metaphor for playing hard to get all her life, had reduced Daisy to a limp puppet with too many strings. She was a bit of a pushover. A pair of magic scissors would free us both, but our game of hide-and-seek had to end. What was left of me didn't care much.

My only chance for survival lay in navigating the whole board. I took control when Daisy slept and whispered *'sweet everythings'* in her ear when she was semi-conscious. Much later, I especially enjoyed inspiring her credit card spending sprees.

I wrestled with traditionally inflexible soul dynamics knowing that even grandmasters can land on slippery snakes and the swiftest boomerangs often lose their will to fly.

Reincarnation had unceremoniously advanced me from seventeen to old age in a single heartbeat. Considering the universe played fair, what was I to make of such a horrendous mistake.

I had no recollection of volunteering for hospice duty and there was no explanation for such a catastrophic detour on the high road to finding Sam. Nevertheless, I congratulated myself that I'd been savvy enough to bring my enlightenment with me for what threatened to be a roller coaster ride ahead.

But it was pointless to deny the facts. My new body was sixty-eight years old, and my newborn bad temper had unwittingly awakened my ego, now determined to dethrone me. The me-of-me was headed down the slippery slope towards Daisy's comatose days.

Don't get me wrong. I grew to accept Daisy. She was my star pupil. I just loved Sam more.

21

THE DAISYCHAIN EFFECT

"And so it goes, tiddely pom
The more it snows, tiddely pom
The more it goes, tiddely pom, on snowing."
A.A. MILNE — FROM 'HOUSE AT POOH CORNER'

- VIOLET –

As our day of reckoning drew closer, I discreetly observed the 'potential Daisy', respectfully retreating out of sight and mind and even showed willing by agreeing to attend a tutorial with Celeste, her departing soul, to bring myself up to speed. It was sink or swim. In hindsight it was a brave mix of both.

Celeste materialized as a sphere of light and introduced me to Daisy as an embryo experiencing jolts of hateful neural shocks while still in utero. The toxic maternal thoughts of Lily, Daisy's mother, had sent Daisy's embryo into spasms of adrenalin spikes.

Daisy flinched, curled tighter into a ball for self protection, her heart thumping out of control.

Inflamed blue veins pulsated erratically under her transparent skin. Such a relentless battering of soul-destroying cruelty took its toll for nine months. After a traumatic breach birth, Lily's disgust turned vicious. It was no wonder Daisy required a fresh soul. Sixty-eight years of unrelenting child abuse had taken their toll.

I turned away, sickened. I could do nothing to change the past.

"On a clear day one can dream forever," Celeste said. *"You were lucky enough to be conceived in love."*

I returned her gratuitous insight with flippancy. "Love has

nothing to do with luck," I said. "Love begets love. If I ever had knowledge of my father, I've forgotten it."

"Sometimes, karma must make things worse to create a balance," Celeste said clearly miffed. *"Time always enters into it. You owe it to Sam to watch and learn from Lily's mistakes."*

"Are you threatening me?"

"How could a soul such as me possibly threaten the likes of a master soul!"

"Have we met? You look familiar but I don't remember when."

"I'm sure it will come to you at the right time. Please pay attention. I can't stay much longer. But you need to see this!"

Lily Price, Daisy's teenage mother, lay soulless, huddled in the center of an unmade bed, hugging her knees, curled in the pose of an unborn child, sobbing her heart out.

Several empty pill bottles were arrayed in a perfect row on her bedside table. Lily had formed a meticulous blue grid from their contents. It was clear she was about to take her own life.

Lily's demon arrived as a deeply offensive odor accompanied by an oppressively scorching wind and the sound of crackling of flames. It hissed at us from the ceiling and sprinkled us with ash.

Celeste hovered over Lily in the guise of a winged moon, waxing and waning, biding her time. She acknowledged my presence with a nod and gestured with a finger over her lips for me to remain silent.

I caught the echo of a familiar love song *"I know not how I'll sink or swim,"* and waited.

Lily let out the deep growl of an injured animal and howled. "My life is ruined. I CAN'T do this! I WON'T! I hate this thing inside me. I'll kill us both!"

Daisy flinched.

Celeste glared up at Lily's demon daring a response.

The demon accepted the silent challenge and swooped to attack as a cloud of smoke and ash. But Celeste's silvery breath rendered it harmless by forming a sticky cocoon around it. *"You already have, Lily,"* she whispered in Lily's ear. *"Death can occur long before it takes place, even before birth itself. The power of intense grief can 'survive' several generations."*

Lily reached for the nearest pill but suddenly jerked her hand away as if burned.

She raised herself and sat cross-legged staring at them as if the pills would swallow *her* and swept them to the floor. "I HATE my life," she shrieked. "I wish I were DEAD!"

Dropped pills bounced on the wood floor like raindrops. Daisy trembled in fear.

Celeste loomed full for an instant and blinked out before resuming her spherical shape. *"Dearest girl,"* she warned, Lily. *"Be careful. A death-wish lasts forever."*

Celeste coughed slightly and addressed me from behind the sun, eclipsing the pitiful scene of maternal misery recently played out against my struggling mission of mercy.

The scene dissolved, shifting to a vision of Daisy, a gloomy teenager, staring with obvious contempt through pill-shaped raindrops on a cold windowpane. She traced a heart in the mist and erased it savagely with a swipe of her hand.

Her impulsive gesture aggravated me in a way I hadn't expected. I came to know the feeling of rage that dangerously precedes physical violence. I needed to get away from her, fast.

"Daisy is an unworthy recipient of my higher vibration of consciousness," I spat at her moony ex-soul.

"Suit yourself," Celeste replied. *"I suppose you think you have all the time in the world at your beck and call. Did you know, by the way, your ego is a nasty little snob?"*

I felt compelled to set my record straight by demanding the universe detach my impeccable credentials from Daisy's pathetic excuse of a life. I expressly used the word forthwith. A word I would never have used had I been centered.

"Daisy is emptyheaded," I shouted. "Literally, brain dead according to her doctors. All too spineless for me to bother with."

Celeste's eyes widened. "I know you didn't mean to come across so heartless considering your" *she coughed,* "mighty status. So, by the same token perhaps I should be calling you meanspirited. Her mother, Lily …"

"Ahh, the lovely Lily. Perhaps it's more appropriate to say Daisy is *Lily-livered* rather than spineless. Whatever the case, Daisy is an old dear void of energy. Her continuance is pointless."

Celeste would have flapped her wings if she'd had them. "By any other name, void of energy means spiritless," she sneered. "And I predict a time is soon coming when you will eat those words."

The quality of the light shifted around me. I found myself sitting zazen on a beach. My shoulders relaxed as a deep humming sound levitated me from the sand.

Against my will, I felt a twinge of compassion for Daisy's painfully slow climb from a pit of inherited suffering. The laws of karma were clearly in play, and as such, had to play out in millions of unrehearsed moves on a gaming board of a trillion squares.

Daisy had entered a loveless world expected but unwanted. Not one for endearments, Lily referred to her as 'The Princess' in such a manner it was clear she despised princesses.

To cope, Daisy made herself as small as possible by joining cat world, hiding out under beds and tables.

I watched her, a fragile child of four, brave pouring rain to run away from home with her beloved cat, Lucky, her 'Beauty' book, four shillings, and an umbrella, determined to hide until her parents' ship sailed without her, resolved to stay with her only non-feline source of affection, a new paternal grandmother.

But it was being forced to leave Lucky behind that sealed Daisy's war with parental oppression. It was the beginning of independent rule without the tools to cut her way through a jungle of despair.

In 'high' school (*an ironic misdirection in terms*) Daisy majored in 'Wallflower 101' for three years, advancing her to the status of *professional* Wallflower.

Secret crushes confirmed she was romantically cursed, and well out of the social loop with one notable exception. She was talent spotted as an artist with a future career in graphic design.

Serendipitously, a small, unexpected, legacy arrived.

Daisy's parents were over the moon to be well shod of a daughter they best described as a morose wet blanket.

Prospects for Daisy's success were no longer gloomy, considering they were placed under the stewardship of one Phillip Moon, a spritely instructor in human form, deliberately appointed by a source I dimly recognized as universal intervention.

As it turned out, I was completely wrong. He was a spiritual injection of energetic creativity from the Goddess Flora.

Mr. Moon, an aging dynamo, famous for taking tea with seven spoons of sugar, buzzed about the classroom in a teaching frenzy with Daisy towed close under his wing.

So, Daisy had had a distant helper who strategically sweetened her days. And while connected, I learned there was one other greater gift to come.

The new option to attend art college in Daisy's beloved 'old country' that Mr. and Mrs. Sinclair could now afford, played out in real time. A significantly opportune time due to the significant presence of Mr. P.V. Moon, who impressed Daisy with his impeccable drawings and his tweed jacket with leather patches on the elbows. The poetic lyrics reflected in a popular song were ringing true. *'The times, they were definitely a-changin'*

Daisy shed her body. She kicked it aside with contempt and walked away light as air. I caught a brief whiff of lotus incense and a split-second vision of an Egyptian soul found wanting after being weighed against a feather.

"And that's when all hell broke lose," the returned Celeste said. There was a shrug in her voice. *"New humans can be insanely selfish from the off. My hands were tied. But rules are rules. Passes and failures count on the final exam."*

I got snotty to win a point. "Romantic love is the ultimate mental breakdown of human wisdom," I said.

"If you say so," came Celeste's unconvincing reply.

To be perverse, my priorities never waivered. Somehow, I knew my energy would eventually draw Sam to Daisy. I would do my duty, see Daisy safely through her inevitable death from old age, and meet Sam on the other side, free as a bird.

And so, not long after I arrived in 2020, my youthful energy spiked Daisy Sinclair's miraculous recovery and Saint 'M' whispered in my ear. "Within the year a stranger will call Daisy from out of the blue. Sam will be at his side."

22

CELESTIAL VISIONS

*"Nurture strength of spirit
to shield you in sudden misfortune."*
MAX EHRMANN

- VIOLET -

I had sixty-eight years of catching up to digest if I was ever going to find out why I was in hell. I couldn't reconcile such punishment, nor could I easily dismiss Daisy's relentless decades of self pity. Her bad memories flooded my brain. I was furious.

This woman *wanted* to die; *I* wanted her to die!

But to grant both our wishes I had to subject myself to Daisy's endless bouts of despair, resolved to listen and watch every thought and detail of her wretched past to find an escape hatch. Daisy wasn't worth the effort, but I *would* do it for Sam.

I became the impatient student of 'a life in retrospect'. Even had I wanted to, I was unable to change the past. Sadly, observing the average human life is a tragic spectator sport.

Together, Daisy's moon maiden and I watched Daisy confidently swan forward into art college, take a dive into a detour with a frightful marital bully, and miraculously experience a brief excursion in an exquisite garden of light.

Accordingly, we rose above her to see a vision of primeval forest and a beach with a spiral of stones marking a maze. I recognized the Scottish eco-community of Findhorn laid out below – an unfolded map of the New-Age showing an abandoned air force runway like a concrete river winding through the rare atmosphere that smelled of flowers and love.

Souls drifted below with imaginary diaphanous wings forming and reforming on their shoulders. Clouds of lavender-colored energy clustered around each majestic tree and exquisite flower.

Ethereal fawns and unicorns looked at home prancing through the forest, but they were, in essence, fanciful projections playing through the minds of the residents.

But as enchanted as they were, Daisy's childhood fairy tales sadly eclipsed Findhorn's genuine mystical vibrations.

But I have raced ahead of Daisy's timeline eager to be well-rid of her. I am obliged to backtrack.

Daisy's fading moonbeam of a soul and I retreated to a significant jumping off point where three happy years of art college were drawing to a close.

Daisy hung her paintings for her final grade.

Behind her loomed a telltale pile of unopened letters from Ms. Lily Sinclair. The telegram on top fairly levitated with dark orders, and in panic mode to counter the parental threat, Daisy grabbed an even darker solution that presented itself out of leftfield – that ominous direction where suffering enters the world disguised as perfect timing. The classic fairy tale of a 'red shoes' trap was sprung.

The demonic art of seduction in all its mischievous alchemy possessed Daisy as surely as a killer virus. It would seem, setting love and happiness aside, a determined creative girl could avoid going home by dating her way to a wedding ring and the perks that come with residential status.

Daisy plunged herself into an Eliza Doolittle makeover to wangle her way into the winner's circle – performing as a common garden daisy in the guise of a hothouse orchid wearing the trendy fashions of a Carnaby Street cover girl.

Thus, unprepared, Daisy headed to the Scottish Highlands to wed a stranger after a whirlwind flirtation on a dating site where the high-speed internet inevitably degenerates to the lowest vibrations of human depravity.

Daisy was essentially homeless, an uneasy creature – a wallflower without walls, a paper doll wife, alone in a strange country, the remainder of her college fund signed over to a man who made her skin crawl.

It took three hellish years until a chance walk in the moonlight delivered Findhorn to her door.

- 23 -

SANCTUARY

"With all its broken dreams, it is still a beautiful world"
MAX EHRMANN

- VIOLET -

Back in the hospital, I made my own leftfield mistake.

The thought occurred to me that when Daisy's life monitors neared flatline levels I had a window of opportunity to safely test the waters inside Daisy's body. What was it like? Could I communicate my mission more effectively from within? She was certainly not cooperating when semi-conscious. Our ongoing debate had stalemated, and truth be told, I would rather move on to my own next life as soon as possible.

I hadn't reckoned my energy would jumpstart a powerful chain reaction of intense aggressive behavior. All mine!

Daisy remained comatose but entered REM sleep that violently ejected me out of her body and slammed me across the room. Apparently, she had an invisible bodyguard to defend against intruder attacks. Ironically, her body recognized me less as a rescuer and more as a variant of the Covid 19 virus.

I tried again the next day. Daisy's comatose body startled from the sudden exclamation of joy that escaped me when the grey landscape of Daisy's dark night of the soul burst into a magic garden where elemental nature spirits frolicked through acres of flowers.

At first, I thought it was an hallucination brought on by the sixties, but it was not so. I'd forgotten Daisy's transcendental

94

experiences in the mystical garden of Findhorn. Daisy had been swept away on a heady spiritual trip where swinging London collided with the New-Age movement, curtesy of Dylan's 'changin' times.

When the marital ground stopped shaking from yet another scathing lecture on the domestic rules of servitude, Daisy called "I'm off out for a walk," over her shoulder to her spouse bully in as neutral a tone she could fake.

She strode from the marital cottage at a normal pace but once out of sight, she ran in slow motion down the winding track to the cliffs overlooking the Moray Firth.

Quite by *calculated chance*, Daisy's suicidal intentions were eclipsed by a display of lights in the sky traveling in a V-shaped formation. A flock of geese turned into a squadron of airplanes flying low to simulate combat in a deafening roar.

An unearthly voice shouted, *"life after death!"* so clearly, Daisy forgot to be afraid. *"Drive south,"* it said. *"Drive slow. Watch for the rabbits on the road. A rabbit will set you free."*

Daisy turned back to the cottage and drove towards Inverness in an altered state, thrilled to have heard the voice of a ghost that had made no pretense of ordering her to save her soul.

At Beauly, Daisy pulled over at a public house for the restroom, passing under the swinging sign 'The Enchanted Hare' that promised a bed for the night.

The barmaid was chatty. And in the lull of her blathering, the sound of low flying planes roared overhead. The woman checked the clock. "Aye, they're allus on time, that lot. We set our clocks by em, so we do."

Point made; the barmaid dutifully pulled a dog-eared road map from beneath the counter she shared with every lost traveler. She traced a small triangle over the map with her finger.

"Now see here," she prodded the paper. "That's us." She stabbed the paper again. "And that's the air force base, Kinloss. "

Her voice took on a storyteller's tone with her final, "And THAT… that is Findhorn. Fourteen miles across the Moray Firth if you've a wee boat. I have a friend who lives there. It's worth a visit if you've a mind for miracles."

The barmaid's voice sounded from far away as if underwater. She proceeded to tell a tale Daisy knew by heart: the fairy tale adventure of Findhorn's founding members and their miraculous experiment with universal intelligence that had caused a stir when a televised documentary touched a nerve with the rising New-Age consciousness.

"If yez were a wee crow it would be 14 miles," the barmaid continued. "Of course, by car it's nearer seventy." She nodded sagely and wagged her index finger. "Mind now, our highland roads tend to take the scenic routes. So, ye'll be stopping fer the sheep of course, and some roads are that narrow they require laybys for oncoming traffic. So, watch yourself."

Daisy resumed her trip the following morning, arriving in high spirits, surrendered to the universe, and stayed ten years.

In retrospect, give or take, her journey took ten years, four hours, or a dozen lifetimes, depending on one's perspective.

The Findhorn foundation, Daisy's spiritual beacon during art school was an express freeway to her New-Age dreams – a remote Scottish eco-village community, where one was welcomed into the finer arts of inspired imagination.

Daisy freely explored the organic side of spirituality as well as delving into the fanciful side of sane psychic phenomena.

I likened it to a hybrid pre-hippy movement – a benevolent international retreat, diversified by equal quantities of innocent hocus pocus and sound ecological principles merging into a narrow scientific bandwidth. It had blossomed into a residential sanctuary where kindred spirits sharing idyllic intentions championed the trinity of ecological peace, compassionate scientific evidence, and paranormal experience into a family of universal empathy.

Findhorn was and remains a sacred Scottish locale honoring the highest good that actively celebrates a mindful healing center for alternate therapies, and a magnet for guru workshops with intensive programs for opening the heart and engaging the soul.

When Daisy's financial realities opened a can of worms with teeth, it wasn't expected. At least, I saw it coming due to my privileged soul's eye view. Daisy had been born under the proverbial 'bad star', the 'soul' bearer of truly toxic karma, thanks to Lily Price passing a contaminated baton to her hapless daughter.

To make it worse, Daisy's rented fairy godmother waved the universe's tainted magic wand of choice over a sleeping beauty. Daisy wore her rose-tinted Findhorn glasses to the ball.

With a flush of embarrassment, I realized I was guilty of the same affliction of nearsighted insight. The universe's creed of being cruel to be kind was a dirty whitewashed lie!

In her enthusiasm, filtered through rose-colored glasses, Daisy returned to Canada but failed to grieve the death of her best Findhorn life.

As to my earlier run-in with Daisy's bodyguard, I concluded later; I was in fact a literal antibody. As such, I gained new respect for Daisy's natural survival response which inadvertently led me to search my memory banks and review my last hour as Violet Seaborn fighting a vicious plague with attitude.

It was then I was stunned to discover that I had given the Spanish flu virus permission to take me!

24

THE POINT OF NO RETURN

"Out, out, brief candle!
Life's but a walking shadow, a poor player,
That struts and frets his hour upon the stage,
And then is heard no more."
WILLIAM SHAKESPEARE

- CELESTE -
(time out for questionable behavior)

There had been early Nova Scotia days when Daisy blossomed but sometimes on 'New-Scotland' days she fell back, a weed pruned out of all recognition.

For a time, Daisy fooled herself as the poster child of a renaissance woman living off an endorphin high.

She was proud of moving heaven and earth balancing parallel Scotlands, but the energy Daisy expended to 'hold it all together' pulled her apart. Writing a diary was the watery glue that temporarily pasted them back together.

Daisy's writing was barely legible from the succubus therapist that took possession of her writing hand. She concentrated on death, withering from the outside in, passing me, her bookmarker soul clawing towards the light on my way out.

Romance as conceived within the old courts of royal privilege were love poems scratched on thick creamy parchment, delivered by servants known as 'pages' – gushing torrid messages fanned smoldering body heat to inflamed passions, evolving into the hot mail of today's virtual lovers.

For a time, fictional fantasies run amok on human chemicals awarded Daisy momentary distractions of pleasure/pain, no more joyous than feeling calm for a day was everlasting peace.

For the most part, Daisy sweltered in her attic bedroom, visited by frantic dreams, and woke gasping for air several times a night.

The top floor held summer light all year round and remained cozy from electric fires when it rained for days on end, or when the oil-fuelled radiators pumped forth belching heat on snowy blowy days. But on the more numerous, flat, flavourless days, Daisy lounged on a balcony against cushions listlessly clutching her Beauty Book while an incessant symphony of insect-droning lawnmowers played in the background.

Daisy had her empty house on a hill, serenaded by maniacal crow laughter squawking curses. But to shift depression, she first had to physically move her body.

For a short time, Daisy seemed to make steady progress, but her anxiety levels spiked from too many years of playing dead, meant her advanced state of self-loathing returned. And when Daisy's ability to feel anything remotely cheerful rapidly evaporated, leaving her in the predicament where bad temper was about to commit a crime. She snapped at loose ends – a housebound spinster shrew. She watched the Covid 19 virus approach and closed her eyes waiting for impact, wanting nothing more than to disappear from the world. And then, she did. And this is where you come in, Violet. If you know what's good for you, you'd best clean up your act.

25

THE TRUTH DAWNS

"In the middle
of the journey of our life
I found myself
within dark woods
where the straight way
was lost."
DANTE ALIGHIERI

- VIOLET -

When the moment arrived to join body and soul to Daisy, I defaulted to a spoiled child deprived of sugar. I watched from the sidelines unimpressed and entitled.

Celeste gasped and popped like a surprised balloon. Her warning *'passes and failures count on the final exam'* played like a cluster headache. I screamed obscenities at Celeste which achieved nothing. It amused her to see me suffer.

I stood by, out of body, watching my seventeen-year-old self stamp her foot. "I'm not going in there. It's not fair!" she screamed. And in all honesty, I couldn't defend her violent reaction without lying.

I sided with my right to a life with Sam. If all was fair in love and death, who I haunted was my business and Daisy's bad luck.

Did I have a choice to help Daisy? No. Never would be soon enough. Sam hadn't deserted me, the universe had. It was war!

So, when I pretended to retreat in favor of Daisy using my soul's not inconsiderable energies and hard-won spiritual maturity, I wondered what her old moony soul made of being displaced by a cunning teenager.

I needn't have concerned myself. The moon maiden had waned into a hairline crescent that fair beamed with joy. *"I'm positively thrilled to death,"* she assured me. Celeste tipped sideways as a princess might dip in a fine curtsey, thanked me profusely for helping her escape and rose into the night sky to what I supposed was her next assignment.

Half moon or full, it was all the same to me. The Moon I knew was a loving mother – an unceasing source of protection and wisdom.

I'd been raised on moon magic. Evie had taught me there never was nor ever would be a man-in-the-moon who ruled fate. Destinies written in the stars were watched over by Lady Luck.

I counted what lucky stars I had left and later, took great pleasure watching as my memories of Sam clouded Daisy's newfound peace of mind as a spiritual master.

I couldn't recollect a formal request to enter Violet's body, but I must have done so. No such takeover would have been possible or cosmically legal had I not of my own free will consented to the events that now leave me on the inside looking out.

I had no intention to stop searching for Sam. I proposed, if nothing else, to use Daisy's stolen higher vibrations to find him.

And then Sam sent me an image of himself grown into an old man named James, Daisy's estranged earth mate, and I felt chastened, briefly obliged to wait in the wings and not cause any further trouble.

If nothing else, Evie had taught me the value of patience. Somehow, somewhere, some *'when'*, Sam and I would have a second chance. Such is the benefit of having second sight.

I trusted the new Sam to keep his old promise.

It was then, he spoke clearly in my head. *"Silly goose. We've always known how to meet in dreams. This is no less true now. I may be James Eriksen but I'm still Sam Watts. I adored you once for your sweet soul and now it's my delight to co-create a future with you at the universe's pleasure.*

Time is not the same for us who float free. We are 'old' souls, you and I, and for a while we will simply be 'old' bodies.

Celebrate what-is, Violet, for it is through unselfish service to Daisy Sinclair and James Eriksen that you and I will win eternity.

Evie used to say there were rewards in heaven – a slightly convoluted take on the whole truth I admit, but near enough to be a cause for divine trust. In the meantime, we are free to work with Daisy and James as partners. As equals. As friends.

Like us, they've been searching for each other for several lifetimes. We have the great privilege of serving them. You and I were never thrown together by chance. We have been travelling towards each other for eons. A few more years won't matter. Regardless of how it may appear, our souls are incorruptible. I am your Sam, now and always. Wait and watch. Be compassionate. Daisy deserves your boundless spirit. It is safe in her hands. As safe in her heart as you are in mine."

I should have taken his advice to heart, but my decisions weren't entirely my own.

A NEW WORLD ORDER
the book of Daisy

26

FIRST LIGHT

"And from this slumber you shall wake,
when true love's kiss, the spell shall break."
'SLEEPING BEAUTY'

- VIOLET -

Daisy's wakeup call'ing dawned fairy-tale perfect on a dark day. I woke her like Prince Charming, with a 'kiss' of life by stepping into her body and locking the door after me.

I hadn't expected the initial sensation of drowning in love inside an old woman's body, confronted by the breathtaking scope of a brilliant new world.

If this dazzling white hospital room was to be the new norm, Daisy would need state-of-the-art sunglasses to navigate it safely.

There existed no clear delineation between crisp clean shapes or the wobbly shapes between them.

Five heightened senses made me sneeze and blink, along with a sixth that knew how the universe came to be and where it was going.

Daisy became a human kaleidoscope. Together we felt the sharp contrasts of dark against light and saw heat emanating from animated edges glowing hot and cold.

Colors and textures shimmered to life still vibrating into form.

I took stock of stillborn air in need of an open window and a hissing facemask flung to the floor. The steady drumbeat of liquid medicine dripping into the clear pocket suspended over Daisy's, and now *my* head, sounded like the ticking of a clock, marking seconds resounding like rifle shots. Golden energy flowed into a vein in the back of *my* hand.

The sudden urge to sneeze from antiseptic and bleach made my eyes water, but a serenade of crystalline birdsong cleared my head.

A delicious sense of wholeness radiated from my solar plexus as a resonate humming from toe to head. Reincarnated bones, and pumping blood filled my arms and legs.

I tasted bitter metal on my tongue, but it was not my tongue or limbs or flesh. It was the woman, now smiling in her sleep whose flickering eyelids heralded a return to consciousness.

I relaxed in the seat of Daisy's soul faced with a vicarious chance to savor her life as my own. Not as fun as it seemed.

It was out of character to think I had almost exited from an open door that manifested in Daisy's hospital room, but much to my surprise, I couldn't budge, frozen as I was in a love/hate matrix.

After I settled in further than I intended to, I retreated into my thoughts while Daisy slept, to understand why Lila had selected me for a mission any soul in-waiting could have done. Instead, she'd chosen to insult me by denying me a gentle rebirth. Why?

At no small cost to my comfort, what I experienced was a one-way ticket to an old folk's home that had pushed me off course, when my soul spontaneously skyrocketed to Daisy's aid without saying goodbye to Sam. Lila was inconceivably bad mannered.

I admit to being sorely used. If nothing else, my misadventure with an umbilical cord in 1901 should have earned me the karmic right to be reborn a gurgling infant in a safe environment.

And then, Daisy woke up happy and all heaven broke loose!

Even so, I didn't completely surrender. It was me inside her that aggravated her fluid retention and caused a prolonged bout of serious indigestion.

I remain deeply aware of fighting a nagging gratitude for Daisy's new world view, courtesy of my own unrequited soul.

27

DREAMSPINNER

"The Owl and the Pussycat went to sea
In a beautiful pea-green boat.
They took some honey, and plenty of money,
Wrapped up in a five-pound note.
"O let us be married! too long we have tarried,
But what shall we do for a ring?"

They sailed away, for a year and a day,
To the land where the Bong-Tree grows
And there in a wood a Piggy-wig stood
With a ring at the end of his nose.
"Dear Pig, are you willing to sell for one shilling
Your ring?" said the Piggy, "I will."

So, they took it away, and were married next day
By the Turkey who lived on a hill.
They dined on mince, and slices of quince,
Which they ate with a runcible spoon.
And hand in hand, on the edge of the sand,
They danced by the light of the moon."
'THE OWL AND THE PUSSYCAT' - EDWARD LEAR

- VIOLET -

So, I played a trick. I found a loophole I could use. Something was missing. Even running on my undiluted confiscated joy, Daisy needed a loving companion. But thanks to my spiritual advancement, the hostility I transmitted to her daily was neutralized by her new love of life. That needed to change for both of us, and I knew how.

Guilt compelled me to concoct a dream from the one thing I knew to be true. Daisy had a soft spot for cats.

I sent my creation to Daisy, proud of my ingenuity for earning universal brownie points. At least I thought it was mine. More the fool, me.

While Daisy napped, soaking in her (*my*) best life, I tracked a strong presence of a cat in trouble. Pitiful waves of cold and hunger came from the local garbage dump.

The cat was already looking for me. It opened its mouth in a silent meow, tail up unafraid, and friendly as I approached.

I spoke lovingly and picked it up. It responded in purr.

That night I toyed with Daisy's dreamtime. I sent her images of cats and whispered a dream scenario until it caught fire.

Daisy's natural affiliation for cats was a given, and in her new receptive state, I suggested they were her totem animal. "Be alert," I prophesized. "A cat will bring you a message from your soul." She took the bait.

I laid it on thick. I must have sounded like the ghost of Christmas future. "Daisy," I said. "A cat encounter is shorthand, for you alone, tantamount to a direct message from the universe."

I wanted Daisy to believe in her own power and leave mine alone. What better way than to set up a dream I knew I could make true!

I never imagined for a second, I was dabbling in mind control.

I watched Daisy dreaming from the foot of her bed. It was like being in a movie theatre with me directing the film Daisy was experiencing.

I warmed to the game. It was harmless and if she died of shock, no matter. I would be released. I had a checklist for movie beats and set the opening scene. Roll camera, I thought. Look out, Lila, I'm about to play!

Daisy and a tabby cat travel together in a car. *Check.*

Mission – to attend an unspecified ceremony. *Check.*

The car crosses a rusty bridge. *Check.*

A passing billboard splashes the words: Welcome to the City of Lost Angels. Population desperate. *Check.*

The ceremony turns out to be the cat's graduation from a prestigious art college. *Check.*

Daisy wears the cap and robes of a professor. *Check.*

She passes out diplomas to graduates as they file by. *Check.*

But when Daisy turns to pass a scroll *cum laude* to the cat, it is gone. *Check.*

Anxious to find it, Daisy makes her way back to the car and cruises the streets, but the car becomes enshrouded in a whiteout snowstorm. The car engine dies, leaving Daisy abandoned, freezing in a white box. "Look at your feet," I direct her. "Why are they so warm?"

Daisy glances down to find the lost cat sleeping soundly there, in a gesture of feline protection and devotion.

Before she gets all warm and fuzzy, I send Daisy to a new location, recast from the cat's point of view of cold and fuzzy reality. Daisy-cat is chilled to the bone, lodged in a crawlspace under a large metal container as big as a room.

She takes in a cat's-eye view of a wintry world contaminated with the smell of carbon monoxide, and a slithering noise of something heavy sliding against steel. *Check.*

Scene change: A human Daisy rouses her spirit body and makes her way to the well-appointed kitchen of her cavernous house, where her lady's maid, Bast the Egyptian goddess with the head of a cat, wears a stethoscope shaped like a crucifix. She's boiling water in anticipation of her mistress's needs.

Bast fills a hot water bottle, shepherds Daisy back to bed, transforms into a regulation housecat purring with unrestrained enthusiasm, and takes up residence at the foot of the bed where I sit cross-legged. Daisy-cat settles herself in my lap.

Present time: Daisy-cat wakes, hugging a cold hot-water-bottle. I cruelly remind her of the time barely three months since, when after toying with suicide for over a year, she specifically invited Covid 19 to release her.

That little haunting jab shook her. Daisy sprang from her bed ashamed of revisiting her past.

"It's garbage day," I hinted. "The perfect time to make a profound gesture. Show the universe your stuff. Throw out your metaphorical garbage with the stinky bags of accumulated waste in your rubbish bins. There's a Christmas gift waiting for you at the dump if you hurry."

Daisy's car was as hard as the bricks of meat in her deepfreeze. Her abandoned horsepower was trapped in a glacial ice-age like a green mastodon.

Winter light bruised Daisy's eyes as she adjusted to the outside reality of digging out her vehicle from the ice hills left by snowplows that blocked the end of her driveway.

Hermit snow, better known as virgin snow, meant no footprints had disturbed its surface for over a week but a pre-Christmas thaw had teased the snow into melting before wickedly shapeshifting into a herd of icy misshapen creatures. I distracted her by showing her animal faces in the snow.

Daisy pried open the driver's door first and started the motor which came to life instantly and collected the small garbage bags into one enormous regulation plastic bag to satisfy the local garbage police.

Daisy wound her way down Electric Street to the outskirts of town. Snowplows had made a narrow pass through the deep snow of the route, little used so early in the morning, and it was only eight o-clock when Daisy pulled up to the drop-off point to jettison her load of garbage on the way to buying food.

She'd made a list of her favorites, including chocolate, rollmops, wine gums, and potato chips that made my tummy grumble.

Daisy's regular procedure was to dump and run. She waited by the safety rail for the sound of impact, as the weight of the bag slid down the metal ramp of the dumpster's maw, to hit the accumulated mass in the pit below, and as she skated back towards the car a dark shape caught her eye on the far side of the lot. It sat, ears perked, from beside a smaller dumpster reserved for compost. Daisy's mind read it as 'cat'.

Huddled against the cold steel was my grey tabby, staring in her direction with the desperation only a starving animal can express.

This cat was feral and wary of humans. Daisy called to it expecting no response, fully prepared to walk the distance even if it *was* going to hare off into the woods, but on it came towards her, tail up in the bitter wind, scrawny, thin, and invited her to pet its head. Daisy felt its pitiful skeleton through hardened fur mats and adopted her on the spot.

"Okay, sweetie please don't go anywhere," she ordered. "I will be right back."

Daisy raced to town, bought a used cat carrier in the second-hand store, and scored the last rotisserie chicken in the market, her new pet's first meal which she would share when the carcass was rendered into soup.

The snow, heavier and wilder than before, made her drive faster than she should, skidding down the track now almost lost in the new fall, silently chastising herself for not buying groceries before her trip to the dump. Precious time had been wasted, perhaps compromising her mission of mercy. The cat would be colder now and hungrier and likely gone to ground for shelter beyond her reach for the rest of the day, or even forever. Damned snow!

The lot was bare of cars. Only a trail of smoke from the workers' hut showed evidence of human habitation. Unbelievably, the cat was in the same place and approached without fear as before. This time it carried a white kitten in its mouth.

Daisy took no chances and pushed mother and child into the waiting cage.

The howl of protest that went up was pitiful, but it was only to be expected. Freedom has its price and captivity its fears. After all a cat's instinct is to struggle, being unable, quite rightly, to distinguish between the rescue of human compassionate or attack.

Her name came easily – Sophie after Sophia, the Greek goddess of wisdom, and her kitten, Summer, for the warm life ahead.

Hours later, while Sophie slumbered on a full tummy, Daisy smugly recalled her dream from under the umbrella of a miracle, grateful for her intuition – the only language the soul understands.

I had Daisy where I wanted her, convinced she was plugged in to the unmanifested and that the universe was her willing partner.

I was *almost* jealous. But then, as it became obvious Daisy was growing into her role as a spiritual leader, I realized my days as her prime dream-keeper were numbered. I was outraged. Ironically, beside myself with envy yet oddly proud of being inside Daisy at the same time.

I felt my power drain into her body unable to staunch its flow. Her newfound radiance showed. Daisy had progressed. She was accessing my energy without me. I fell into a funk of feeling mightily sorry for myself.

And then out of the blue came the vision of a Viking waving an axe. I was too weak to protest and watched in horror as Daisy's custom movie degenerated into a Scottish memory, long since buried by someone I used to be but couldn't remember.

I grabbed Sophie and Summer for a healing cuddle. "And what about you two," I asked. "Who did *you* use to be?"

Sophie purred loud as a diesel engine and nuzzled my hand. "I'm your mother, Evie," she replied in cat-speak. Summer is my daughter. I guess that makes her your sister. You may remember her as Sister Veritas. "Goodness, child. You took your time. I thought you'd never come."

28

SOLE IDENTITY

"Speak your truth quietly and clearly;
and listen to others,
they too have their story."
MAX EHRMANN

- VIOLET -

Daisy wasn't vain but she spent a long time studying her face in the bathroom mirror like a scientist. She turned her head from side-to-side checking angles, her thinning grey hairline, and the new swirling patterns in her pupils, thinking, have my eyes changed color?

I looked back unimpressed disinterested in my new-old-face. It wasn't as if we were having a proper staring contest, so, what happened next surprised me. And by surprise, I mean profoundly shocked. Daisy sensed me! "Hello," she said. "Are you still in there?"

I blurted back without skipping a beat. "Of course, you are."

"I know *I* am!" Daisy said, irritation evident. "I'm speaking to *you*. The radiance I see shining under my skin. Who are you?"

For a heartbeat I was flattered. "My name doesn't matter," I said. "I'm sharing your body. We're essentially, pardon the term, *married* for better or worse."

"Obviously you don't want to be in here *with* me."

I took a deep breath. "Well, it was a shotgun wedding!" I shouted deciding to spill a few beans. "It's best we're truthful, Miss Sinclair. I can speak freely knowing you won't remember this discussion because you're in a trance."

I was loath to admit that Daisy and I seem to have exchanged personas. "I am experiencing your past emotional pain and you are experiencing my recent joy of life. Quite frankly, you have the better part of the bargain."

Daisy continued to brush her hair. "Are you depressed?"

"I deserve better than being reduced to a resentful servant girl. I may look like a teenager, ma'am but I have a thousand lifetimes behind me. I worked hard to acquire my enlightened state. After I increased my spiritual vibrations tenfold, I was promised a life with… with someone else."

"What did I ever do to you?" Daisy asked.

"I think I'm here to find out."

"Me too."

I tried a new tack. "You're feeling sleepy," I said.

"Are you trying to hypnotize me?"

"I don't have to. You've already hypnotized yourself. Staring overlong into a mirror will do that. It's not recommended."

"You must hate me."

"I don't hate you… not yet. I *resent* you. I don't need a new best friend. I just need to find the one I had."

"Do you have a name?"

"Not anymore."

And so, our conversation rattled on until Daisy lowered her drawbridge eyes, and I was able to rise several inches above her body. The open door was tempting but pointless. I stayed, unsure where to put myself. Daisy was determined to quiz me and so I allowed her to drag me into a conversation. I lowered back into her body determined to put her, as odd as it sounds, in her place.

Our mind play of duelling images started out like playing a game of snap. Nothing strenuous or competitive. Child's play. But in the end, we advanced to kindergarten chess where an invisible time clock compelled us to 'Q & A' in rapid kneejerk moves.

Daisy's first question startled me. "Who is Sam?"

I played it cool to test both of us. "Who? Can you describe him!"

"Is he here now?"

"He's always here. He's part of me so, he's always inside you. Think of us as nesting sarcophaguses. He and I are twin souls."

For a moment Daisy shared her interest in archaeology and I reminisced about Sam and I finding a Roman brooch. I pictured Sam in the height of discovery until the face of a stranger pushed in.

"I see him too," Daisy said. "He's with Sam. Who is he?"

I answered unruffled. In her dream state, Daisy had things to share I needed to know. "A third sarcophagus?" I suggested.

A sudden smile took years off Daisy's sleeping face as if she knew the stranger. "It seems so. I expect we'll know soon enough."

Daisy was using my superior powers of reasoning. I'd have to watch my step and pay attention. I sent her a random shuffle of mental snapshots. But she changed horses in midstream and soon she was sending, I was receiving, and we were deep in a multiple-choice exam.

Daisy stretched her arms wide. Moving them like wings. "I'm floating in a foaming bubble bath," she said clearly delighted.

I recognized it immediately. "That's the North Sea."

"I see a girl holding my 'Beauty book'. She opens it to show me, but the pages are blank. The illustrations are gone."

"The girl is me. An open book represents honesty – a true story. The blank pages are your new unwritten life."

"Now, I'm back in the hospital. The halls are filled with nurses walking in single file like a parade. They're wearing black floor-length hospital gowns and stethoscopes around their necks shaped like crucifixes. They are sightless. Dazed. They have empty eye sockets."

"The nurses are the sisters of Immaculate Deception from the convent where I lived. They paraded as a matter of course. Dazed describes living-dead zombies. Sightless attests to being blind to reality."

"I hear hoofbeats. A pair of armored knights approach me on horseback. One rides a black stallion, the other a white mare."

"A dark horse is a deep secret. A white horse always carries a lover."

Daisy relaxed into her movie. "A beautiful fairy godmother is waving a wand over the sea."

"The fairy woman is the Goddess Flora casting a spell to dispel the virus that ravaged my homeland. Its twin ravaged yours."

"I'm in a grove of sacred trees where many people have left tokens in the branches for the fairy folk in exchange for help."

"Fairy assistance is the lesser reality of celebrating yourself."

Daisy laughed out loud. "Wow. Now I'm water skiing behind a powerboat. We're going so fast it's like flying. The boat is telling me not to be afraid. But I can't swim."

"You're traveling through time by way of a powerful water sylph who will never harm you."

Daisy's brows furrowed. "Now, I *am* afraid. I'm out of my depth floating in a corridor of rushing water. There's debris all around me."

"The corridor is your birth canal. The flotsam is harmless; it's leftover afterbirth."

"There's loud hissing in my ears. I can't breathe. The umbilical cord around my neck tightens like a snake."

"That's your oxygen mask leaking after the cord is removed."

"I'm walking over a war zone of blood-soaked ground."

"That's easy", I replied. "Blood is always blood."

A rapid-fire exchange of questions and answers slowed as Daisy moved into delta sleep.

And then I heard a bloodcurdling war cry. A storm of hatred

surged ahead of a Viking hoard wielding axes dripping with blood. They swarmed over Horse Hill and came to a full stop, voices strangled dead in their throats, and fell to their knees before the chalk outline of The White Horse newly-risen from the turf as the holy terror of a spindly skeleton with fire breathing eyes.

TIME OUT FOR BAD BEHAVIOR
the book of Violence and Peace

29

BRUTE FORCES

A clash of clans in 1518 destroyed the church.
But the real troubles for Portmatilloch
began much earlier in the year of someone else's lord,
for ours had clearly forsaken us in 901 A.D.

901 A.D.

- VIOLET -

History repeats itself, so I was not surprised to learn Daisy's inherited 'point of no return' arrived by ship, like mine, in a particularly rude awakening of white-hot grief and insatiable need.

Perhaps, after all, she and I shared a common ancestry of death and doom. I summarily dismissed the notion out of hand.

Surely, Evie would have told me!

I had to know for sure, so I spontaneously traveled back to the day in question when mountain-sized warriors were unleashed on a community of innocent sheep with orders to ravage at will.

Images of a Viking raid in Portmatilloch came into focus fast and vicious.

In close succession, I am aware of innocent laughter distorted as if underwater. Next, I witness a clattering mob of Viking invaders, clambering up Horse Hill at the speed of death that awarded them the first glimpse of a village waiting to have its throat cut.

Time awards me consecutive scenes that form and reform.

Women lay in shock hoping to be absorbed by the mud reeking

with gore. One has the strength to groan, the others erupt in a wail so terrifying it frightens the creatures at the bottom of the sea.

Women slowly regain consciousness, cold and wet, shivering, impregnated but strangely disembowelled, vomiting poisonous memories of cruel blue eyes, foul breath, and grunts of cruelty pinning them to an earth running with blood.

New rain bathes their wounds. One by one, they claw themselves upright, grateful for the rain as if a Sky-God could cleanse them of horror.

What had happened? Was it over?

The beast may retreat to gloat; the victims barely have time to count their dead, account for the survivors, and assess their injuries.

With broken arms dangling slack, the women rake broken skulls and spilled brains into piles for burning, silently dragging their own flesh and bones with an ear alert for the rattle of shields and returning swords.

Multiple funeral pyres of sons and fathers are seen from across the firth. Portmatilloch looks like a hill on fire.

Most of the women huddle under the goddess's empty shrine and ask for guidance. But some grovel under the stars at the feet of an absent warrior God for an explanation why they were forsaken by the new promise of a divine Father. They don't see the invisible cross I see in the sky. Both shrines remain silent.

Women get busy mending clothes and hearts and the broken promises of religion.

But in the shadows, a few women sit apart from the others, feeling distant enough to steal smiles of relief from being relieved of a bullying husband, quietly grateful to their attackers even as they mourn the broken land and a happy sensation of loneliness.

The significance of this shocks me but I also understand. Even now the human psyche is still in its developing stages.

It's impossible to ignore a collective of traumatized village women pretending not to fear while searching the sea for the first sighting of a dragon-ship's sail, secretly yearning for barbarian sex.

One such guilty heart, Lilith Ross, dares to speak her truth and the relief of like minds unfolds into a secret sisterhood of joy. Tales of wonder are shared, and the ancient Clan of the Horse remains safe.

Two weeks later, lazy smoke curls from chimneys accompanied by the melodic clanging of cow bells.

Women take turns on the cliffs scanning for dragon ships and rally their muscle memories to stir soup and bake Bannock.

Throwing themselves into domestic work, barely able to look each other in the eye, is a way of creating solidarity yet in the evening they huddle together for psychic warmth as one woman with a dozen guilty hearts and exchange memories safer to tell in the dark.

Months go by. Deadened abandoned women bereft of religion, go about their days, collecting water and wood, clutching bellies swollen with foreign life.

Nine months after the raid, the screams from a second battle of mothers giving birth to fair-haired blue-eyed children is a common sound. They call Lilith's daughter a monster for her freakish transparent skin. I recognize her as Daisy in utero, barely formed, inside a membrane of invisible skin. The words transition and parent strike me as meaningful. A conversion is begun.

A few old women silently boil bitter herbs and turnips to nurture the first life signs of unborn Vikings.

Rain continues to wash away the evidence of war. Wooden crosses rot into memories until only a few stone cairns remained as grave markers.

I witness their future after many generations of innocent sons and daughters jumpstart a community of conscious single mothers mindful of the dirty lie perpetrated by the arrival of a new church founded on the immaculate conception of a woman overpowered by a male God.

Christianity builds a stone church. Many Portmatilloch survivors are swayed by a bigger picture that emerges and they shift their allegiance from trust in each other to the Christian God.

For these women who align themselves to a heavenly father, subsequent raids require the wholesale replacement of saint's finger bones, candlesticks, and bibles that act as salve, so, instinctively they make more salve. Bones are always easy to find.

In retrospect, it's obvious that a few crushed trinkets have shed their divine auras to be sacrificed, melted down for armour and rivets in the thieves' fierce unforgiving homeland of ice and snow.

Not surprisingly, Lilith's free lifestyle ushers in a divided parallel village, signifying a permanent parting of the ways from masculine authority to feminine sensitivity.

A secret ballot belies the surface compliance of servitude shrewdly displayed by Portmatilloch's resourceful wisewomen hidden in plain sight.

As long as no one rocks the boat, life on the surface resumes as sham equality. Savvy wives and daughters obediently defer to new husbands and fathers. Laundry, housekeeping, childcare, cooking, and procreating children are accepted without protest and the true power behind the apron strings reigns as secret princesses, queens, and goddesses biding their time.

Artful women slip underground to lead double lives – the best of both worlds: magic with the freedom to enjoy their natural feminine omnipotence vs. the indignities of female servitude.

Somewhere between the lines of higher power, menfolk join fake brotherhoods of masculine authority and rest smugly within an age-old hierarchy: the God-given right of kings.

Dormant magic rallies, stronger than ever under the leadership of a female clan member appointed Mistress of the Horse, chosen for her purity of spirit worthy to serve the ancient goddess inscribed on the hill.

The restoration of the Green Gods: Pan, his consort the Lady Flora, and the primeval 'Clan of the Horse' gains ground, albeit in secret.

The fully awakened eyes of the women for whom being ravished represents the singular joy of being valued, grow in number yet equally diminished by fear.

From the first experience of violent lovemaking to the wild orgasm of primal coitus, the sexually awakened recognize one shiny new thing: that carnal union with a rutting dragon means the thrill of being taken and giving oneself freely occur at the same time.

"I tell no lies," Lilith secretly confesses to a friend, "Being ravaged by a horny dragon is worth going to hell for."

Sadly, fearful ears are often attached to mouths that spew unconscious gossip to the cruelties of unconscious power.

So, from out of the mouths of guilty women, Lilith was sentenced to death for witchcraft in an execution worthy of the name, hell.

Her tortured cries echo down the ages until Lilith's reincarnated spirit, Lily Price, gets knocked up by a bad boy a thousand years in the future. Ironically, it's Lily's daughter Daisy who pays the price.

But where did I fit on that terrible day? Had I killed or been killed? Nothing made sense. And then I was alerted by a mewing sound carried on the wind.

A twelve month had passed.

I immediately recognize Grace – a crying infant, three months old with blond hair, transparent as glass, casually dismissed by three words faked on a church register: cause of death… *failure to thrive.* She had been a sacrificial peace offering to appease the God who had abandoned Portmatilloch – a lost soul left exposed to die in the wind and rain on Horse Hill.

The me-of-me was still a mystical spell waiting to be born at sea. But I saw again, my mother Dorota, and the cowled pinched face of the demon soul who would one day leave me for dead.

I had pause to regret my outburst declaring Daisy was an empty liver-lilied soul. I had damned myself no better than the reluctant soul who'd left me to die. An old voice rebukes me. *'So, what,'* my ego crows back. *'All's fair in fight and flight.'*

Celeste interrupts my poison. *"Incoming travel documents for Miss Violet Seaborn. "I hate to be the bearer of bad news. It's your passport to hell."*

PEACE AT LAST

- VIOLET -

I couldn't help but feel sorry for Daisy. It's hard to shake hands with a woman who isn't there. Harder still to thank a ghost for the loving kindness she may have only imagined.

Daisy was reborn with a fantasy, waking from her coma in a spotless room cleaned by fairies as she slept. No footprints, fingerprints or the imprint of a soul remained other than a vague notion that wouldn't go away. She had been visited in the night. All she knew was her sad memories had popped like soap bubbles and left her giddy with happiness.

Of course, Daisy felt better. She had an enlightened soul, me. She had Sophie and Summer which meant she also had Evie and the essence of Sister Veritas!

The delightful scent of violets filled the air that the doctors and nurses couldn't smell. Daisy's first order of business after being discharged from hospital rehab was special ordering an old-fashioned nosegay of violets that she carried close under her nose the way women in the old days held plague germs at bay.

In short order, Daisy honored the ghost of me with page one of her new diary and began a new life. She printed: I'M A DIFFERENT PERSON NOW, in bold caps and underlined it.

But I continued to plague her.

THE AGE OF REASON

*"Avoid loud and aggressive persons;
they are vexatious to the spirit."*
MAX EHRMANN

- VIOLET -

I cared nothing for Daisy's appropriated triumphs or her inexhaustible state of joy. Mine and Sam's ambitions outshone them all. I'd been tricked into sacrificing ancestral promises of successive lifetimes only to be cut short of true love by a witless microbe.

I saw my purpose as being born to expose a lying thieving universe I believed to be a waste of virgin hydrogen. Lila played high stakes games pitting humans against impossible odds. The women of the Horse Clan were found guilty, punished for conquering body *and* soul which was apparently a worse crime than being a Viking slaked with lust.

I had been roughly treated, volunteered for Daisy duty, coerced, and subsequently punished. I needed to understand why I had forfeited my future to a thieving virus.

Daisy Sinclair died spiritually from severe depression when low expectations and bad timing claimed her life years before she died physically from the low spirits that compromised her immune system.

I arrived as a free agent, sucked into the vacuum caused by Daisy's induced coma from Covid 19.

Celeste's identity as moonbased was flawed from the start. I got right to it when she returned to check my progress. "As Daisy's *acting* soul, surely you have a stake in the nature of her eventual demise," I whined.

"But I'm NOT a soul! Never was never, will be," Celeste insisted. "I'm a placeholder. I stood in as Daisy's guardian and waited for her soul to come but it never showed. I'm a moon maiden. That's why you see me as a globe of lunar light."

"I thought you were being coy, in disguise for a reason. What do I look like to you?"

"If you must know, I see you as a spoiled princess who is utterly impotent and insubstantial."

She was hedging.

"WAIT! Does that mean? Are you saying that Daisy Sinclair has *never* had a soul!"

"Not until *you* came along. You can see my predicament."

"And what about mine?"

"You've maneuvered yourself into a rock and a hard place."

"But Daisy lives, yes?"

"Daisy was depressed from gestation. As such, she was born only half-alive."

"Why me?"

"You were the only soul with the right... *ahem*... connections worthy to take her on."

"So, you've been her babysitter!"

"No, genius. I'm YOUR babysitter. Your mother hired me to keep you honest."

"As far as I know, Daisy and I share no connections."

"Easily said by someone who doesn't think very far. I shouldn't have to remind the likes of you that Karma is a slippery business. And you, Miss Bossy Boots, are walking a tight rope. I suggest you step carefully. You're surrounded by psychic landmines. Why are you so hell bent on destroying Daisy?"

"Not destroy, surely only to educate. I will ask Lady Flora if I may to speak with the 'old one'. She loves me."

It's an eerie sound when the moon sighs. "Entitlement is an ego thing," Celeste chuckled. "The same is true for arrogance and jealousy."

"I'm a master soul. Time moving on is not an unknown concept. The Universe needs to expand. Joke intended."

"Don't you see? That's your ego talking. Your ego is in control now. And since when has that ever proven to be the goal of an enlightened being such as yourself? The answer is never. I would have thought you'd toughened your resolve to dump your ego long ago when it reared its ugly head."

"I didn't think it could anymore."

"That's the most honest thing you've said. YOU DIDN'T THINK! And you're still not thinking now. But you *can* turn things around. It's not too late although you're not in the Universe's best books. From what I hear, and I hear a lot, Sam's energy is, excuse the crude term, *saving your bacon*. But as your twin soul, if you're banished, so will he."

"I'll reckon with Sam in the light of day. You are the moon. What can you know of the truths seen in daylight?"

"I know that the nighttime rules secrets and all matters of clandestine malice. I used to keep close council with the Mistress of the Horse and together we watched over the goddess in the water."

"Then you must be aware of the prophecy naming *me* the next Mistress of the Horse."

"And you must have forgotten that because you predeceased Evie by a heartbeat, there has been *no* Mistress of the Horse in Portmatilloch for 100 years. The 'old one' has retreated to the depths and the land suffers terribly. You, Violet, have some serious soul searching to do!"

32

WHO?

*"Daisy, Daisy, give me your answer do
I'm half crazy all for the love of you."*

- VIOLET -

A dozen times a day, Daisy shouted "Who goes there?" into every silent corner, flickering electric light, and pregnant shadow. She startled at every imagined sound. The unsettling feeling of not being alone haunted her as I intended it should.

A ghost hovered in plain sight… but that ghost was me. My plan was going well – better than I'd hoped because suddenly Saint 'M's prophecy came true. James Eriksen appeared in a dream, and I knew I would get to see my Sam again through Daisy's dreams.

Once again, Daisy's boy was there, waiting… sitting high in the elbow of a grandfather oak, swinging his legs, dreaming of puppy dog tails. He was thinking of her… creating them… and Daisy took form according to his every mood. She left the illusion of sixty-eight years behind. For now, happily, she was nineteen.

Dream-sharing was maddeningly random. It had been eight months since their last tryst where they'd been playing a Rumpelstiltskin game of guessing their names. So far, all Daisy could get from her boy was the letter J written in sand, and all he remembered from her was the sound 'day'.

So, she called her boy Jay. He was her Knight, and she became his Day.

James is always three years younger than Daisy, but he has more faith than she does and always dreams her better on his restless days. They connect best when he's close to exhaustion. When they're teenagers. Today James is sixteen.

All the while they wander dangerously unchaperoned under storm clouds, their shadow monkeys chattering incessantly of great expectations.

James jumped down from the branch as the sun came up… traced Daisy's name in the sand… D…A…Y… and listened to the wind for signs.

We watched James from behind a storm fence placed there by the invisible shamans of this sacred space who knew full well that dream molecules touching out of divine sync caused counter-productive turbulences to human progress.

Forgetfulness keeps dreamers honest.

Lucid dreaming permits the illusion of an eternity or a few seconds. Depending on one's inclination to accept time as it plays 'outside the sphere', James and Daisy have shared a single heartbeat that has lasted eight months.

Their eyes searched for details.

Whether Daisy was a woman grown to plus three of Jay's earth years whispering to a boychild, or Jay was a teenager with stars in his eyes, they walked slowly as through deep water, side-by-side, inches apart, without touching. A pleasant charge of electrical static pop-crackled between them.

James stood to Daisy's left. A violet halo pulsed over his head as he valiantly repeated his earth coordinates.

"Yes," Daisy answered. "I will remember."

Such is the ecstasy of out-of-body contact; Daisy felt the ghostly presence of her lover's aura. A gentle atom-fuzzing spirit-boy shimmered on her left pointing to his tree where the letters J and D entwined were now freshly carved inside a heart.

She felt the loss of her beloved the same way I missed Sam.

Bittersweet waking-pain is the universal legacy of transitional consciousness between dream lovers.

Reality requires molecular adjustments for re-entry… turning back, tuning out, coming online, marking time under each other's skin.

Daisy woke with love blushing through her as a delicious sensation of goosebumps. James's *"I adore you. Tomorrow, then. Don't be late"* followed her like a warm shadow.

Walking for hours in a blissful daze suddenly prompted her to send Jay a message. "Daze," she shouted aloud, startling a passing pedestrian. "My name is Daisy!"

Her jubilance was ashes in my mouth.

BROTHERS IN ARMS
the book of James & Sam

33

VIRTUAL GIRL

"Remember tonight
for it is the beginning
of always."
DANTE ALIGHIERI

- SAM -

James used to be a morning person. Now he startles awake with his hand already reaching for the computer mouse. He taps his fingers impatiently while his PC whirs into online life. I see him bathed in the monitor's muted aqua light, accompanied by its comforting chirping bleeps and deep electronic sighs.

"Good lad," I whisper. "That's where she's likely to be.

Searching the profile galleries of internet dating sites was a hit and miss technique, a logical lifeline albeit a fragile one.

But now and then, Daisy traveled the jumbled code-roads of virtual space for signposts and probed the interference with her headlights on high beam: 'Virtual Woman Seeks Ghostly Lover'… and then, one restless night, as James's dreamcatcher, I took control of his hand and turned on the radio.

James used his radio like a tranquilizer. Without it he stared at his ceiling rose with far more attention than it warranted – an activity that bored me to distraction.

Retirement had gifted James ample time for a multitude of pursuits with the added curse of insomnia.

The legacy of insistent career buzz and jet lag had once made it so. Right brains care nothing for clocks, nor do they respect the limitations of the human body. Fatigue was never enough to close the gap between work and sleep.

James's body, irrevocably set to overtime, transformed his reclining armchair into a bed; it was so much easier to flip a lever than alert me, the night watch, whose job it was to connect his body and soul to the dreamtime.

34

SEARCHING FOR DAYLIGHT

"Go placidly
amid the noise and the haste
and remember what peace
there may be in silence."
MAX EHRMANN

- SAM -

Where once the wide hallways and living room carpet of James's bachelor pad had been strewn with maps, camera equipment, and half-packed boxes of provisions, it was now the pristine bachelor space of a retired scholar.

James ate his dinner on the balcony but retreated inside when a generation of new mosquitoes baptized by a late afternoon downpour, hatched under the warmth of the sun, and rose in a desperate swarm of bloodlust. He kept the doors open but I pulled down a white fall of insect netting – an essential carry-over from living in the deserts of Sakkara.

My presence drew an exorbitant number of mosquitos into a halo over James's head which I continually had to wave away.

A gentle breeze blew in the September perfume of maple bark, wet leaves, and red apples, and rustled the flimsy net curtain into a ghostly apparition of crushed gauze. James fretted, trapped inside it – a white cocoon to incubate his dream girl.

Dusk was James's favorite time of the day, and an autumn dusk rated the highest of all. It was bliss inside a parenthesis of time, lodged between the drudgery of life's petty maintenances and working the nightshift search engines of the love computer.

Searching for the elusive Ms. D by day was impractical. Years ago, James had allocated entire evenings hypnotized by the screen, but now he assigned himself a thin hour from eight to nine to scan internet dating sites in what was now a somewhat automatic response, searching for a pearl within a million loose grains of soul. Such was the tenacious work ethic of a Capricorn with attitude.

James stood at the window nursing his wine and absorbed the last rays of the setting sun. I kept him gazing transfixed at the sublime sunset of violet cumulus tipped with gold because it reminded me of Violet.

When it faded to orange James settled into his reading chair, and restlessly opened the latest half-read book subscription offering to give it one last benefit of the doubt. But within ten minutes it passed the point of no return, where one can stop believing a story is going to pick up and become interesting, and he set it aside in favor of the radio.

Partly from my boyhood dreaming in the fields I had taught James to love the passive nature of absorbing information without using his eyes. He willingly switched to the art of listening, bypassing the whiplash of negative news, and caught the tail end of an interview.

We heard a voice which paused his fingers searching for CBC International and listened to a woman describing an artist colony for retired painters and writers in Nova Scotia.

I recognized the faint echo behind that voice.

James followed my lead and grabbed the nearest scrap of paper. He wrote: capstone - - colon - - ox - - nova - - day - - sin, and a 902 phone number just as it fizzled out to music.

James resumed searching for his favorite station which promised to drone well into the wee small hours and settled the dial on the deep serious monotone of British interviews which made a soothing intellectual background chat.

It was the ultimate electronic sedative. There were no promotional emotional outbursts of hype, just gentle elevator decibels beneath closed eyelids where most nights he followed the captivating voices to alpha.

James heroically skimmed a few more pages of his book but it weighed like lead in his hands. When I caused it to fall, he didn't bother to pick it up. His mind latched on to the presenter's voice like a lassoed calf. Down it went without protest.

James was primed for astral travel... an exacting exit strategy for balancing exhaustion and karma. He floated lightly out of his body like a zeppelin anchored to an umbilical cord.

Gaia sighed once, and her white beaches cracked open groaning with the creaking bones of an ancient guardian. The underworld chasm was dark and familiar illuminated by Middle-Earth's midnight sky hiding underground. A pinpoint of light shimmered in the velvety blackness of REM sleep as a shimmering pearl blinked open with a starry rush of beckoning electrons.

James emerged on the other side savoring the steady call of a name inside his bloodstream that amplified the sound of his quickening pulse.

The fates decreed he would land softly into a replay of tender courtship, and within its bubble he was privy once again to the logic of universal mind in a crossover landscape so familiar and dear.

There was no urgency. I reassured him Daisy would be there at the tree.

Violet would make sure she was there.

35

I THINK WE'VE MET

"You have been mine before —
How long ago I may not know."
DANTE GABRIEL ROSSETTI

- SAM -

The national anthem caused James to stir inside his dream, awakening from the disturbance of intense crackling interference under the weight of white static.

It was 2 A.M. He switched off the unconscious radio and I drew his attention to a scribbled message on a slip of paper. It read: *capstone - - colon - - ox - - nova - - day - - sin* encircled by a coffee ring from a wet mug. A strange message to have left himself... but there was a phone number.

The word 'day' jarred James's mind. I stayed close, ready for action. He had just left another 'Day' dream and was still in tune with her. The note was an automatic response stimulated by a waking dream. He'd had a history of sleepwalking in college.

Doctors speculated it was spontaneous self-hypnosis because the intensity of his study techniques occasionally sent him into a trancelike state. I knew better. James had always been in denial of the psychic influences of universal love.

James strained to recall the dream before it went the way of all the others. Fortunately, he had me to remind him.

James's obediently replayed his latest dream as a ghostly mirage behind a plate of frosted glass.

He'd been sitting in a tree looking down on a farmer's field, a square of grey blanket on a bed of wheat grass, a sprawling picnic, a girl looking up. He saw a dark cherry-red sports car, and a green wine bottle shaped like a fish, and recalled shy talk saturated with serotonin and laced with dizzy surges of pure adrenalin.

A wind had picked up the corner of a paper napkin and moved a stray curl of the girl's brown hair. Both were crystal clear things. The bent handle of a spoon made into a friendship ring linked to a future promise, and a dust devil of leaves blowing in slow motion like a mini cyclone of gold and orange bees spun around the girl, obscuring her childlike delight, reaching and laughing to catch one before it turned into a white butterfly.

A sleeping cat pinned down one corner of the blanket, and a lilac shadow passed over them. James heard the sputtering engine of a plane overhead and witnessed the sharp trail of a white jet stream that cut the blue sky in two. *Flightpath streaks heading east… muffled sounds…* She said Jake? Jason? James? And he stopped her with a yes... remember James! She told him her full name street address and phone number. Then there was the familiar cold howling of a rocky mountain wind, a black bear waving see ya later, a first hello linked to goodbye forever, the honk of a car horn that sounded like a crazed goose, rain, a wet rooftop, and a spinning fan-vent shaped like a Chinese lantern that turned in lazy hesitation like a top that couldn't fall over. The girl blew a kiss in his direction, and he was awake.

Images crowded his mind, but when forced to the surface they crumpled like dust under the strain, until all he had left was the strange note, and the lingering presence of the D girl. I made sure of that.

If one had to be haunted, she was the kind of ghost he would choose. And as all dreamboat confections go, she always hovered in the shadows for days, full of unearthly sweetness with none of the abrasive substance of a real woman.

James made strong Turkish coffee and considered the code. Capstones meant achievement, a crowning glory, the best… the highest. It evoked the missing crown of the Great Pyramid of Kephren.

The coffee took control and for a caffeine moment he savored exquisite bitterness laced with sugar and cream. The dream was gone again... quicksilver words made of ice melting on an Indian-summer morning.

"Is it going to rain?" I shouted, louder than my usual hinting voice.

Out of habit, James flipped on the TV for the weather, and channel-surfed till he found a swirl of map half obliterated by cloud graphics swirling in a protoplasmic blob and weatherman babble: *long range... maritime storm... moving east... low pressure... freezing rain... Nova Scotia.*

Ox?... nova? ... colon? ... day?... A long beat and some deep brain synapse connected nova with Nova Scotia, and the rest of yesterday's cryptic message unraveled quickly. Colon? ... *colony.* So much for the art of abbreviation.

Laziness was rarely an excuse for James's actions or lack thereof, but the morning seduced him into a reverie where he wanted to sit quietly and assimilate a delightful dream. Business didn't have to wait. Retirement decreed the absence of business.

I repeated the name Daisy in James's ear as many times as I dared. It was against Lila's rules for a soul to overly interfere with romance this late in the game.

I suggested the sound zee. James came up with Daisy. It was a neat play of words working within the rules of free will.

The number was not in service.

36

BUSY SIGNALS

*"I am forgetful of everything
but seeing you again –
my life seems to stop there –
I see no further. You have absorb'd me.
I have a sensation at the present moment
as though I were dissolving"*
JOHN KEATS

- VIOLET -

I heard the phone ring long before Daisy did.

She was content, languishing in the astral sleep between the dreams I played for her, loathe to leave the romantic liaison behind where she and a boy loved each other so desperately.

"You should get that," I whispered in her ear.

"It will only be a wrong number," she replied, pulling a blanket over her head. "Leave me be."

I spoke louder. *"No really, pick up. It's important."*

Daisy drifted back to my memories of Sam, the boy of our dreams.

I watched a bee land on Daisy's arm and swatted it to stir it up before I recognized Pollen, who was not impressed. I'd known him in Portmatilloch. Pollen often droned fairy gossip in my ear to pass on to Evie. "I hope I didn't alarm you. I would never have hit you," I explained. "I needed to wake Daisy. That ghastly ringing noise is a life-changing miracle. If you give Daisy a wee sting, she and I will be forever in your debt."

"That ringing makes my ears buzz," Pollen said, and obligingly backed into Daisy's bare arm.

As it happened, I bore the brunt of Pollen's stinger, but post phone call, Daisy rubbed her arm where an angry red bump should have been. "Something bit me in my sleep," she complained.

"It's a love bug I shouted back," winking at Pollen.

I jerked Daisy's blanket away and pinched her arm, so mine regained its feeling. *"Wake-up,"* I shouted. *"It's your dream boy, calling... our boy! Yours and mine."*

I sent her a mild headache accompanied by a thirst for Earl Grey tea and made the third ring whistle in her head like a boiling kettle.

Daisy bounded off the sofa so fast she left me behind and grabbed the receiver. *"Don't look back,"* I called out, although I doubt in her haste, she would have seen me.

I caught up to her in time to hear her say hello. She jiggled the receiver. The warbling dial tone sounded stressed. It was a false alarm.

Someone is trying to get through," I said. "I feel it."

"Another wrong number," Daisy said. "That's the third one this week."

Later that night I got to hear James's soppy opening line: "I believe we've met."

While James stuttered through the rest of his awkward preamble, Daisy absentmindedly rubbed the bruise on her arm where I'd pinched her. It was clear the bee sting belonged to me alone.

I sensed the familiar echo of Sam's voice as James stumbled through his dragged-out apologetic introduction. He couldn't have been more embarrassing if he'd greeted Daisy with the famous quote when Henry Stanley greeted Dr. Livingston: "Daisy Sinclair I presume."

James continued to burble nonsense, but Sam sent me a message between the lines. *"Violet? Is that you? I heard you on the radio."*

"Sam?... SAM!"

"It's us. We did it," Sam crowed. *"Well, YOU did. I was never as powerful as you. I've been with James since his birth in 1953. I sense you and Daisy are only recently acquainted."*

"Aye, a few months. Do you know what this means!"

"We have forged the connection we were destined to have. My memories of you have already imprinted in James's psyche as I hoped they would. I assure you it wasn't for lack of trying. If Evie was right, old souls reincarnate from new memories."

Knowing Sam was somewhere nearby, helped. At first our connection was barely audible, but we soon triumphed creating stronger astral forms from the residual psychic DNA of 1918. We hit old age running, inside bodies ready to die. And I learned that a bee sting is painful even if one's body is ethereal.

But even through our renewed joy I came to view the universe as unjustifiably perverse. As young unconsummated lovers, Sam and I faced a new world, apart yet together – a pair of old souls reborn on the same planet, possibly thousands of miles apart.

Daisy and James had met in dreams forgotten by morning, but I felt Sam's loss like a phantom limb. Mornings became 'mournings'.

It took Herculean strength to hold up a sky full of miracles, to write the final chapters of someone else's life, to get up some mornings, to leave or stay… to make friends with a strange face in a funhouse mirror.

It came down to uncommon sense. I thought I could make the supreme sacrifice by deliberately erasing my previous lifetime and accept what-was. Game, set, and match. But I could not. I was at war with what was. Sam and I were twin souls – immortals charged with connecting a pair of trifling humans.

For a long groggy time afterwards, I dreamed two uncertain beginnings, trying to remain thankful that Sam and I only needed a single happy ending.

We had no choice but to wait because Daisy's miracle became too heavy to carry around and my spirit kept wafting back to Neverland like a helium balloon.

During those times I clung to Portmatilloch where I wandered through my old life, retracing steps, trailing the scent of happiness from beginning to end in the dank ruins of convent walls and into the hills of transcendent summers.

And when I regained my Nova Scotia presence, I never allowed Daisy to forget the muted colors of the highlands, a pair of loving hazel eyes, or the special 'miracle' that was mine and Sam's – the truly marvellous something that had happened during the sweet days I shadowed him working in the fields.

Because, we had each found our calling after a clod of earth thrown up by a plow changed the course of our future. A future I guarded fiercely. A future I thought I would never forfeit.

But if a recent revelation was true, I inadvertently had. What if I hadn't just *allowed* but *desired* the Spanish flu virus to take my life? What if I'd begged it to!

I blocked the ghastly repercussions of my crime determined to discover the truth, whatever the cost.

I was especially aware of the severity that fuelled my Daisy revolt. The consequences for misbehaving were severe; the punishment of forfeiting immortality was doubly real. As twin souls, whatever I did affected Sam.

I was either a monster or the helpless offspring of a monstrous universe.

Daisy's old landscape was foggier each time I returned.

For years she had been a lonely warrior aimlessly searching for white knights, mistakenly tuned to dreamy fiction and vicarious big screen kisses. As far as I could determine she barely survived her teens on empty calories in a steady diet of fantasies sweetened with cinema magic.

Daisy had been starry-eyed, caught inside many a love triangle of deceit, but she could never be faulted for giving up for long. We were evenly matched on that score. Neither would I.

I had been right. The universe *did* have a perverse sense of humor. No wonder the deadly Venus flytrap was named after the goddess of love.

On occasion, I continue to haunt the graveyards of Portmatilloch reading gravestone poetry. As far as I can tell, epitaphs are love songs stifled in stone hoping to redeem the broken promises of paralyzed spirits. Not much cause for celebration.

Reincarnation was supposed to be the blessing of a return to square one infancy. Why had I been cursed?

I was all too aware of the universe's dreaded 'Void of Emptiness'– a shadowland threat forever hovering in the background, careful to avoid its damnable last resort for good reason.

Naturally, Daisy's soulless body could only host one soul. Daisy woke one morning with no conscious memory of our spirited competition. I had been fully assimilated.

I officially had a body, Daisy had a permanent soul, and my ego mind had taken possession, but none of us was in control. I was of two minds. It was not yet clear to me that my ego would have to die to enable my eventual rebirth which, to me, had never been taken off the table.

It was then, after hearing my no-nonsense diagnosis that my ego doubled back like the slighted fairy from 'Sleeping Beauty' with a spiteful parting gift.

Much to my horror, Daisy's acquisition of my hard-won spiritual energy, had stolen my purest light. Her haggard grey eyes turned violet now and then for an isolated hour just to mock me, and in a childish sulk of meanspirited entitlement I punished Daisy with even more unrelenting memories of Sam.

It turns out a divine bee sting can leave a deep spiritual scar even without a physical body.

37

J-MAIL

"Keep peace in your soul"
MAX EHRMANN

- SAM -

My take was different from Violet's. I didn't respond to James with depression or hostility.

Not having grasped the infrequency of fully engaged providence, humans seldom register the significance of their own spontaneous actions. Rare moments of purified intuition communicated directly via their souls are mostly processed as random encounters. Only hindsight hoists them to a pedestal where they might well stand in awe of a split-second yes or a sudden left-hand turn.

There are times when earth holds its breath, and even souls stop their ears and look away. Too often have their golden whispers gone unheard or unheeded.

The room had been palpably tense when James dithered about phoning directory assistance. Three small numbers separated him from his destiny... *411*... and he had ignored the opportunity twice before.

The number was wrong. The person answering told him he'd reached the city of Oxford, Nova Scotia. He might try checking with directory assistance.

I hadn't been able to tell James what I plainly knew. The word he'd scribbled had been Capstone not Stonecap. Only to be expected since he invariably had pyramids on the brain. Luckily the local operator had heard of it.

Fairy tales never use the 'three-wish' paradigm lightly. A human life is ruled by countless unseen influences, so complex that connecting two individuals is exceedingly rare if they miss the first chance. Three wishes are a common enough occurrence in fairy stories but are generally navigated with some difficulty. Eighty years is the blink of an eye to a divine clock-master, and multiple lifetimes are usually required to complete time-sensitive bytes of predestined fate.

Evie had taught me that sometimes a soul can be too pushy for their own good. And since I needed to preserve every ounce of good karma for my next life, my thoughts drifted purposely to allow James's divinely inspired dream materialize in perfect timing without undue influence. It was James solo flight.

If only humans could be aware of the gravity of attraction, but they are so often filled instead with unrest. Prolonged waiting breeds impatience which spawns delays and denials, until instant gratification destroys the art of awareness.

But when I shifted my attention back to the moment, James had already hung up the receiver after retrieving a seven in place of the one he had copied by mistake, and he was automatically dialing the new number oblivious of its significance.

Violet told me Daisy had vaguely sensed the great stirrings of fate days before her phone rang, but Violet thankfully being one of the pushy souls Evie had warned me about, suggested Daisy cancel a trip to town to await the destiny about to be caught on the flagpole of Stonecap House.

James and Daisy had resonated instantly to the other's voice. Twenty minutes later James asked for details of colony membership, and Daisy witnessed flash bulb images of James as child, boy, youth, and adult aligned over one another.

And after they discovered their common interest in Egyptian history, Daisy's instincts amplified by Violet's willpower, kept the conversation casual to keep James talking about archaeology while the energy behind them charged to full power.

Daisy had answered on the third ring. Violet and I left them alone to celebrate in private.

Third rings and third chances are always more precarious since they've been bargained for with compromises and fear which renders them fragile wispy things easily misplaced under mindless distractions and mountains of unpaid bills.

Letters flew across the internet in rapid succession building momentum carrying missing puzzle pieces. James and Daisy assembled a long-distance jigsaw puzzle the hard way, from the center out, but eventually the calendar released some December travel dates of winter respite.

I had been packed and ready since James's first DAY- dream.

38

CROSSING OVER

The water is wide,
But not as deep as the love I make
I know not how I'll sink or swim.

Late December **2022**

- SAM -

It was midnight when James Eriksen, retired Egyptologist Classics professor, hoisted a pristine backpack into the overhead luggage carrier of a Greyhound bus.

He acted confused as he blindly shouldered his way to a pair of empty seats near the back of the bus.

Instead of gracefully taking his seat he landed heavily, momentarily dislodging me, wedged a rolled sweatshirt between his neck and the window, cracked open a book on photography, and adjusted the reading light to maximum effect.

He faked the casual pose of a bored traveller. I would have to be vigilant. His book was upside down.

Too keyed up to sleep, James immediately drifted off against his will from the intense relief to be underway.

I left him to his semi-conscious panic attack and imagined how I would feel if it was me on my way to Violet, which was easy because I was.

The giant skyscrapers of Vancouver silently slipped away like adrift icebergs.

Nearing the open highway, a snow plough lumbered out of a side street. Its taillights glowed like the red eyes of wild things at the edge of the Eriksen homestead after dark. It pushed the weather out and away from the main streets, scraping a path for the cold bus grating its teeth against the road surface.

It was my sworn duty to nudge James awake as the bus pulled into the first rest stop, even though I knew he would hear the hydraulic hiss of the bus's door opening from deepest sleep. "Time to check your bags," I said. "The driver is opening the luggage compartment under the bus."

Suddenly, my fanatical James was back like a neurotic guard dog to defend his property.

Thick snow surrounded the bus, insulating the interior, trapping the sounds of human prisoners. The drone of snoring passengers merged with a sluggish engine pushing against ice pellets, grinding them into slush, dragging its weight of forty-three humans and their assorted emotional baggage.

The rocking of the Greyhound spaceship hummed a crude lullaby: *Daisy Daisy give me your answer do.* And sometime around 4 A.M. James woke from what passed as a sleepy headache.

Snowflakes the size of cornflakes fluttered in the night sky rather than fell, and James wondered how the driver would see the highway but assumed he could and thought no more about it, relishing the hypnotic effect as quite lovely, knowing he could nod off at any given moment in total safety. My relentless presence had given him that level of confidence.

I thought it sad that the luxury of letting go that James might have experienced at any time but never had, was no small thing. And yet for all James's legitimate aura of a learned man, he was a terrified child.

The bus continued to progress in a straight line from Vancouver to Oxford, Nova Scotia with no icebergs in sight, while James nurtured an image of Daisy making a Mount Everest out of a million snow cones.

This uncharacteristic whimsical thought gave me reason to believe James's terror may be something worth cultivating.

James was as permanently suntanned as a cowboy from desert adventures in the mother of all sandboxes. We had cross-trekked the Sahara and trailed the Valley of the Kings enough times to almost take the romance out of the name Egypt. But even so, the tinted sands of Sakkara never failed to cause a tug on his navel as if an umbilical cord from a parallel life extended internally, attached to his soul, ME.

He hadn't created his passion for archaeology, it blossomed the first time I drew his attention to the sound *Egypt* made in the air. With my attentive industry it wasn't long before ancient names rolled off his tongue. I knew I'd done well the day he rebuked an ambivalent student with heartfelt candour: *"Mister Jones, anyone who fails to taste the exotic spices between the hieroglyphics or hear the mourners of pharaoh wailing in the wind, has no business messing with Egyptology. Please take your seat."*

I was taken aback with the depth of his romantic outburst that had erupted unbidden from his subconscious without being edited by his intellect. And I thought: my boy is stepping up.

James's love affair with paper maps was mine. He 'read' each pastel shape, ignoring placenames in favor of the topographical delineations he knew so well.

Memories of women with painted cat eyes inhabited James's dreams. He knew the feeling of scorching flesh-colored sand against a calloused foot and was able to summon archaic images indelibly imprinted on the part of his primitive brain that reacted joyfully to the shriek of monkeys with great longing.

In the end, after much creative obsessing, I appointed myself

James's brazen internal poet for the selfish joy it brought me. He was in a bit of a quandary about how to begin, but after I helped him out with a first line, he was away to the races.

In a good way, James taught me to pay closer attention to his needs. He'd been internalizing his negative thoughts, but I'd heard them so often sometimes I failed to listen.

Looking back, James had been eager to express himself on our first dig in Thebes. Even now, I continue to whisper an inspirational prompt for a diary entry in his ear at least once a week. So, I credit myself with transforming James's tediously flat travelog into a journal bursting with vivid impressions.

Once he wrote: *'Today, an overwhelming impression of awe rippled through the shimmering mirages palpable heat of the ever-present Aten as it threw orange shadows over the glint of tomb gold in the afternoons and turquoise shadows across purple pyramids in the evening.'*

He documented the joys of plaster walls still wet with pigment, white bleached stone, green papyrus, and the red painted palms of scented ladies.

Spellbound audiences became so enraptured by his presentations as to be transported through the unlikely time portal of a stage podium. The students who could, followed James making fresh footprints together across a landscape of ancient power and three-thousand-year-old dreams.

Not one to spend hours surfing and canoodling with the internet's fickle charms, my boy kept his laptop closed, deferring to printed maps.

James planned to experience this trip as a traveler of old: cell phone, camera, and internet were silenced for the duration. Falling into a map was the best he could do for entertainment.

Despite years of reassuring therapy, we had flown to faraway digs enough times for James to feel he had probably surpassed his limit for safety sky-passes. Crashing to earth in a fireball was an image too cruel to consider beginning this final chapter of his life. He was programmed to obsess over tragedy.

Fate had some mean tricks up its sleeve and although not overly superstitious, James's heightened senses reasoned that caution was the better part of wisdom.

I was mildly concerned that he blithely ignored the dangerous winter driving conditions driving an icy highway at night.

One large duffle bag, a guitar case, and a shopping bag of gifts rode in the luggage compartment beneath the bus. It was James's nature to disembark at every pit stop to insure they stayed put.

Being happy made him nervous.

Even in the countries where it was common to be permanently separated from one's *stuff*. Such was the power of his vigilance; James had never lost so much as a roll of film. He put it down to focus. I put it down to me as his obsessive loudmouth travel guide.

Sleepless on an exciting journey made me suggest rather boldly that James capture his thoughts on paper. I tipped over his backpack and eased his diary out of its pocket. 'Write Daisy a poem.' I suggested in his ear. To my surprise he automatically responded in a loud NO I CAN'T! Not to me precisely but certainly towards my interference.

"I'm half crazy," he sang to himself, *"All for the love of you."*

THE END OF DAYS
the book of Comeuppance

39

STONE HOME

Human animals must follow their true nature.
Wolves never meow. When you find the howl
you were born to make you are home free!

CHRISTMAS EVE – **2022**

- SOPHIE -
Oxford Nova Scotia

Daisy crossed over the narrow country sidewalk side-stepping the largest patches of black ice, looking for a break in the hardened slush hill at the edge of the road.

Home loomed close through a chilly curtain of soft December flakes, and I felt her surge of happiness that always arose when she approached the wrought-iron gate marking the entrance to Stonecap House.

Stonecap was set far back into the curve of a low hill – a precious pearl in a row of sister buildings culled into an artists' colony on Electric Street. It's a residence of delightful artists who love animals, but, quite rightly, recognize cats are infinitely more sensitive than dogs.

I watched the street from a diamond shaped window on the third floor with my daughter, Summer, peering through a small opening in the layer of frost coating the inside of the glass. My mouth moved in the silent cat natter of recognition at the sight of Daisy.

I had a job to do so, by the time the key turned in the lock, I greeted Daisy, tail up, chirping like an excited dolphin.

Visitors were welcomed by the fragrant aroma of lemongrass, but being a cat, the scent of lemon was somewhat painful as was the irritating sound of wind chimes that alerted today's cook from the kitchen. Each artist took turns at culinary duty. I gravitated towards the ones who erred on the generous side when portioning out fish paste and kibble.

Florence pried shopping bags from Daisy's numb fingers, eagerly searching for signs of cinnamon and cloves before she disappeared to reclaim the kitchen in the spirit of yuletide.

Daisy fussed me, a besotted ball of fur winding impatiently around her legs, but the phone shrilled like a demented creature, and promptly ended my human therapy session. The severity of its ringtone, deliberately calibrated to reach the far corners of Stonecap House, a rabbit warren of hidden cloisters, always rattled me.

Static issued from the receiver… another missed call. But I heard Sam shout "Hello, Violet, I'm nearly there!"

Indigestion from the first ice storm of the season had dumped 30 cm of wet snow and brought the heavy power lines drooping low to the frozen ground.

I headed off while Daisy took a nap, to calm my nerves in a cozy spot in the *living* room, a strange name for a house bustling with spirits, to celebrate a dream come true where Sam, Violet, and I would be together again.

Daisy came downstairs flushed and groggy. She joined me beside a blazing hearth fire that had captured Summer, and a gentle old collie, named Ginger. I leaped on Daisy's lap. She gave me a sideways glance as her eyes sought the mantel clock. Daisy rubbed her nose into mine and looked more closely into my face. "Sophie, have your eyes changed color again?" she said. "I never know if I'm imagining it or not. One of your green eyes was distinctly sky blue for a moment there. And now they're both sea green."

"It means I'm overexcited," I purred back. "My eyes, as you well know, are a striking *emerald* green and when one of them reflects the blue sky it's a sign of something good arriving out of the clear blue. But when they turn aquamarine, it means Epona is calling me."

Daisy still had a few hours before meeting James and my Sam in Amherst. Sam had never seen me as a cat before, so I was in a playful mood. And now that I knew my eyes were changing color, I was keenly aware of a healing power surge that I shared with Summer. That's when her eyes changed from gold to violet, and the phone almost rang.

It was my cue to meow loudly enough to remind Daisy she had a bus to meet but Violet was ahead of me. Sam was the love of her life; I was only Sam's dear old Mam who had taken the form of a cat to teach Violet a lesson for the best of reasons. One of which was high tea served at four o'clock on the dot when sardines and saucers of cream were the main feature.

40

WE

"Just when at that swallow's soar
Your neck turn'd so, some veil did fall —
I knew it all of yore."
DANTE GABRIEL ROSSETTI

- SAM -

James's nerves were firing so erratically I took control and forced his attention on Daisy.

She was there, sheltered out of the wind inside Amherst market, where the Acadian buses pulled in once a day – a slip of a girl aged sixty-eight, materializing from a swirl of snow. Her form emerged from a Christmas postcard and waved.

She and James shook hands and didn't let go.

I didn't pay much attention to them after that. I was too busy feasting my eyes on Violet whose form alternated from the nine-year-old girl I knew to a beautiful woman in her twenties.

- VIOLET -

I read Daisy's first impressions, and while James found his tongue, I encountered the lost love of my life.

"Sam? Is that you?" I shouted to a Sam older than I remembered who immediately shapeshifted to my eighteen-year-old sweetheart. "Oh, there you are."

Sam grinned, looking best pleased with his older form. "I think we're meant to choose how we see each other and stick with it," he said. "I expect there are rules for this sort of thing."

"We're not teenagers anymore. It's entirely up to us. Obviously, we've moved on. I say we explore our latest forms."

"Agreed."

And that was that, despite our appearances we hadn't changed. Our 'December Song' began when Sam drew me into his arms. I snuggled into his neck after a long kissing session.

"Wait until you see Evie," I said giggling.

Daisy and James hadn't needed Sam and I to get acquainted.

Daisy was immediately wowed by James's style that gave an overall impression of casual faded blue denim even though he was wearing an eclectic long black wool coat and tall leather boots. He was too handsome. She was besotted at first sight until her confidence vanished. Suddenly she felt drab and provincial, entirely unglamorous.

She chided herself. This was the man who had won her heart and he hers over the course of endless telephone conversations.

Determined to recapture her happy mood, Daisy announced "Welcome to Shangri-La," a little too brightly. "The blizzard parted for you." What she thought was *oh my god, this man is out of my league. I'm an old fool.*

James's reply "a good omen" was awkward but his shyness pleased her. Despite his celebrity good looks, he was down to earth. But then James smiled, and she felt giddy again.

Daisy was tongue tied. Caught off guard. "I didn't expect, that is, you… um, look so, well, *different* than I imagined," she stuttered.

"You're beautiful," James countered, used to the effect he had over women. He blushed, terrified he had lost her. And then he drew Daisy into a hug and kissed her. Daisy melted and decided not to fight fate. James felt right as long as she kept her eyes closed.

James kissed Daisy's hair and face until she felt beautiful. "It's all right," he said. "I knew you would be perfect." They clung to each other after that, holding hands like a couple of timid kids, sneaking sideways glances at each other, afraid they might wake up.

- SAM -

Standing next to my Violet grown into a tall stunningly beautiful woman was like having a psychic blood transfusion. I stopped guiding James and looked away as he bravely put his foot in his mouth several more times.

Like me, he couldn't stop grinning, his unused smile muscles responded to an automatic memory of mine. I remembered the way I used to greet Violet every day and wondered if James's face would hurt from the strain later, as mine had done.

James tossed his luggage and packages into Daisy's car with such enthusiasm he lost his balance and slipped but Daisy caught his arm. Once upright, holding hands was no longer enough. Daisy gave him a bear hug to which he surrendered. He mumbled a silly excuse into her hair that somehow between two coasts his belongings had doubled.

He finally broke away. "Well, that's everything," he said hanging onto the car door for support. "The rest was on the truck."

"Yes, it arrived shipshape," Daisy said. "But I already told you that over the phone, didn't I. I've arranged everything in your room. I hope you like it."

More self-conscious ice breaking ensued with much stamping of wet snow.

- VIOLET -

I was miffed at Daisy for using the word shipshape which she knew I detested. "Let's leave these two alone," Sam said. "It's too painful to watch."

Daisy noted James's impressive backpack with pockets and zippers like a Swiss army knife.

They sat back, leaning against the headrests, content to let the parking lot empty.

- SAM -

But for the promise of future adventures, the two would have happily expired there and then, but I reminded James he was cold and hungry. "You're having trouble focusing," I said. "You need food. Relax. Daisy is crazy about you."

Violet prompted Daisy's response. "Let's get you warm. I expect you're starving."

While James and Daisy negotiated the excruciating pitfalls of small talk and self-conscious looks, I had a chance to speak with Violet.

"We work well together," I said. "They're very obedient aren't they. James usually has his head in the clouds, so this is a nice change."

"Only nice?"

I used James's grin as my own. "My dearest love, I am over the moon to be with you."

"They're in acceptance right now," Violet said. "Love, if it comes at all, will arrive later."

"I do hope they keep hugging. I'm going out of my mind to kiss you again."

Violet's sarcasm was evident. "No worries on that score. Daisy is leading him there as we speak. She's quite knocked out with him. And despite her demure looks, she's quite the formidable controller."

"I wonder who she gets *that* from," I said meaning to be funny. Violet was not amused.

Surprisingly, James hadn't bothered to do a mental recount of the extra packages he'd thrown willy-nilly into the car. He was not functioning at his optimum intelligence.

Daisy's voice broke through, but I still barely registered her words. "We're making a short side trip for supplies, a storm's closing in tonight and we also have to pick up my laptop from the repair shop," she said.

The word 'we' made James grin even harder. "Lovely," he answered, taking in the white snow crystals dusting Daisy's dark hair, casually twisted in a tortoiseshell clip.

Loose tendrils of escaped strands softly framed Daisy's flushed cheeks. Her eyes were an extraordinary shade of violet.

"She has your eyes, sweeting," I said to Violet.

A shadow passed over Violet's face. "Yes, she *does* love to borrow things without permission."

I chose to ignore her vexation and sent James a *'you're doing fine'* heads up as Daisy's car skated along through rush hour traffic.

The computer tech had bad news. "We seem to have lost some of your data," he said retreating into his default position shrug of 'not-my-fault'.

Daisy sent him a dazzling smile, unmoved.

Violet reacted with a choking sound. "This is *so* not Daisy," she said. "She's showing off for James."

"Today, everything is shipshape," Daisy said. "No worries."

Violet responded with a shiver. "Sometimes I think Daisy

chooses words to deliberately upset me. Ships fall apart. Ships deliver killers. Ships are haunted by ghosts that live forever."

James was impressed. Back in the car, he waited in silence expecting an explosive outburst. By her exasperated sigh, so did Violet.

Daisy inhaled deeply. "What seems a mistake, often proves to be a gift," she said sweetly.

Violet snarled. "Atta girl. Just let the Universe do its thing I always say. It's not like we have a choice."

- VIOLET -

Daisy eased her small car out of its cramped space, maneuvering slowly over the compacted snow, yet untreated with salt and sand, concentrating on the laws of traction over attraction.

"Your James seems good for Daisy," I commented, cattily. "It's doubtful but maybe she'll become the gracious spiritual leader she's becoming famous for."

Our hosts rode in silence the rest of the way to Oxford, but James couldn't help but comment on the prominent eight-foot-tall blueberry mascot made of cement as Daisy turned off the highway. He shuddered. "That's kind of creepy, isn't it," he said.

Daisy made a wide turn off Main Street onto the sheer ice of Water Street. "I've always thought so. It used to give me nightmares when I first moved here."

The car entered the welcoming embrace of Electric Street and headed up the steep hill that always made me nostalgic for the White Horse. I stared at Sam and imagined my beautiful Epona of the good old days, swimming ashore to me as I enticed her with a sweet red apple.

- SAM -

James's first glimpse of Stonecap House was flashing strings of cobalt-blue Christmas lights beckoning atop a hill on the aptly named Electric Street. But while James and I had spent many hours imagining a winter postcard, Violet and I shared a picture of Portmatilloch's Horse Hill with the outline of a vibrant blue horse captured in a flickering strand of electric Christmas lights.

Violet and I stepped out of our human hosts and held hands. Somewhere behind us stood the aged boy and girl who'd delivered us from west to east. By the way they stared at each other it was clear that neither of them needed us to fan their flames of desire anymore and so we fanned our own.

41

THE INVISIBLE MAN

Yesterday upon the stair
I met a man who wasn't there.
He wasn't there again today.
I wish I wish he'd go away.
HUGHES MEARNS

- SAM -

I suffered for James's bruised ego. Whenever an ego is attacked there's trouble.

In Daisy's world James was an invisible man with zero credentials. The media immediately dismissed him as a trophy husband. A hanger-on, stealing Daisy's stage presence – an interloper in need of attention who had shrewdly smitten a vulnerable woman. Obviously, he was a calculating womanizer after a free ride.

It was a sad sight watching James's clenched fists open and close, furtively searching his mind for a means of escape.

As James's invisible agent and bodyguard, I fully understood.

In the old days, the competitive nature of James's rapt audiences vying for attention had bordered on idol worship. And now his position was reversed.

He was no longer James Eriksen, archaeologist. He was James What's-his-Name, a two-dimensional silver fox. How dare he usurp a spiritual leader of Daisy Sinclair's standing.

James's iconic popstar looks had awarded him the aura of a charismatic celebrity – more of a performer than an academic speaker, thrown to a crowd of insatiable female students clamoring for a proverbial touch of their master's robe. James had to contend with frenzied fans hoping for a vicarious brush with what passed for fame.

There had been nothing dignified about being catnip in a lecture hall of feline students.

But next to a box-office spiritual teacher, an archaeologist, albeit a sexy one, remains ordinary unless a spectacular find advances him to the spotlight of front page news. Fame, as always, was as fickle as the weather.

James's old muscle memory of unworthiness returned, eclipsed by Daisy's newfound confidence in the limelight. In a perverse way, embracing insignificance next to Daisy offered him a second chance to identity with the anonymity he was comfortable with.

There had always been days when James, the center of adoration, wished himself back on his parents' homestead – an overlooked child whose only friend was a dog named Buster.

Both he and Daisy's origins seemed destined to live lives as anonymous shadows, but James was able to find his true calling from birth with me as his guiding soul.

Other than being born breach, Daisy had had no soul to recommend her as special. But for reasons neither Violet nor I could fathom, Lila had intervened in her favor late in life and rewritten the rules of fair play.

Daisy's new incarnation, belatedly graced with Violet's extrasensory abilities, had sent Violet into a tailspin. I was left, torn between an injured party who was depressed and angry at the same time.

Violet, sensed James's instinctive failure to shine had been imprinted during a traumatic event. As such, she grappled with revisiting the Viking raid, unwilling to risk the possibility of further delaying the lives of her ancestors already denied for centuries. It occurred to her that perhaps James had been there on that fateful day.

Daisy's 'Professor Sinclair' persona instinctively understood that particles acted out in aggressive patterns but moved in passive herds aligned to the sentient dynamics of their observers.

And now that Violet and I are James and Daisy's designated prime observers, all four of us are affected. Something has to give!

My take on human consciousness or lack thereof, is that neediness is attracted to power, frightened people beg to be saved, atheists want to believe in a higher consciousness, and hard nose pragmatists remain forever terrified of the paranormal.

For a long time, the only link James had to imagination was a flirtation with science-fiction. Theosophy was absent from his curriculum. Being a purist, alchemy placed first in his academic choices as the original source of chemistry, Khem being the ancient name for Egypt. Meanwhile, quantum physics called from a lonely mountaintop he was uninterested in climbing.

But after James separated the math from magic, a compelling blend of anthropology and ancient history made sense. After our 'transparent' meeting it was easier for James to unravel mythical from mysticism, but true spiritual awareness required a leap of faith only Daisy could give.

Seeing his own textbook 'Sands of Time' on Daisy's bookshelf shocked James until he remembered they shared a legitimate passion for all things Egyptian.

Daisy painted Egyptian art; he sifted Saqqara for artifacts. He almost reached for it, but he closed his eyes and allowed me to select the book he *needed* to read.

That night when James fell asleep on the sofa. He dreamed the painted floorboards of Stonecap House creaked and groaned like an old ship.

I studied his pained expression. "James, I said. "When you were born you had no choice but to obligingly follow your aging parents as sheep children are wont to do until they remember they're tigers.

It's time to roar, now!"

THE WATERFALL WEI

- VIOLET -

The full moon cast a mauve beam across Daisy's face. She flinched with a start already sitting up in bed, awake, strangely fearless. The hair on her arms tickled pleasantly with positive ions reminiscent of spray from a mountain waterfall. The sound of rain drummed seductively against the window.

She scanned the room for ghostly forms to explain her happy shivers. "Who's there?"

My voice in her head responded clearly *"silly goose, it's only me."*

Daisy crept towards the call of midnight sugar like a cat but instinctively changed course and made a beeline for the living room bookcase.

A feeble green glow from a clip-on booklight drew her attention to the couch. James lay there sleeping, clasping 'The Great Gatsby' to his chest.

Without thinking, I called out "Sam?"

James smiled in his sleep. "Precious girl, I must be dreaming," he answered.

"I must be, too," Daisy said, snuggling up beside James so they could stay dry while Sam and I walked in the rain.

INNERMOST SANCTUMS

"Exercise caution in your business affairs,
For the world is full of trickery"
MAX EHRMANN

2023

- VIOLET -

The voice of St. 'M' woke me with a prophecy: *"James's identity is the missing key. After you find him hidden in the Viking raid, everything will fall into place."*

"Duly noted," I said and drifted off to thoughts of the day ahead with Sam.

I only took my mind off Daisy's thoughts for a moment. She wriggled away chasing a grey rainbow with James. I welcomed her growing independence and mine.

But her role as bride-to-be made her giddy for more attention. Her ego had gone to her head, and she wandered down a road to disaster dragging me on her coattails.

Unharnessed power always attracts the wrong sort. And to prove it, Doris Chapman, a well meaning Stonecap resident chose that precise moment to shine under Daisy's limelight that resulted in a total eclipse of innocence and ignorance.

Sophie shadowed me. "Spirituality and psychic awareness, while related, vibrate at alarmingly different levels," she meowed piteously. Her eyes changing color should have been a clue. When they turned white it was too late. "Completely out of control" she mumbled. "Dangerously out of control. Think quick."

I *was* quick. "Daisy is growing up. It will do her good to feel her oats," I replied confident I was right.

Sophie's pupils turned midnight black. "You misunderstand me," she said. "It's *you* who are out of control. And Daisy is NOT a horse! You leave Daisy to her own devises far too often so you can spend time with Sam. I don't begrudge either of you some stolen moments of happiness unless it conflicts with your prime mission."

I listened more closely to Daisy and caught the echo of a new obsessive thought. At long last, Daisy had her eye on the prize as a woman of importance, intent on basking in the attention she'd thought would never come. Spirituality be damned!

"Tread softly," Sophie hissed. "A woman making up for lost time is an unstoppable creature on a mission her own. It may already be too late. In which case, be prepared for negotiating a truce between heaven and hell." And with that, she did what all cats do to restore their power. She took a nap.

James's welcome home party was hospitable enough during the welcome speech and cake, but rapidly disintegrated to a lively debate over the origin of conscious souls.

Doris Chapman tapped her wineglass for silence. "Please keep it civil, dear hearts. I'd like to propose a toast to our newlyweds," she said holding her glass aloft. "Here's to true soul mates!"

James grimaced. "Please don't call us that. It reduces us to a ridiculous New-Age cliché. And we are not yet married."

Murmurs of dissent circulated in protest.

"But my dear James," Doris responded. "You're spiritually mated which is far more important. How else would you describe the two of you meeting in shared dreams. Surely such events cannot manifest without divine guidance."

James strengthened his resolve bravely. "Spirituality is a relatively unknown territory for me. I don't profess to know how Daisy and I met in a dream. But I will most heartedly join in celebrating whatever it was, whether it be luck or a form of serendipity I don't yet understand."

A look of certainty transformed Doris's face. "Then, I have the perfect engagement gift," she announced aloud to herself. "I will give the happy couple a past-life regression. It's a special talent of mine. We'll do it tomorrow."

James's protest was immediate. "NO! Sorry, absolutely out of the question. I don't believe in such things." Then added a sheepish, "but thank you for the kind thought."

Doris backtracked seamlessly. "Just for Daisy, then. And if your past lives are as connected as I believe they are, the reading will deliver a message for both of you, and no harm done if you choose to look the other way."

Sophie sprang into action, tearing around the room in frantic circles, leaping erratically from the furniture to the window ledge and back again. I made an excuse for her. "She's fine. She's just got the wind in her tail."

Doris's theory was more ominous. "Cats are sensitives. I expect there's a restless spirit in the room who needs help."

"By all means feel free to fling open the doors of the afterlife," Sophie grumbled. "What could possibly go wrong."

James's jaw clenched. "You've missed my point, Doris. I'd rather not look at all if you don't mind."

Doris had no intention of minding. "So be it. As our guest of honor, we shall graciously defer to your wishes," she said and promptly ignored James's request without the faintest hint of grace.

Daisy's curiosity would not be denied. In her heart-of-hearts she believed a past-life regression was a bit of a lark – a harmless party trick and being tipsy from the previous day's excitement she winked at James. "Actually, I *have* had some fairly lucid dreams, so there are a few twinges of the past that I'd like unlocked," she said. "So, I happily accept a reading in the spirit of generosity in which it was offered. Thank you, Doris."

UNLEASHED

"If you compare yourself with others,
You may become vain or bitter,
For always there will be greater
And lesser persons than yourself"
MAX EHRMANN

- SAM/JAMES -

The day of the regression arrived. Doris our dipsy 'therapist' reassured me it was safe, nothing more than a natural extension of intuition blocked by too many thoughts. I could relate to such a state but remained alarmed by Daisy's eagerness to what she casually referred to as laying a few ghosts.

That should have been my clue to quash a fanciful session contaminated with residual vibes of soul mate twaddle, something I'd learned to supress around the woman I loved – a recently ascribed spiritual teacher.

My future wife was fast becoming famous as an eleventh-hour wunderkind and the latest mystic for reactivating dormant consciousness.

As I understood it, hypnosis of a sort was required to set the participant in touch with their inner-self, and hopefully a meaningful connection, that could never, under any circumstances, degenerate into a tacky séance – a regression being incapable of deteriorating into farce, let alone anything life threatening.

Daisy appeared curious, albeit no longer enthusiastic. I had my doubts but that's just me so, I kept them to myself. I saw it as a chance to enjoy a cup of tea and watch a performance that was, if nothing, an upbeat fairy story contrived to lift Daisy's spirits.

- VIOLET -

Doris arranged the seating in a circle and went about the room waving a smudge stick into the corners and under each chair.

James paced, arms crossed, fuming. "Is this mumbo jumbo really necessary?" he said.

Doris kept smudging. "Mumbo jumbo is an essential ritual to cleanse the air of curses and negative energy – lurking demons and suchlike," she said dismissively.

Doris sat across from Daisy smiling seductively, moderating her voice to an hypnotic monotone. "James and Daisy, please pay special attention to the area above and behind your heads – the seat of the soul where souls are reputed to reside," she droned.

Doris's parroted wisdom evaporated on contact with the sage smoke, and I considered that since the epitome of human wisdom is known as 'sage advice' the herb may be divinely inspired.

Sam hugged me in a spontaneous burst of rapturous energy that surged up Daisy's spine, flooding her extremities before radiating down from the crown of her head to her toes. It manifested as a white-hot body halo extending three feet around her causing her to blush.

Daisy patted her flaming cheeks and pretended to examine her toes, but she was angrier than she'd ever been, and her anger was with me. *"This is you, isn't it! Why are you still here? Whoever you are, you need to go. Leave me alone. I've had enough!"*

When she looked up from her toes she was in a trance.

It was then, the woman I once deemed stupid, firmly put me in my place, deeply unhinging me with her profound observation.

Daisy channeled me and addressed the assembly!

She came of age, gazed vacantly into the past and confessed my truth. "Regression is essentially meditation where you listen to silence," she said. "In 1918 James and I died young in a parallel advance of Covid 19. We were expecting to receive hard-won rewards for dedicated service, but instead we were volunteered without notice to neutralize the karma that continues to plague us still.

Sadly, my initial resistance devolved into a veritable power struggle with the universe, and I retreated behind my ego that was only too willing to play the lead in an evolving passion play.

There are dire consequences when a soul defies its overruling divinity. But there it is."

Daisy woke abruptly; unaware she had spoken. James left the room.

Doris clapped, clearly stunned, encouraged the confused guests to join her in polite applause. "Everyone please remain calm. Could one of you fetch Daisy a glass of water."

She coaxed Daisy into a chair. "Sweetheart, you weren't yourself just now. Do you feel all right?"

"Who else would I be," Daisy replied. "I feel fine. Where did James go? Has something happened?"

While Daisy waited for James, I entered her deepest unconscious to have it out with her. If I was to save her, our kindred, and my mission she had to accept the part she played in her own self destruction.

I knew regression was not the best way to reconfigure an

abandoned path quaintly referred to as a 'dead end' but under the circumstances, it was the quickest.

"You need to let go of this needy 'poor little me' game you've been playing your whole life. You're not the only child to have been unloved. You could have overcome your self-indulgent wallowing," I said. "I can't truly be your soul until you grow up and stop feeling sorry for yourself and honor who you really are without using my energy. I'm no longer your 'get out of hell free' card. Tell me you understand!"

Daisy paused before answering. She looked deeply into my soul before speaking. "Have you considered that I might be yours?" she said.

James returned white as a ghost to comfort Daisy who clearly didn't require comforting. She had an unrecognizable quality about her and then she burst into hysterical tears and the fireworks began.

- JAMES -

Looking back, I can only describe the ensuing chaos as an invasion of *'body snatchers'* laying in wait for the opportunity to hijack Daisy.

It was as if a hoard of restless souls, relatively connected, had been waiting in the wings for Daisy's spiritual awakening in the hopes of a chance to (*excuse the term*), reincarnate, and move on.

Again, in hindsight, I grossly misapplied the term relative considering they failed to pinpoint the correct saviour they had come to petition. Daisy was not their intended target. I was told later, the past life of a girl named Violet, was.

45

THE UNPLANNED PLAN

"They shall be one
With the man in the wind
and the west moon
When their bones are picked clean
and the clean bones gone,
They shall have stars
at elbow and foot.
DYLAN THOMAS

- EVIE -

Saint 'M's message sunk in too late for Violet to avoid the oncoming confrontations: "Low-life surprises always undermine spiritual progress," she warned. "Look to Sophie more often and you won't go far wrong."

A nauseating smell filled the room. The air darkened with smoke and a cloud of ash clung to the ceiling. Each of the entities milling about the room paused to examine Daisy close up and finding her insignificant, moved on.

I recognized them at once. Most were easy for Violet to identify. Sam knew Daisy but had not been privy to Violet's visitation to 901 A.D. nor meeting Celeste.

Lilith, Dorota, Lily, and Saint 'M' clung to Violet's aura like sheep. But Lilith bravely opened her eyes wide enough to register the presence of Aaron Harper Witch-Hunter, and a nameless priest who by his own declaration was to remain eternally anonymous as his *God intended.*

Doris was out-of-body looking guilty. Various confused Viking ruffians needed no singling out; they had merely attached themselves to a distant memory and requiring no direct intervention, soon dissipated.

And when they were gone, the brisk wind died down to a gentle breeze, occasionally whipped up by Lilith's demon or Lily's ego who attached themselves like shadows to their hosts.

Violet's ego was off in a sulk, but Daisy's was far too timid to make a fuss.

One by one, the doppelgangers approached Violet and made appointments to meet her alone.

I advised her, through Sophie, to think of herself as an unsuspecting victim caught in the crossfire of 'psychic contamination by association' and to revisit the Viking raid when the worst was over to discover essential missed details. "Sam must tag along as your bodyguard," I insisted. "I will help him. Listen carefully to whatever he says. His semi-corporal presence will be a vital means of emotional support."

46

OUTMATCHED

"Keep interested in your own career,
However humble; it is a real possession
In the changing fortunes of time."
MAX EHRMANN

- SAM -

Doris Chapman's reading broke its banks venturing into the paranormal territory of a forbidden séance, out of James's area and smack in the middle of Daisy's. It was not an 'I told you so situation' it was a moment of truth.

James was a bull in a New-Age crystal shop when it came to metaphysics, never more insensitive than blurting a timid comment to his Daisy-love meant to ease the tension. "All right old girl?" he said but it wasn't a question.

The inevitable clash between their worlds had occurred in a full-on mystical event, unexpectedly expected, the like of which Daisy had frequently opined as divine interventions arriving at the right moment. She was eventually thrilled to put herself (along with James) in the hands of the universe. Since her misdiagnosed near-death experience – an actual brain-dead death according to science, she'd referred to their time together as her next life.

Not surprisingly, logic was nowhere in sight. Daisy was too dazed to take in a miracle she professed to believe in. All she managed to impart was "It's no use, James, too much has happened we can't explain. I need to be alone for a while."

Doris looked as if she wasn't breathing. I envied her apparent coma.

I took a seat a little apart from Daisy, but James, somewhat clumsily made contact with me – an invisible manifestation he once assumed was his conscious mind. There was no way around it. Scientific investigation was all that was left to him.

He gathered his courage, left his scepticism dead on the floor and dived into a casual one-sided conversation that quite honestly was an embarrassment to him. "Sam?" he said, "Your name *is* Sam, correct? Please bear with me and don't answer back until I've had my say. Look here… *um*… Sam. I'm a dyed in the wool non-believer faced with… well, *you* and whatever *this* was.

I've never believed reincarnation was more than wishful thinking. I always deemed it as pointless navel gazing – the sole invention of creative speculation rather than a proven convention.

The ghastly thought occurs I have been physically separated from my soon to be wife. Have I been parroting her spiritual convictions to keep our boat steady? I just don't know.

I proceeded to play along against my better judgement to please Daisy. I've always considered myself solidly anti-spiritual," he said. "So, your existence is an electric shock to my system, quite the new awakening. Another entity sharing my body will take some getting used to."

I maintained a silent presence.

"I see you as a ghostly apparition, but if what just happened is true, it occurs to me I've been passively listening to you all my life as my personal oracle. A constant idea machine. Not a casual acquaintance but incredibly, a mortal person who once lived and died. Not a god as such, but perhaps, in my wildest atheist dreams, an internal connection to the source labeled God that I vehemently deny. Are you a parasite or a neurosis I've been chatting with as the personal go-to psychotherapist in my head?

I've relied on you for advice and sympathy my whole life. I don't mean to be rude. Please excuse the irony but right now I'm feeling literally psyched out."

He took a breath.

"I suppose it's time you joined this conversation which is funny because I've always talked *to* you. I just thought it was me answering back. So, if we're to take whatever *this is* to a new level, I need to be sure of something. Are you there?"

James experienced a pleasant buzzing in his ear and tingling in his solar plexus unprepared for an answer.

"Brave, James, I am always here," I said.

Despite being in shock, James was quick to reply. "Thank you, Sam, although, I think, man-to-man, you may be a great deal braver than I."

"I do not plan to confront you, James. I'm not your father nor you, my son. I'm neither judge nor jury. Not technically your friend but another human vibrating at a different speed than yours sharing the same road you travel for a while.

We're kindred spirits, moving though life buffeted by emotional ups and downs and reflections both harmful and inspiring. The afterlife is a waiting room with no waiting. It was not my conscious choice to join you. Events after death unfold pretty much the same way they do in life: Out of the blue, from frying pans to fires and back again."

James breathed more easily, relieved 'his' Sam had a sharp lucid mind. Indeed, a mind of his own. James was clearly a rational soul with legitimate unanswered questions. After a brief exchange, he judged me a worthy companion. The positive thought occurred that if James remained open and civil, he would teach me something important.

He hesitated and spoke shyly. "I think I could use some space to get my head round this for a while."

"Agreed," I said. "I need that too. This is a learning curve for both of us."

"Then I hope our journey is one of mutual evolution," he said.

I wisely allowed James the last word. I was proud of him; I was proud of both of us.

47

A FAIRY'S TAIL

"Once upon a time you made a wish.
No need to thank me."

- VIOLET -

Daisy zombied off to be alone, curiously in the most appropriate place where we could formally meet – at the bottom of the garden where fairies are said to dwell. She was clearly put out – the perfect counterpoint to my pushing in, the day she died from Covid 19.

We stood on common ground, far from solid. Ironically, she was out of her element, just as I was finally getting into mine. Her speech had startled me. It was the second time she'd consciously spoken to me out loud as if I was another person. I felt guilty but relieved.

Her bitterness was tangible. "So, it seems I have you to thank for my sudden cure," she said. "I'm only a spiritual teacher by proxy. A fake. And my love affair with James was merely an afterthought of yours and Sam's."

"We've both been used," I said.

"You're a sprite. And I have been pixie-led. Literally down this very path to speak with the me of me I meet in meditation. Your silence has been strangely reassuring.

It makes sense now. You've been mocking me. But now I miss you, again. I say again because I always wanted a sister, and I missed you all my life. But we are not that. My mother was right. I was never enough. I'm an old fool."

The long pause where her terrible disappointment threatened to 'unseat' me meant it was my turn. "Yes, yes, yes, sort of, no, no, almost, absolutely not," I answered, meaning to be honest from the get-go. But even I heard myself as superior. I had given her my best 'glib and condescending' answer. I tried again.

"As for being a punishment, I'm not yours. But for the longest time I believed you were mine. And as for siblings… we seem to be distant cousins. Birds of a feather with broken wings and now we must move on with one good wing between us."

Daisy choked back a tear. "I thought I hated my life, but all the time it was you hating me."

"I did at first. I don't now. But it was not *all* your life. We only met a few months ago in the intensive care unit. How's that for irony. Old habits die hard, pardon the pun. Supernatural events never happen without a reason. From where I sit…"

"Right. Somewhere in the back of my head," she said to herself. "Floating like a helium balloon."

She wasn't far wrong.

I changed tack. "From where it *feels* like I sit, in the subconscious afterlife, ironically, now during someone else's life. Daisy, please believe me it's not lofty up here. If I sound arrogant it's because I was a spoiled child."

"Me too." It was said automatically. Sadness, surprisingly without bitterness. She checked herself. "Not in the conventional sense but spoiled as in broken and useless."

"If I'm perfectly honest, Daisy, I don't think I'm your soul. I assumed I was but now things are different. Sorry. It's impossible to make such a long story, short. I take the blame for our odd start. Apparently smooth transitions are not my strong suit. Perhaps, we should consider ourselves as long-lost friends meeting on shaky ground where we can stay until we get to know one another better."

Daisy walked over to frozen lilac bush, snapped off a long branch, and waved it slowly like a magic wand.

I felt lighter as her *spirits* lightened. "So, we've reached an impasse," she said raising the branch to the sun. "I surrender. I offer you this olive branch. Here's to reincarnation."

"Yes," I replied. "But in my case, it's more *'hands across the sea'.*"

And then a thought occurred to me. Daisy couldn't have a broken spirit. Nor could she own a spirit that grew lighter or a troubled soul that grew darker (although I was certainly troubled) because she still didn't *have* a soul. And if I wasn't her soul, who was I!

48

DARK SIDE OF THE MOON

Though they go mad
They shall be sane,
Though they sink through the sea
They shall rise again and death
Shall have no dominion."
DYLAN THOMAS

- EVIE -

Sam had kept the search for Daisy alive by convincing the skeptical James, forever dreaming across physics, of an afterlife that heralded the end of playing dead. But ironically, holding James's together meant shaking his fears apart.

When Daisy materialized no-one was more surprised than James, but being a practical scientist, he brushed the miraculous element aside as luck.

Now he sits bewildered, staring into space, aware of Sam, but thankfully blind to what I can see down the road. He flinches as if stung by a bee whenever one of the troubled spirits wanders close. Now and then he tilts his head straining to hear a voice.

James sighed deeply and squeezed Daisy's hand. "I can't think straight," he said. "This situation has opened my mind to… *he paused...* to nothing, no possibilities, absolutely nothing I can prove."

Daisy rested her head on James's shoulder. "Please try. Do it for me."

"Perhaps I'm insane," James said. "I was seriously *mad* to put your mental health in the hands of Doris Chapman."

Violet needed to feel responsible. "How did a wedding gift get so out of hand?" she asked me.

My harsh reply was an unsuspected slap in the face. "More importantly, why did *you* let things get out of hand. Daisy thought Doris was well meaning and was up for a bit of harmless entertainment," I said. "It was a simple courtesy. No one was prepared for All Hallows Eve, least of all Doris. And sadly, neither were you."

New-Age literature had hooked Daisy on soul mate stories. Having no romantic success as a teenager, psychic phenomenon was a natural progression from fairy stories to pie in the sky dreams.

Sam eventually convinced James there were synchronicities within archaeology that begged the existence of a supernatural force holding sway over us.

Violet's ancestors circled like predators and bombarded her with questions.

Doris stopped breathing and joined the other spirits in the guise of a gnarled old man with a battered hat, causing a disturbance wherever she drifted.

Lilith cursed Aaron Harper in a shrill voice. "Witch hunter!" she spat. "If we are truly in hell together it will be my pleasure to watch your reckoning. I'm happy to stay here to cheer your payback."

Aaron circled Doris's body and pinched her viciously with no response. Instead, he had to rub his own arm now sporting an angry bruise. He pinched Doris a second time, gazing in disbelief at a second bruise added to the first.

"Pinching a dead woman won't reveal a witch," Lilith sneered.

"You'll need to do better than that or have you lost your special covenant with your God."

Doris stirred. Aaron examined her closely. "Mistress, how came you here? I don't recognize you." Doris's silence displeased him. He turned away and took a menacing step towards Lilith, but she crossed her mangled fingers and held them ahead of her like a crucifix. Her body bore the telltale scars of recent torture. "I curse you," she screamed. "Where's your lying magic now!"

The room's furnishings collapsed into dust and swirled away first, the walls of the room disappeared next, leaving a pattern of fast-evaporating wallpaper roses suspended over Horse Hill slowly wavering into focus.

Sam stood by Violet's side, searching a long-ago horizon.

"Stay close to Violet," I ordered. "Don't disappear like the day you died."

"Mother, I don't mean to be rude," Sam said. "I've explained to Violet many times that I didn't *leave* her; that the universe parted us without warning, and we flew off like frightened birds, Besides, if anything, Violet left *me*!"

"Did you mention to her that nothing happens without a reason?"

"I never got a chance. The sky was empty when I got there. There was no trace of Violet *to* follow."

"Chances aren't handed out like sweeties," I said. "You have to *take* them, Sam. Love always leaves a presence of the beloved. You have to listen to the silence for a sign. You left too soon." I hadn't meant to sound so harsh, but both my children needed an abrupt awakening if they were to prevail.

- SAM -

I left James to himself and went to find Violet. She was alone, having escaped Daisy. She looked the part of a long-lost ghost. "Like minds," I said. "And speaking of minds, James's was too jumbled to fully understand me. He needed some space. How are *you* holding up?"

Violet seemed strangely subdued. "Surprisingly, not as well as Daisy."

I slapped my knees and stood up. "Right. We should get Daisy and James away from here and settle them down… maybe settle ourselves down as well. James is sending me distress calls despite himself. He doesn't know it, but tonight's business has helped him make a significant start towards growing up. I understand him well enough to know he'll require a few more 'starts' but what he feels right now is huge.

Right now, he wants to go for a drive. It's a thing he does to center himself."

I enclosed Violet in a hug. "What say you and me do a disappearing act. I don't mind saying Stonecap has changed this night and not for the better. It isn't safe here. Tell Daisy that James needs her help. I'll make sure he ends up at the coffee house. We need to shake off the vibes in this house until Evie clears it."

Doris sat motionless in a corner, back in her body with her eyes closed, beyond the capacity to be thanked. "That's what you get when you dabble in the supernatural," I shouted in her face. "There's a correct procedure for these things!"

The atmosphere was toxic. A light sprinkling of ash lay on every surface.

Sophie and Summer appeared at my feet. They were in effect a pair of industrial strength 'canaries' checking for *poisonous mine gas*, entering a minefield of psychic disturbance.

I felt as nauseous as I ever did with the Spanish flu, but the touch of Sophie's fur cleared my head. "That's because psychic disturbances have the same vibrations as the flu," she said. "I'll do what I can, here, but I need one of my potions to permanently dispel a hangover of this magnitude.

These souls were not accidents waiting to happen like the ones who gravitate to amateur seances; they are a severely traumatized group soul. I only hope this incident hasn't destroyed their chance for rebirth. The New-Age has a lot to answer for," she hissed and disappeared.

Summer spat at Doris and swatted her ankles before sniffing the room for leftover demons.

A deflated Doris sat hugging her knees, rocking back and forth. "Is it over?" she repeated dully, unsure of where she was. "My head is thumping. I don't remember. Is something over?"

"Something is definitely *not* over," I said to her. "You're going to need a ton of smudge sticks to exorcise the damage this little party trick of yours has unleashed."

I left Summer dispatching low-lying blobs of dark ectoplasm like a plague of rats, and rejoined James.

49

SECOND SIGHT

*"Time for you
And time for me,
And time yet
For a hundred indecisions,
And for a hundred visions
and revisions."*
T.S. ELIOT

- SAM -

Violet and I were clearly in need of revisiting the past to put the present into perspective. A trip to 901 A.D. was the best place to start.

I abandoned James and stayed close to Violet like I promised Evie, but for once Violet didn't want my company.

"Why do *you* need to watch this? You *weren't* here," she snapped. "I was alone. I never saw you when I was here before."

I kissed the tip of her nose. "I'm here at Evie's orders to support you, so, I'm staying. No need to thank me."

I felt Violet's shame when she admitted she'd dismissed the exposed child as soon as she discovered it was effectively a version of Daisy. "I thought the infant was me," she said. "Daisy was expendable. Sacrificed. It seemed unimportant. The worst had already happened. It was over."

"It wasn't over then and it's not over now," I said. "Sometimes we're given a second chance to do something for the first time. I'm taking that chance, now."

- VIOLET -

There was no moon when Lilith fought her way to the horse. She carried Grace swaddled in a shoulder sling, blindly inching her way through the stink of charred flesh and choking black smoke. I felt Lilith's pain, clawing the turf, hand-over-hand, listening her way to a pocket of silence within the outline of the White Horse. Lilith's fingerbones snapped, barely knitted together, crushed as they were, after weeks of Aaron's torture.

Sam felt me cringe when I cried out "I've seen all I need to see, I'm off home."

He stayed my arm. "Evie wanted us to watch. She especially wanted you to see it twice. We're not leaving until it's over."

Dorota followed Lilith, hunched, weaving drunkenly up the hill. She counted in repetitions of ten under her breath. "Ten little fingers," she whimpered. "My child has ten little fingers and ten perfect toes." A twisted arm hung limp at her side. "My lover has ten little fingers and ten perfect toes," she panted. Her face blackened by soot and dried blood, showed one eye swollen, sightless. But the sanctuary within the horse called her to rally.

Lilith tried to stand. She reeled back, veering off course. "Lilith, don't look back." I shouted. "I can see the horse. It's straight ahead. You're almost there. May the goddess be with you."

Lilith heard my voice as Dorota's and answered Dorota with a curse. "Go to hell foul witch. I've given you up to Master Aaron. So, you're next."

But then, Alba overtook Dorota and quite accidently knocked Lilith's arm, correcting her course. Alba grabbed one of Lilith's ankles as her arms reached into the horse's flank.

Dorota tore at Alba's hands, but fear had turned them to steel.

Evie's proclamation carried over the wind like thunder. *"Pity the lad. He loves Lilith but he needs a first kill to wash away his shame and appease his father. His life depends on sacrificing his daughter or swapping Lilith's life for his own. He has chosen to die with Lilith, but sadly, the fool believes there's still time to save his daughter."*

Lilith inched her way forward pushing her bundled infant further inside the belly of the horse and loosened the swaddling. Grace's seagull cries rose and fell on the wind. Alba heard nothing but his own failure and surrendered, blinded by fear and the congealed blood in his eyes.

The roar of torch flames flared higher above a circle of hatred. Warriors mindful of losing their virility to a goddess known to castrate gods for her amusement, twice celebrated for threatening to geld Thor, were careful to keep a distance of three axe lengths from the outline.

The screams of a dying horse silenced their war cries. But Epona was not dying; she was calling her sisters to rally until every loch and river boiled with fury. A narrow channel of seawater pointing the way home lay in wait, serene as glass for the dragon ship.

Alba, pulled by his father, brought Lilith with him until they were set upon as one creature by the mob. Alba's father cheered them on, consumed with shame, determined to destroy the weakling who'd defiled his name. It was over when the cheering ceased. The torches were lowered. The men had their blood sacrifice. Alba and Lilith were silenced.

Dorota was too weak to protest.

In the aftermath of victory, the men milled about looking lost, suddenly spent from hours of screaming and posturing with heavy weapons. Scraggly bands of warriors drunk on bloodlust wound their way down Horse Hill heading for their ship. For a moment, the dragon ship silhouetted against the returned moon looked like the sea monster rumored, in Daisy's century, to inhabit Loch Ness. I shivered. It was uncanny knowing too much history.

A highland gale strong enough to ground Flora's fairies roared over Dorota, left in the dark weeping over the body of Grace. It lifted her best friend's charred sacrificial bones and ash in one hand and dispatched them hissing into the sea where a spout of red water surprised the warriors settling into their appointed rowing places.

The last retreating voices of men singing, blurred into what sounded to me like the low grumble of thunder. The last semblance of snaking torchlight stumbled and bobbed in the dark. Oars splashed.

Thor was asleep at the wheel when a giant horse's head surged from the water, glared into the dragon's mouth, and capsized its body with a single thrash of its tail.

Dorota slept as if dead. The blood-red gash on the Hill showed the horse's outline as a gaping wound protecting the goddess's womb – a white circle of moonlight still warm where Grace once lay.

It was now clear why there had been no moon. The goddess Celeste had burrowed her mother deep into the heart of the hill where her light escaped through the cut lines of the horse as a ribbon of white fire seared into the blackened grass.

And I knew without a doubt, that James had been Alba, and Dorota had been my first mother followed by Evie, my second.

I had been born under a double curse to reconcile two friends made enemies by a lie. Dorota had reincarnated as Saint 'M' and the higher truth of it all was that I was in essence, the love child of Epona.

I was Sin-Thea *and* Violet, and in a strange twist, Daisy Sinclair's ethereal cousin. Reincarnation's 'no rules rule' had smudged the thousand-year map of our fragile connections. Oddly, our ties had grown weaker with time but rallied stronger with distance.

I learned the full measure of sadness. I could be born in 901 A.D. and in 1901 – as Dorota's spiritless lovechild – the bane of Lilith's demonic anger.

The goddess Karma had a perverse sense of humor. It wasn't the last time I reflected how alike the words friend and fiend were.

Goddess only knows what year it will be when Daisy and I are rid of each other or how much of the present world survives.

But that night I remembered to bless Dorota for conceiving me in the healing belly of the horse where I steeped in Epona's good graces under my given name Sin-Thea.

It was the measure of Epona's unconditional love that she allowed Evie to set aside my divine name and rename me for the color of my eyes.

As for Daisy: born of Lily; born of Lilith and Alba, she had been the sacrificed infant Grace, transparent and unfinished, and I now had the power to grant her a long-denied life of love and happiness with her twin soul, James.

It was my decision, but St. 'M's voice visited me. "Sam is your savior," she said. "Trust him with your next life."

THE MOURNING AFTER
the book of Evie

GUARD YOUR QUEEN

*"Take kindly the counsel of the years,
gracefully surrendering the things of youth."*
MAX EHRMANN

- VIOLET -

Evie prophesized Daisy's accident months in advance so I knew it was meant to be. Still, Evie felt required to issue a warning even though, ultimately it was Daisy's choice to live or die.

"In case James hasn't noticed," Evie said. "Daisy is a tad wobbly on her pins. Not to be maudlin, but there's a death in the wind so be prepared." Then she upset my applecart.

"How will you feel if Daisy clambers up the same slippery cliffs that were treacherous for you even as a wiry child?" she asked. It felt like a trick question. I was being tested.

I was cagey. "Fate always worries me, but you taught me to honor Daisy's choice to accept death when her time came. Besides, James is now her go-to sherpa. Ever since the séance Daisy's head has been in the clouds. In any case, Daisy and I have agreed to disagree. She grows more infantile every day. As such, I've become the perfect babysitter for her second childhood. She insists on playing hide and seek so I humor her by hiding, but Sam reminds James to keep an eye on her. And since I wanted Daisy to die for such a long time, it's best I look the other way."

ICEBERG AHEAD

"You are a child of the universe,
no less than the trees and the stars;
you have a right to be here".
MAX EHRMANN

- EVIE -

Violet had been born many times before she came to me. Souls like Violet, singled out for greatness, arrive at my door immaculate having proved themselves to be inviolate over thousands of incarnations. I've guided many an old soul to meet their destiny but none so unique as Violet's. Each one was a special case where a strong-will was an essential requirement.

By the tender age of seventeen Violet had made amazing progress towards her bizarre destiny. She was born delightfully headstrong; she had to be to honor the great purpose for which she'd been chosen. So, although I knew the first time our eyes met that Violet's training was never going to be clear sailing, I assumed it would be a joy and the brightest jewel in my crown. And so, it has been.

I was in awe of Violet's perfection. All I saw was the multiple blessings surrounding her that blinded me to the curse lingering under her skin.

Violet's current predicament is clear. She has committed crimes against a soul she was entrusted to serve – a vulnerable old woman, in crisis, no less. For which, by law, Violet will be severely punished.

So, when word came in 1917 that Violet's lifespan would be cut short, I consulted with Epona, Lady Flora, my handmaiden fairy, Celeste, and Violet's beloved Sam.

We deliberated how best to compensate but our solutions must have been blocked by an unprecedented dark force because none of us saw the trouble ahead. Surely, an iceberg of doom loomed in the waters ahead.

Somehow, we weathered the unpredictable storms of Violet's extreme hatred for Daisy in shock and surprise. And it's taken me all this time to see the truth that had been hidden in plain sight. Which leaves me with the conundrum of how to save Violet from my grave error of careless naivete I hadn't thought possible.

The solution is simple but not easy. Universal laws are fixed to preserve a flawless state of consciousness. End of story.

The so-called tests of time are impossible to breach. And since Violet's credentials were entirely above reproach, I chose to finally inform her gently by way of her favorite bedtime story. even though the barn door had closed after the horse was gone.

I visited her while she was dreaming. "Violet," I began. "Perhaps you recall my telling you the story of 'Sleeping Beauty' when you were a child."

"The one you read to me at *least* a million times? Yes," she answered groggily. "I believe I've heard of it."

"It's a fable that has endured because of its magical appeal about an innocent newborn princess who suffered a curse of sleep after a jealous uninvited guest overturned a celebration of birth into a party of horrors. Ring any bells?"

Violet crossed her arms in her sleep. "I see where this is going," she said. "But I *was* uninvited, Evie, and it wasn't *fair*! The universe had no business hijacking me from an incarnation I earned. It was an award for being a perfect soul!"

"Dearest girl, you weren't sent to Daisy Sinclair just to be her soul, troubled though she was. You were sent to save your own," I said. "Higher purposes require extreme procedures."

"Higher shmigher, I was clearly hi-jacked. Someone might have asked my permission."

"But you may have refused."

"Obviously."

"It was a decision necessary to complete your training. You came into this lifetime at the direct bidding of Epona."

"I gather that, *now*. But it would have helped me more if I'd been informed *before* my death."

"You were being tested. It was a test of your capacity to selflessly obey the karma of cause and effect. You weren't *supposed* to know the answers in advance. *That* wouldn't have been fair.

If you hadn't intervened, Daisy's untimely death would have had tragic repercussions that may have jeopardized several troubled souls trapped in fear and torment. You were the only one who could save them.

Need I add, if you can help a troubled soul find their way, it's your duty to do so.

You've always been a *headstrong* princess; Daisy has been a *troubled* princess – a sleepwalker all her life. As the afflicted souls approach a narrow bandwidth of rebirth, the recovery of a rare group soul lies between the two of you.

For the record, your downfall was ego. Except it wasn't entirely your fault; you were distinguished by your faultless credentials. And by the way, a dormant ego is always half awake until you graduate with full honors. It can't follow you around like a hitchhiker. You're the boss. You must effectively pull its plug and make peace with the universe that only *appears* to have excluded you from a list of invited party guests."

"Are you saying you're the good fairy and I'm the bad fairy in this scenario?"

"I'm saying *you've* been both! I'm saying *I've* been both. I'm saying we're the mistake that sunk a thousand ships.

While you've been guarding Daisy, I've been monitoring the claims against you. Damage control means reversing the image of you as a sinking ship. What's done cannot be undone but it *can* be atoned for with honest cunning."

"If I'm not mistaken, that's *your* forte, Evie."

"Yes, I'm proud to say it is. But whatever works to save you is good. We reject nothing."

Souls need to make a lot of impromptu decisions conducted from a neutral zone for the best results. In soul terms, could an inexcusable blunder ever be excused? Part of the group soul negotiation was Violet being the only one who could turnaround a mistake pinned to her failure to act compassionately. She was royally screwed.

"You may be an old soul, Violet, but each time you're reborn you're given a new ego – a young impetuous dragon eager to fight. Its function is to survive at all costs. It lives in fear of death, quick to anger, quicker to blame, and even quicker to fight for its life at the at the exclusion of everything and everyone else. Once activated, a new dragon seeks out its enemies. And once maligned it will defend its territory to the death.

I invite you to view me, now, as the good fairy who arrived unfashionably late to counteract a bad fairy's temper tantrum. Lately, you seem to enjoy identifying yourself as a bad fairy."

"I know a bad fairy from a wicked one."

"Cleverly put but you're not off the hook. Manipulating a human host for your own ends is tantamount to murder. We must assume the worst."

"You refer to being recycled via the void of no return?"

"Stage-managing a human in crisis is a clear violation of protocol."

"Can it be overturned?"

"If it is, it will be the first time."

"Then what can be done?"

"It's time to deploy an S.O.S flare. To save your soul I must spiritually prostrate myself before Lila, and if I can save the day and more importantly, save face, Lila may see the error of my ways and save *both* of you."

Sometimes conversing with Violet was more effective when she was semi-conscious. But Violet's immature ego, the sleeping dragon, awoke and declared war.

I had failed Violet as well as myself.

The truth, the whole *unvarnished* truth, was that Violet had been temporarily possessed by the reluctant soul who wanted to punish Dorota back in the day. I had dismissed it as an irrelevant temper tantrum and assumed when it dissipated through the side of the ship, it had departed, as in deceased. I was wrong. It was in league with the demon flu that took Violet's life. I see it still, in corners lurking and cackling, ready to pounce.

Close association with Daisy, meant it took custody of Violet like Daisy's deadbeat mom.

Ironically, as Daisy absorbed Violet's pure energy, the more Violet was drained of power to withstand its attacks. Phoenix power was duly eclipsed by fresh dragon fire.

Sam believed Violet's forgiving nature would prevail, but he was sidetracked helping James process a spate of distracting dreams as Alba-FirstBlood that featured Lilith's madness. As a result, James ignored Daisy when she needed him most.

Violet's plan was to wait for Sam, considering James wasn't immortal.

Celeste agreed with Sam, but I had been robbed of such surety, and Epona had sent Violet so much white light she was in danger of disappearing.

ANNUS PERFECTUS

"We two have run about the hills,
and picked the daisies fine;
But we've wandered many a weary foot,
since auld lang syne."
ROBERT BURNS

St. Valentine's Day – **2023**

- VIOLET -

After Doris's party, there was nothing James could do or say to deter Daisy from choosing Pormatilloch as their honeymoon destination. Daisy referred to it as *'the Perfect honeymoon for the perfect us. Absolute Perfectus.*

"It's our second childhood," she insisted. "Sam and Violet will be thrilled."

Well, I wasn't thrilled. And if anything, Pormatilloch turned out to be a disastrous second honeymoon for Sam and I. Sam had been against the whole thing. But I was slightly carried away by the romantic notion of revisiting the home where Sam and I met and planned our future life of perfect bliss.

Portmatilloch was the same and not the same. Our highland paradise turned out to be a wasteland of spiky charcoal-tipped grass, the perfect setting for a disaster. Its soul was away under the cold bleak sea.

I searched in vain for a black shape in the water and suggested

Daisy buy a quantity of apples I needed for a ceremony. More of a ritual, I told her, but I said please in such a way that Daisy was bound to say yes, all right then.

"You'd better grab a cardigan," I said to her, "or better still, a warm coat. It can get nippy on the hills and in the forest, although out of the wind the land rather exudes a specter of death. Not to be too gloomy but that's the truth of it. You can walk under that thing that passes for a sun, later, should it deign to appear."

By now she and James were used to including Sam and I in their plans, but we left them soulless more and more. Daisy bought the apples and explained to James. *"I don't know what Violet wants these for, but she does. She has to deliver them to someone named Epononomus or something. She said it won't take long. It's the least I can do, and it's a good excuse for an explore. Violet's feelings are mixed. She's not having a good time. I feel we've been selfish by forcing this visit on her. Her trips down memory lane are a tad dark."*

Daisy was right. By the same token, a woman on her honeymoon didn't need to be distracted by negative thinking. She and James were happy to be together, anywhere, especially without my past hanging over them like a damp pall of death and regret.

Sam and I felt like children again, but that guise only worked its magic for a few hours. We had moved on in ways I would never have imagined. And so, we strolled hand-in-hand as if we were besotted teenagers on our first date, slightly nervous and self-conscious.

From the time Daisy glimpsed Horse Hill she failed to listen to me, for no other reason than she was obsessed about her new walking shoes that pinched cruelly. She constantly battled with deciding the best time to take her pain medication for old swollen feet, hobbling along, propped up by James who was feeling queasy from multiple headaches. It didn't bode well for a great day.

Sam directed James to the grey stone church which blended into grey streets lined with grey shops. They poked around the deserted stables and workshops while Daisy sat on a bench massaging her toes. My old phantom white scar on her left big toe reminded me she was in danger.

I left Daisy's side, drawn to Saint M's semi-demolished cell, nearby. It lay exposed to the elements from a hundred years of latter-day pilgrims, blindly searching for magic according to the famous legend of Sister Mary's mystical powers. They'd carried off as many souvenir stones as they could.

Despite the sad condition of Portmatilloch, Scottish flavored memorabilia steeped in mysticism were popular items to sell at the highland games and in the psychic fairs, increasingly focused on travel guides pumped up romantic ambiance of ancient highland myths.

Words to describe my old home escaped me. Later it came to me. The word I'd been searching for was lacklustre. The spots where nature should have shone, had blended into locations robbed out of all power. The locations of the goddess's shrines I knew from memory were overgrown lumps of blighted cairns reduced to moss covered rubble.

It was hardly surprising that barren landscapes bereft of spirit were devoid of color. Even the apples Daisy brought me looked grey.

When the four of us took a stroll on the beach the day was overcast, chilly as were most summer months.

In my time, the seashore held an aura of celebration. It

symbolized my birthplace where Epona had lovingly deposited me. Even the time my ejected spirit circled over it when I'd said goodbye to her, it had never been completely gloomy. I reckoned, since Sam and I were back together, it should have regained a spark or two from our presence, but it was not so.

The adage 'one can never go home again' held a ring of truth. James and Daisy wrote their names in the sand and Daisy performed the tasks I asked her by rote. As promised, she left a row of apples at the edge of the sea and several more around the rim of Epona's spring – a sad indentation full of dead leaves in the heart of an ailing forest.

It was sweet when she spontaneously rubbed her forehead after I recalled a vision of Evie and I tracing wet stars on our skin.

James rubbed his forehead for less pleasant Viking memories, so Sam showed James his treasure field while Daisy took off her shoes to fight the losing battle of rubbing life back into her numb toes.

Naturally, James was experiencing cluster headaches. As Alba-FirstBlood, Grace's teenage father, his few happy memories of Portmatilloch were overcast by terror and shame.

Thankfully, Daisy seemed immune to thoughts of James failing to save her, which was odd because I had recurring visions of the terrible raid at every turn. Daisy wasn't blocking me so much as dreaming of the new house she and James were planning to build in Oxford.

Sam said there was a pain-free moment when he'd shared James's glimpse of a lovely girl heavy with child. An innocent enough dream but not a happy-ever-after Viking tale. This was the place where his comrades bludgeoned him to death with their axes. James's latest headache was severe enough to warrant the temporary end of sightseeing. Their picnic trek was cancelled, and while Daisy and James took their afternoon nap, Sam and I went for a walk as the happy couple we once were.

Sam strolled over his field of earth that could now only best be described as dirt. Such a lifeless word. But this had been the spot that delivered a vibrant crop of Saxon memories and Roman finds.

It was far enough away from the slaughter site to feel reasonably deserted and yet I could still see the faint disruptions of plumes in the air like lost heatwaves where dispossessed souls still searched for their mislaid possessions.

After the accident, Sam told me he'd shared James's spontaneous vision of a descending axe at the time Daisy screamed. My thoughts were hazy after that. But in the early moments while Daisy fought for her life my mind was clear enough to feel remorse.

Daisy went climbing remembering my happy escapades climbing Horse Hill and decided to make it up the rocky approach and wave to James below. I should have been with her to warn her that my delightful recall edited out the dangerous slippery nature of rocks that were now lodged in an unstable matrix of bone-dry soil.

Daisy was barefoot when she stubbed her toe. I felt it in my foot. Reluctantly she had forced on her unyielding new shoes.

She limped forward dislodging a clump of dead grass that sent a scree of gravel tumbling her backwards towards the spectre of death waiting beside a large boulder. Death caught her in its skeletal arms. I felt the impact of Daisy's skull cracking on stone from my location daydreaming in the belly of the white horse.

THE SLIPPERY SLOPE

"Out, out, brief candle!
Life's but a walking shadow,
A poor player that struts
And frets his hour upon the stage,
And then is heard no more.
It is a tale told by an idiot,
Full of sound and fury,
Signifying nothing."
WILLIAM SHAKESPEARE

February 18 – **2023**

- VIOLET -

There was no expectation. No pain. I merely pitched backwards out of Daisy's body when her head met the rocky outcrop. I was swooped up to a position above the incident as it continued to unfold.

James wrapped his jacket around Daisy's head and mopped the blood from her eyes.

I was undone, dizzy by association and sat down on the summit to calm Daisy's nerves. But they weren't Daisy's; they were mine from the old days when my nerves were immune to the shakes of any kind.

My left big toe fairly pulsated with pain. My name, Violet, evaporated. I had no idea who I was.

OVER HER DEAD BODY!

*"Love is gentle, love is kind
The sweetest flower when first it's new
But love grows old and waxes cold
And fades away like morning dew."*

- VIOLET -

I accompanied Daisy to the hospital, riding beside James, following in the ambulance so I could talk with Sam.

Once installed in the intensive care ward, both Daisy and I stood outside her body waiting for the clinical end.

I reached out for Daisy, but she refused to feel or see me.

She murmured the words black beauty over and over with a beatific smile on her face. I held her hand anyway.

Daisy was fast-tracked to deathwatch status, examined, put on life support, and given the regular length of allotted time necessary to calm the next of kin into a state of mind where they were compelled to make a life and death decision.

Daisy tagged me. "You're it!" she shouted and ran off giggling. I followed in hot pursuit in and out of operating theatres and nurses' stations.

I couldn't catch her so I retraced my steps to the cliff where Daisy fell, clinging to the hope that someone would tell me who I am.

ABANDON SHIP

*Merrily, merrily, merrily, Mary Lee
death is but a dream*

- VIOLET -

I was privileged to share Daisy's final moments, but although I was there, I was most definitely not *all* there – a state that was thoroughly unnerving until I caught up with Sam and James in the ambulance.

I worried myself back under Daisy's skin to say goodbye, but she'd already left. We spoke now, from the same side of death.

My spontaneous ejection from Daisy's body had momentarily propelled her skyward prompting a weightless descent as a seventeen-year-old girl to make me feel at home. She landed beside me on a trampoline made of snow where she bounced me, giggling like a wild child.

Daisy embraced the hologram of death, and the ironic aliveness of it, taking to it the way a launched ship embraces the sea, which may account for her flying dream of free-falling from a blue sky into a sailing ship. There had been a friendly bump followed by a memory of underwater turbulence (*one of mine, I'm afraid*).

Sixty-eight years melted away as we made snow angels. Swaddling clothes of flesh were released until Daisy was a newborn who aged into the old woman I had grown to care for.

Daisy's atoms reassembled into colorful globules that hummed in a jelly-like suspension melting and reforming like a human lava lamp. She was clearly experimenting for she rose next as a cloud of playful snowflakes.

As Daisy's substitute soul, I shared her Kaleidoscope senses. Layers of emotion painted with light nudged each other, revealing familiar faces and places. Our roles reversed. Daisy was now my host who delighted in being out of my control. I, in turn, delighted in her saucy nature that had been hidden under sadness and fear. We continued to play hide and seek through the halls of the hospital where she was attached to life support, a déjà vu moment for me. She flew to James's side as he consented to let her go. Sam acknowledged my presence but said nothing.

The instant the monitor flatlined, a first chakra mist ascended through my bone marrow, and I found myself floating in a sea of stars swimming and diving with Daisy like a pair of dolphins united in pure consciousness.

Gaia sang Evie's lullaby from light years away: *There is a ship that sails the sea. She's loaded deep as deep can be. But not as deep as the love I make. I know not how I'll sink or swim.*

Champagne air effervesced our liquid forms bathed in lemon soda pop. Each iridescent bubble snapped with electricity tingling the place where our skin used to be.

We burst into sparks as we gained speed, and I was hypnotized by a pearly spiral of DNA that unraveled from my navel at the speed of light. When I left her there were no goodbyes, only love.

That evening Daisy visited James. She bid him sleep in her bed and to wait. She would fly home that very instant. She told him seven times, and then she kept her promise.

56

GIVING UP THE GHOST

Though lovers be lost
love shall not.
And death
shall have no dominion.
DYLAN THOMAS

- SAM -

James's first glimpse of Violet's ghost was a flash of white nightgown in Daisy's mirror. I know Violet saw him because she always liked to hide behind curtains. I can't be sure whether it was curiosity or terror that drew her out. But this much I *do* know. Violet pretended James wasn't there to deliberately unsettle him to counteract her own unsettling experience of being no 'where'.

"Hello," I said gently.

Violet startled and made a beeline for the door but when James looked in the hall she'd gone. "It's all right," he called after her. "It's me, James. Don't be afraid. I know who you are. Violet, isn't it? I think you may be looking for Sam. I can give him a message if you like."

Violet shouted back. "I… DON'T… know… anyone… named… Sam!"

I counted to ten out loud the way Violet and I used to play hide and seek.

Sure enough, it triggered a memory and Violet crept back keeping to the shadows. She placed a hand on James's shoulder and whispered directly into his ear although she remained invisible. "I'm looking for Daisy," she said.

"Daisy passed away in the night," James replied.

Violet's vacant expression puckered into a frown. "Then SHE'LL be looking for ME. We were playing hide and seek. So, as you can guess, one of us is seeking and one of us is hiding."

James played it cool. "I promise I won't give you away. Violet, I'm new to this soul thing. But I believe Daisy has gone wherever it is humans go after they die."

Violet was clearly surprised. "No no no! It's impossible for her to leave without me. Besides, she would have told me unless she's still not thinking straight."

"Why wouldn't she be thinking straight?" James asked.

Violet flounced into an armchair, clearly flummoxed. "I'm a bit muddled myself. Daisy was injured. That is, WE were injured. I heard the doctors explaining to you that she had brain damage. We've more or less been twins you see, so whatever effects Daisy affects me. Anyway. How should I know? I'm only a ghost."

"You're an old soul," I said.

"And you are?"

"I'm James but mostly, I'm Sam."

"My mother said I was extraordinary."

"Yes," I agreed. "Evie was proud of you."

Violet barked "Who's Evie?" and evaporated.

James examined the vacated chair. "Okay, Sam, I could use a little help here. I don't know who *I am* anymore."

"I'm your soul, James. Remember? No worries. I'll sort this out." I spoke to the empty room. "Hello my sweet girl. Please come back. It's me, Sam."

Violet heard me. "I already told that man. I don't know you."

"Give it time. You'll remember. You've been through a bit of a mix-up. I will wait here with James. Call my name when you're ready."

"I don't KNOW your name!"

"It's Sam but if it helps you may call me James."

James addressed me, his voice lowered to a whisper even if it was only a thought in his head. "Could a soul even *sustain* a concussion?"

"Of course not," I replied. "Only a physical body can be injured. An ethereal one has no brain *to* damage."

Violet gazed at her reflection in the mirror. James's stood directly behind her. He smiled as best he could. I raised his hand and waved. Violet burst into tears, walked into the mirror, and disappeared.

"That is NOT my Violet," I said. "She's not herself."

James staggered away from the mirror holding his head. "I think I may have taken too many tranquilizers," he said to himself. "I feel rather queasy." And then he addressed me. "Seeing a ghost isn't all it's cracked up to be, Sam. She really got to me. Besides, shouldn't DAISY'S ghost be here."

I reminded James. "Violet IS Daisy's ghost."

James flopped into the recently vacated chair. "So much for tranquility," he said. "I need a drink."

While James slept off the effects of a stiff double malt whiskey, I spoke with Violet. I'm afraid I was a bit gruff with her. "Do you play hide and seek often?" I asked, "because it seems you're still doing that with me. And I'd like to understand what's going on. I'm here to help you. We're old friends."

Violet answered calmly. "Nothing is *going* on... no-one is *moving* on. I will find Daisy when she decides she wants to be found. That's how we always play. We've been playing hide and seek all around the hospital and this house for weeks."

My voice changed the way one speaks to a lost child. "There there, it's all right, now. I found you so the game's over. I won, so let's get you home, shall we. You used to tell me I was your home."

"I live in Portmatilloch. That's where I belong. Please, Sam, take me home."

225

DEATHWATCH

"Many persons strive for high ideals,
and everywhere life is full of heroism."
MAX EHRMANN

- SAM -

After Daisy's death I slept about the same number of hours James usually did, less than eight, more than three. It was the quality of rest that changed. But I could never be sure afterwards if he was sane.

When the vortex of despair claimed James, he was grieving. As his designated observer, his image in the looking glass reminded me of a framed painting. If I had to give it a title it would be 'Emotional Shipwreck' a self-portrait splashed in untamed Van Gogh colors aged by craquelure.

We rose early. Dawn was our thinking time – the time James used to leave for trains and airports. It was also the time James caught the bus to Nova Scotia when he'd been most alive.

James thought he made a list in his head whenever he packed the 'forever suitcase' kept ready by the door. But the truth is, I was his list. I always was. He'd relied on me from childhood.

So many distracting thoughts confused his early days. Because, although James was happy, he never fit in. Like Daisy, his timeline conflicted with his soul. Or more to the point in Daisy's case, the lack of one.

I was in a similar state of limbo, missing Violet. I'd held her close inside James for all his life, so there must have been times he wondered why he always missed someone he'd never met.

Like Violet, I too learned the 'Sleeping Beauty' story at Evie's knee. And it was in this context that wormhole sleep seemed natural and fitting, like a consolation prize for a wicked fairy's curse.

The Goddess Lachesis granted James an extension of his original life thread, which instead of choking him dead, served as a personal lifeline for me to safely navigate the maze of his confused thoughts.

James's astral dreamscapes were built larger than life by me with the help of our hero, the architect Imhotep.

After Portmatilloch, I had come home to roost as baby James's soul, and when he turned nineteen, the same age I died, James experienced an intense déjà vu memory that shifted a bout of common influenza into remembering my last fever dream.

James had also caught my fever for Violet as his own, when both our loves were moving ever nearer to us.

I never proceeded in the constancy of clock time, yet I planned James's days with a psychic calendar in mind.

His story came in nightly chapters, shuffled by an unseen hand. Positive spins spawned from years systematically sabotaging the laws of attraction, eventually conspired in his, and our, favor.

When the dead weight of James Arne Eriksen collapsed into sleep on his first night of grief, I couldn't be sure if he'd sunk through his bed or if the bed had levitated through him.

The compressed density of sorrow drew James tighter into the void, and I was powerless, helplessly drowning in my own terror suddenly separated from Violet.

Molecular integrity flew apart. Everything outside James shifted out of sync. Bed speed, body speed, and thought speed, overlapped in a state of flux.

It's strange how a bedroom, so recently a haven, morphed into an asylum cell.

I floated in the afterlife self-ejected. James lived on without me, soulless in a state of denial. James grieved in blinks of heartbeat time so intensely, I temporarily lost track of Violet – a sensation of amnesia I'd never believed possible.

James and I were like Siamese twins, one alive carrying the dead weight of the other.

But James wasn't dead he only *wanted* to die. His suicidal thoughts ejected me from his body whenever I found a way back in.

It was my responsibility to recover my abilities of possession to serve him and find a path back to Violet.

One surprising thought survived after I recovered enough energy to block his suicidal thoughts: that eyes may actually *be* the windows of the soul.

I retraced his life for weaknesses to find a mental doorway left ajar in his past and encountered a memory of jetlag from his first days in Egypt. The combination of jetlag and the Egyptian sun had created severe insomnia. In desperation, I shouted into the doorway as loud as I could. "Daisy is trying to reach you from the afterlife, but you've locked her out! Daisy needs your help. Let her in. Still your mind. Breathe. Listen. She will hear you."

Mercifully, James heard me. I took advantage of his commitment to Daisy to regain control over his panic attack. He took several deep breaths and in the calm space between medicinal intervention and sleep, fear and guilt worked their magic.

It was a shaky return, but I learned to keep my obsession with Violet in check and gave James my full attention.

It was rocky but we faced his pain as climbers roped together on a mountain. And when James listened, Daisy visited him.

James wore a blindfold to bed to block out emotional storms.

It acted like blackout curtains, muffling the brightness of raw pain into a hush of hospital whites that soothed his skin and evened out his hot dry spasms of survival breath.

James had taken no heavier 'helper' to lose consciousness other than an over-the-counter remedy for mild pain relief, but none the less, waves of endorphins flooded his extremities. He entered natural internal hospice in an altered state separated from the wrath of 'Hurricane James' and found shelter behind the solid doors of a drawbridge dropping on heavy chains creaking with rust.

The sensation of James and I cleaved in two, mercifully retreated. Bereavement came to a full stop. The ensuing silence felt as if we'd dived into a humane pool of holy water.

I allowed myself to dwell as enlightened as James, alone at last, dwelling lightly in the dimension of incubation feeling a delicious sense of resting at the point of no return.

I sensed James was highly alert, so I left him to heal, drifting in amniotic suspension as a compassionate ball of amnesia. Pale hypnotizing threads floated from his fingertips and toes, as a tangle of puppet strings; James was on organic life support.

The curiosity of scientist-James intruded upon the sublime void, and he tried to investigate their source.

Inside the womb he felt a gentle tug at the top of his head where another string latched, making me feel like a marionette on a helium drip-feed. More strings bled from his elbows and knees, as James's directed his gaze sunward.

I strongly suggested he open his eyes, but he replied: "*No. leave me be, Sam. I want to die.*" In the end I coaxed his eyelids open, letting in thick syrupy light that surprisingly restored my depth perception. And so, I regained consciousness and experience the odd sensation of restoring my own soul.

James suddenly experienced rather than remembered, a last cup of companionship with Daisy.

I pointed out the symbolism of a dark Rorschach blot from the thick un-dissolved sweetness of sugar and cocoa grounds in the bottom of his cup.

I suggested, perhaps too whimsically, they were unborn hopes.

We had reached the middle of a movie where the hero turns for home. James's relapse was inevitable, but we surrendered to playing hide and seek with our spouses and each other.

Up James floated, through the center of a sculptured plaster rose on an underwater ceiling, rising through each crystal teardrop of a chandelier suspended in a cloudless watery sky.

He ascended in a graceful swirl of atoms rising like steam – a soul leaving its host for the sun. "Race you to the top!" I shouted.

James's spine straightened in a painless crackle as he swam vertically in the water.

He moved effortlessly from the ankles down on merman flippers, that looked an awful lot like webbed flip flops.

James heaved himself from the sea and into our dreamed rowboat. It was raining gently when he woke up. "You've been gone a long time," I said. "Can we go now?"

"I'm ready," he said. "If Daisy finds me, I will go."

58

LAST KNIGHT JITTERS

"And when I have offered up each fragrant night
Only, from the ashes then thou wilt rise
And thou wilt come to her
and brush the mischief from her eyes"
e.e. CUMMINGS

February 24 – **2023**

- SAM -

As James's soul I serve as the 'soul' executor of his estate.

What happened next seemed completely natural to James but took me by surprise. A great calm overwhelmed him. James's breathing resumed its even pace, as he floated to the ceiling. His prone body below looked as if a ghost valet had laid out tomorrow's clothes on the bed. The essence of James lay fleshless, boneless, ironed flat as a painting.

A dress rehearsal for a future performance had been laid end to end: shirt, tie, pants, socks, and shoes to see if they matched, ready to wear by a three-dimensional James in the shower. Some 'how' he was still attached to them… a vapor of two dimensional will, too weak to protest… not caring he was melting away.

James observed his body cloth below with mild interest, and saw Daisy approach the bed. Then he floated down to greet her.

Daisy gently pulled James from his body and bore him away.

James was dead and I was free.

GOOD GRACES
the book of Surrender

59

LA MAGIE DE LA MER
(the magic of the sea)

Somewhere beyond the sea
Somewhere waiting for me
My lover stands on golden sands
And watches the ships that go sailing.

- CELESTE -

I answered Violet's plaintive call before she called me.

I found her, aged seventeen, standing on Horse Hill, staring out to sea, searching the water in that age-old way humans have, being unable to see the forest for the trees.

But she was still far from finished, and she knew it. She despised her state almost as venomously as she had despised me when we first met.

She was searching for her lost soul somewhere beneath the waves. Every now and then she caught her breath and her shoulders tensed believing it had surfaced but then just as quickly, they relaxed, and she resumed her even breaths.

She sensed me arriving, but her gaze never left the water below. I knew who she was looking for, but she was still blocked by anger, refusing to acknowledge defeat. I waited until we were side-by-side. There was no greeting between us. Not even the tension we usually generated together.

"You don't need to breath," I reminded her. "You're not alive.

Her reaction surprised me. No hostility but defiant, nevertheless. A little girl stamping her foot, crying woman's tears beside herself with despair.

"Defeat is too small a word," she blubbed. "Have you come to gloat? I thought Sam would be here."

I steeled myself for being cruel to be kind. Not my preferred mindset for administering compassion.

"Sam doesn't want to be here."

She wiped her tears on her sleeve and whimpered in what almost passed for contrition. "You've always found me wanting," she sniffed. "Why would you say something so hurtful. Sam loves me."

"Precisely why he isn't here. If you'd only stop feeling sorry for yourself, things may turn out for the best. There's still time."

While Violet whined, Epona breached the surface and swam in a wide circle. It was a silent message of goodwill meant for me, not an order.

I grabbed Violet's shoulders and shook her gently. "I find you sulky," I said in my best schoolmarm voice. "Come child, what nonsense. Surely you can SEE as in SEA?"

Silence from Violet and more sighs from me.

"And so, we meet full circle," I said honoring Epona's wishes.

As soon as I spoke, Epona thrashed her tail and dived deep. I could tell it was deeper than usual from the wake she sent as a thank you. A vast swell of concentric ripples unrolled for miles and the water glowed a delicate aquamarine as if lit below from an underwater moon.

And then I saw the sea through Violet's eyes – a calm expanse of dull green glass and felt sorry for dismissing her so cruelly. "Your ego has a habit of falling short," I said. "It's time to grow up."

And grow up she did. Violet morphed into the beautiful woman she would have been.

She showed no resistance when I took her arm. "Come with me," I said. "We're going to a wee séance. If you want to reprieve your situation and retrieve your soul, we need to revisit your ship.

"I've done that too many times already."

"This time your ego will not be accompanying you; the ship's already overcrowded with ghosts. But this time you will record the sights and sounds you've always ignored. There's nothing new to fear. Nothing will change. But if you do it right, *everything* will change.

We arrived in a heartbeat. Nothing was amiss; everything was amiss. Violet positioned herself as far away from the newborn child as possible. "The basket is not where I remembered it," she said. "I'm standing well back so I will be able to see my angry soul approaching. I know when that happens. I've seen it often enough. Can I go now!"

I was tired of babysitting a newborn coward. "As always child, you are beside yourself with fear. Do try to grow up, Violet. Push yourself. Go on! Or do you suppose quite wrongly you have all the time in the world? Because you most certainly do not."

Violet's anger came out to fight. And for once it worked in her favor. Her eyes narrowed. "I hate you, Celeste. I will look but only to be rid of you."

I felt like a piano teacher with a tone-deaf student. "Start again from the top. Please describe the basket."

"It's wobbling. About to tip over the edge. Condition precarious."

"Better. Now, look at the child. Look into the child's eyes."

"The child is dead. Its eyes are closed. Just tell me what you want me to see so we can go."

"I want you to see what the child sees. I want you to engage ALL your senses. Clearly, seeing from across the room is not believing. That infant is *you*. Aren't you the least bit curious what you felt so close to death?"

"My answer is no. Stop pushing me. If you must know, I'm

staring at the ceiling with my eyes closed. What's left of me has floated free of its body. I feel the ceiling bump against my back. The ceiling is my new home. I shiver in wait for the approaching witch. I feel the need to re-enter my body, but I refuse to go."

"The tug you feel is the child pulling you in. Let go. Listen in 360 degrees."

Violet gave a melodramatic shudder. "I'm inside it, back in the basket. A death rattle gurgles from my throat as if I'm drowning. It's hard to breathe with a rattlesnake hissing around my neck. They hadn't bundled me dry. I'm shivering beneath a damp cloth from wetness above and below and even as I suffer, the flimsy sheet is ripped off me. I lie fully exposed. A draft whistling through the ship turns my skin blue. Satisfied?"

"Who exposed you? Who would be that cruel? Who is the witch? Who is the apprentice soul who delivered an untimely birthday gift wrapped in a curse? I only ask to make a point. It's a soul that hates your mother. Think on that."

"Lilith! Yes, I see her, now. A beautiful lady demon staring down at me. I think she's come to save me from the snake. Her gentle eyes bathe me in the tenderest love but it's impossible to coo back while I'm being strangled. Her hand reaches towards the snake. But she ignores it and rips the blanket from beneath me. Her luminous skin puckers into vicious red welts. She drools hatred from lips black with encrusted blood and spittle. "Is it hard to breath, luvvy?" she snarled. "It's time to fly. Your second death will kill your precious mother."

"I only ever saw her as a blob of protoplasm before. You were right. Nothing new happened but everything has changed.

My mother, Dorota's anxious face is torn from my ceiling. Her pleas echo inside my head. *Goddess, mother, keep my daughter as your own. Free her from this harpy. I willingly forfeit my life for hers. And so, mote it be.*

A thunderous wave jolts the ship. My basket falls, caught by an unseen force. ~~The~~ umbilical cord around my neck is gone. I can breathe."

"There was another face after Evie's. Look again."

"Dorota is crying out not to look. I'm not allowed to look."

"But you *are* allowed to *feel,* Violet. You are allowed to remember."

"Warm breath snuffles my skin. A velvety nose fills my basket and nudges me."

"Describe velvety!"

"Soft. Warm. I grab its hair. No. Not hair. Its mane. Its nose nudges me again, and I behold the eyelashes of a huge animal. A horse. I believe it's crying. The smell of seaweed comforts me. *Sleep my child,* the horse says. *My back will hold your cradle aloft and give you safe passage.*

A daylight canopy of dazzling blue flaps gently in a sea breeze. Sunshine warms my face. Evie's face materializes. She's wearing a crescent wreath on her brow. My fist curls around her finger. Evie belongs to the moon. She always did.

It's freezing but nothing as cold as the icicle bones of the thief who stole my soul.

After that, Evie smiles. She swaddles me in a new blanket. I'm snug and warm. She recites an old nursery tale children know well. "Violet. You will not die. You will live seventeen years and fall asleep for a hundred more. Time brings tough magic that only good magic may soften. Happy endings from curses grow."

"And what of harpy endings, Celeste. Do they grow from pure hatred?"

"Hatred," I answered. "Pure hatred."

Violet called me out. "Foolish woman, there's no need to speak to me as if I was a child. I'm too old for fairy tales."

"How many times must I tell you. I am *not* a woman; I'm a celestial storyteller. Fairy tales are my specialty."

"Then, I assume this infernal story will end. Is there any happiness ahead?"

"There is happiness behind as well as through and through if you would but look. And, by the way. There was never a snake. The hissing was the whistling wind, *foolish* girl."

But Violet was donning her imaginary coat heading for an imaginary door. I called out. "No-one can fill your place, Violet. Tis a grand blessing to be moon-touched. Soulless souls like you are called doppelgangers until they learn to keep their place within the sacred pages of a wisdom story. You are a pale ghost, my girl. Ripe for the void. The lunatic asylum of unfinished souls awaits you. Sam is there already."

"How dare you!"

"The goddess gave me the power to dare. Epona charged me to guide you here. Prove me wrong if you don't believe me. Go on, I dare you!"

60

TO WHOM IT NEEDN'T CONCERN

"Do I dare disturb the universe?
In a minute there is time
For decisions and revisions
which a minute will reverse."
T.S. ELIOT

- VIOLET -

I'd be remiss if I didn't mention that when one reprimands the universe there are consequences.

To my knowledge, nothing had ever been documented in the divine guidelines about a soul losing its temper, let alone, effectively taking the universe to court. But the lopsided distribution of good luck, the overwhelming unfairness of suffering, and the sheer inequality of universal favors, infuriated me.

In my present state of soulful awareness, I remember every misheard deathwish, every pointless power struggle, every former lifetime with Sam, cruelly cut short of consummation.

The last, eventually propelled me to Sam's side in Portmatilloch only to be conquered body and soul at the age of seventeen by a pretentious little microbe no less savage than a Viking warrior on a rampage slaked with bloodlust who randomly selected women for sexual assault.

I was mightily incensed. So much so, that jealousy consumed me. All at once, I cared nothing for the current flowering of Daisy's blossoming libido or the afterlife revival of James's unsung sexual conquests. I lost sight of the big picture and forgot the virtue of humility, the rewards of compassion, and the empathy for humanity drowning in its own self-centered greed.

I'm ashamed to admit I briefly despised Lila for satisfying her creative needs above the dreams of her vulnerable human tenants, selfishly snatching joy from the mouths of her professed children. I once called the universe a self-centered waste of virginal hydrogen behind its back and now I repeated it to Lila's face.

I believe I'm an immortal soul but that the bodies I inhabit CAN die. It's not that complicated when you get down to the basics. But there's nothing basic about the universe.

I have a twin. Not many souls are twins. The trouble is when I'm punished my twin is similarly disadvantaged. Sam is my twin soul but when we take physical form, he and I can die. We've done so with irregular regularity.

A soul cannot love; a soul IS love! But here's the conundrum. Only when born, can a soul experience the joys of human coitus.

I am the eternal yin to Sam's yang – a more advanced state than happy ever after. There is no simple way to pass judgment on my, and Sam's by association, apparent crime spree.

And now I have the unenviable task of justifying my actions to Sam. I am granted a moment in real time to do this. There will be tension but never recriminations. My Sam will understand; what he won't do is REMEMBER!

The river Styx is no childish myth. It's the mind-blowing brainwashing of Now – a phrase that almost sounds comical. It is nothing remotely humorous.

Sam and I may be born thousands of years apart – 'Siamese' souls connected at the third eye. But under the laws of genetic dynamics, wherever Sam's molecules manifest, he will always be male, and I will always be female.

However, to make it more complicated, we aren't always 'born' at the same time. Fluid time is tricky stuff.

My crime means I won't remember Sam, that is to say be able to RE–MIND him or RE–CREATE him for eons, a flimsy definition that may take thousands of years. We may be separated to exist trillions of light years apart.

Our punishment gives new meaning to the term 'dark side': darker than the furthest reaches of outer space, darker than the hideous depths of conscious despair, and infinitely worse, the inner darkness that descends upon a pair of star-crossed lovers punished with eternal amnesia.

What can I say to Sam in the minute or so allocated to me for baring my soul? Sorry, I didn't mean to… it was an accident?... it won't happen again. Because not to put too fine a point on it, me being 'let go' equals total destruction. Sam and I may NEVER EVER happen again. Full stop!

Any way I look at it, I was fired for being fired up.

I plotted against a fellow human being for my own ends. Suffice to say I will have all the time in the universe to reconsider such a reprehensible thing. Essentially, I was granted the power to create any life I wanted just not WHEN I wanted it. Especially *not* in this lifetime.

Would I do it all again? Would I do it for love? Yes, by the goddess. I would!

Being disenchanted with enchantment ends in a time out, pathetically sent to my room in disgrace, in effect, grounded with kindness. It's the height of saccharin punishment for a sensitive New-Age soul choosing to take a stand, determined to rewrite physics.

If we're still around in a million years and if we are cunning enough, we may get lucky. We may become mortal and die.

"Wherever you are, Evie, I hope you can hear me. The universe is more fickle than I could possibly have imagined!"

Evie was close by as I'd hoped. "I am always with you, Petal," she replied. "The universe is more loving than you give it credit for!"

"I remember you telling me to just breathe."

"Think back. Think harder than you ever have, Violet, and tell me, did you see a swinging oil lamp or a naked light bulb in the ship's surgery?"

I searched my memories before answering. "Most definitely, an oil lamp. I've returned to that scene many times."

"And did you not think it strange that a modern vessel equipped with the latest equipment would have such a dangerous light source?"

"I was a child who'd just taken her first breath!"

"Not on your subsequent visits."

"What are you suggesting?"

"You know me better than that. I never *suggest* what's true. It's time you knew that the distance between your sinking ship and Portmatilloch was measured in years. One thousand to be exact.

The goddess Epona guided you true, to the precise spot where you were destined to reunite with Sam. And with, I might add, the express blessings of the universe that for reasons past understanding, irks you still.

But I will say this: if you were fired for being fired up, you must have done something right!"

61

FINISHING SCHOOL

"Speak your truth quietly and clearly;
and listen to others,
even to the dull and the ignorant;
they too have their story."
MAX EHRMANN

March 21 – **2023**

- VIOLET -

Celeste snuck up behind me and delivered a surprise slap on my face. "You need to grow up fast, Violet." she said. "And considering the miracle healing you hope to pull off this morning, it had better be fast!"

I rubbed my burning cheek. For a split second I defaulted to Daisy's defensive persona of a powerless child but managed an anguished comeback. "Well, I've been seventeen years old for over a hundred years!" I shrieked, made more humiliating by Celeste's triumphant laughter.

A scene I'd rather forget replayed in my head. It was the first day I confronted Daisy wallowing in her 'comatose of despair act' begging for attention. But I'd been mistaken, Daisy craved oblivion. She had chosen to suicide by flu. She tried to dismiss me. But I ignored her fragile condition. Instead, I ridiculed her babyish habit of carrying a children's book like a teddy bear.

I blurted out "You're an old lady, so stop acting like a princess! Grow up and die. That's life."

Daisy was unprepared for a vicious attack from who she

assumed was an angel of mercy. She looked at me, shocked. "What are you talking about?"

I couldn't stop the replay and listened in shame to my heartless lecture. "You took your 'Sleeping Beauty' book far too seriously for your own good," I said. "Although I have to admit, the playing 'a princess in a coma, ruse' was a nice touch. It sure fooled the doctors."

Daisy wheeled on me. "My mother never *said* I was a princess; she *called* me a princess. There's a difference," she sobbed.

Celeste made her point. "Violet, you took your anger out on Daisy who heard nothing but you shrieking venom. She was a fragile child in an old woman's body," she said. "I hope you do better today. The souls gathered here are depending on you. You're all that stands between the void and new life."

"I'd only intended to sting Daisy," I said knowing it was a lie.

Celeste rubbed it in. "And Evie only *intended* you should understand the sensitive juxtapositions of fickle curses and blessings and birthdays and times of death. Now you see them; now you don't. Life can change in a fairy's heartbeat or from the title of a book.

Violet Seaborn. *You* were a princess before Evie told you who your parents were. Daisy was the sleeping princess from a book who *you* woke with a kiss of supernatural power. You invoked *her* prince by calling *yours*.

You've changed, my girl. And not for the better. You've become jaded in addition to being an insensitive snob. Well done."

I couldn't argue. She was right, but I defended myself anyway. "Thanks to you I'm less likely to believe grandiose claims if that's what you mean. Whenever I see or hear the word 'absolutely' I mentally replace it with *whatever* in inverted commas followed by a question mark. I call it growing up. So, well done, you, Celeste!"

Celeste condescendingly patted my knee to humor me which always irked me. "Absolutely jaded. No question," she said.

It was time to complete my mission. Celeste reluctantly directed me to the place of atonement on Horse Hill as it was during its holy days. There, Evie, Sam and I, assembled to convene the healing ritual of the unfinished souls I'd *volunteered* to restore.

A bedraggled gathering of the long-since departed were seated cross legged around the White Horse under a low-lying cloud of smoke and ash that clung to the hill. Each person was given a piece of chalk to hold from the horse's belly.

I swore no oath. Celeste sent me a disgusted look, closed her eyes, and proceeded to relate the ancient Egyptian tradition how one's heart is weighed against the feather of truth, clearly directed at me.

She rose with the words, "they're all yours, Violet," and sent me a telepathic message 'and may the goddess be with them'.

My first job had been to brief each soul separately and greet each ancestor as a long-lost friend I hadn't seen for a while, which was true as much as it was *untrue*. I had seen *them*, but they hadn't seen *me*.

I read out a *'you are asked to listen without comment until otherwise instructed* list' which basically asked the injured to remain silent without touching each other or speaking unless to answer my direct questions.

Everyone involved, loved ones or worst enemies, needed to be on the same page for the best outcome. Everyone heard the same pitch. Mostly what they already knew: their soul was in an unstable state of transition from death to life, traumatised by lies and violence, dispirited, abandoned, and inwardly outraged.

Below the surface of their martyrdom, seethed outrageous anger drowning amongst the debris of immoral physical, emotional, and spiritual suffering.

Despite my cheerful: *'all is well, you're safe now, the worst has happened, it's all good from here, your new best friend reincarnation awaits you, and the proverbial River Styx exists to wash your horrors away',* speech, I was met with undisguised expressions of scepticism and hostility.

I responded with a second humble request: Please keep an open mind and control any immediate defensive reactions you may have.

With one exception, each ancestor flinched when I touched their hand. Even Daisy was hesitant to accept me as her recent comrade in arms. James, however, had no misgivings towards Sam who acted as a calming bridge between us.

Even so, every victim noticeably relaxed after looking into my eyes from the spark of love they found there. Each hand resting in mine triggered a weak smile when I gave it an encouraging squeeze.

With Celeste's help I had divided the unfinished souls into groups. The first confrontation was critical because it set the tone for my own assessment which Celeste informed me would be last and definitely *not* least. She made it clear that in spite of my recent progress I was far from complete. Evie would conduct my assessment after the others were released from their suffering.

Celeste gleefully referred to my approaching evaluation as an ominous day of reckoning that, by comparison, likened my upcoming trial, in itself a life-or-death situation, to a small glitch of indigestion.

I knew Celeste to be a brutally efficient teacher who found me severely wanting. I was familiar with her bullying methods well enough to know she had chosen her words explicitly without mercy to loom over me and the day's proceedings like a sword, blatantly another of her tests meant to finish me off which ironically was exactly what I needed.

The old badger often reminded me I was unfinished in ways considerably more complex than my ancestors and that my actions carried deeply profound consequences.

I thanked her for her concern with a chilling expression and curtly dismissed her.

"I have work to do now," I said. "It's time you take *your* place to observe me from a distance and do your best or worst as you judge fit on that clipboard of yours."

I concentrated on the task ahead. The future lives of my ancestors depended on my ability to navigate them through their traumatic storms of shame, blame, and fear.

Sam sat next to me shoulders touching for support. Celeste gave me the stink eye from across the room as she kept score on an already shaky report of my insensitivity to *'mastermind without manipulation'*.

For now, my ancestors were my priority. I would sink or swim later.

Lilith had not only been physically destroyed, but she'd lost the love of her life as well as her newborn child. She'd felt abandoned by her goddess, set *apart* from the truth, and set *upon* by a demon of the worst kind – a recipient of her unleashed rage that had manifested into an entity unto itself that was out for blood.

Lilith's demon was in fiery evidence, reeking as a ghastly smell that by now I recognized as charred flesh. I set aside my personal grievance with 'it' and watched with detached amusement as it circled Celeste and occasionally dive bombed her with a terrifying screech accompanied by a shower of grey ash.

But by ignoring it, Celeste sent it into a tailspin – a spoiled child having a tantrum, whooshing around the room like a punctured balloon.

I had time to assess Lilith's present state of disorder. She'd come straight from her torturous death, burned alive after a violent assault of physical brutality that should have felled her at the first blow.

The conniving priest and his witch hunter accomplice, although physically absent, were clearly in evidence as the palpable spirit of fear emanating from Lilith's trembling body.

Lilith looked about warily in case either would appear. Her twisted broken fingers plucked at her charred dress. She sat cross legged as best she could, supported by Alba's chest. Her poor feet were burned to stumps. A fierce skull fracture revealed an inflamed bulging grey mass trying to escape.

Dishevelled hair revealed patches of bare scalp where raw wounds oozing pus matted with blood clots and fragments of leaking brain matter. Her bruised mouth gaped half open showing missing teeth.

One swollen eye glared from Lilith's ashen face. The other gouged beyond recognition, was lost in a gory eye socket of congealed blood.

I stood abandoned on a bloodstained trail of victims and bystanders caught in the crossfire of vicious attacks.

The heart wrenching sight of three victims of coldblooded hatred unnerved me, but Evie nodded to go on. Her wan smile of reassurance enabled me to proceed.

The non-touching rule was summarily excused. Lilith and Alba – a pair of teenage lovers, victims of unparalleled butchery, sat hunched together. Alba, bludgeoned by an axe, had draped a broken arm over Lilith's left shoulder. His dislocated right arm rested bleeding on his battered knee.

In sharp contrast, Dorota looked on clearly sickened but with a guarded eye to the demon that had hastened her sacrificial death after leaving me, her newborn daughter, to fend for myself.

Evie instructed me to engage my intuition during the healing process. I was nervous at the start, but Epona's voice came through mine with an answer to the first question, and I relaxed knowing what was unfolding was the highest truth.

I knew instinctively what to say. And so, I related the vision of their story as it formed in my mind and waited for Epona's compassionate magic.

A picture clearly emerged of Lilith and Alba locked inside a theatre of terror.

"Allow the screams of the raid around you to fade," I said. "Recall Lilith, how Alba's expression showed concern. He was clearly under duress under his father's critical eye, but his eyes remained calm. The violence abated. Your breathing slowed. Alba's face relaxed. You both smiled.

Lilith, feel again your mouth reaching for Alba's kiss. Remember how you guided his hands under your skirt and gave fully of yourself as a bride to her husband. I see the two of you content, resting fulfilled in the aftermath of bliss.

Alba's weight on your body left you feeling protected. His smile was never an apology; it was a heartfelt *'Hello, all is well, my love. Have no fear. I will never hurt you.'*

Lilith, Alba purposely lay prostrate over you so both appeared dead. Remember the sound of the marauders collecting their plunder, and how Alba placed a finger over your mouth with such tenderness to urge you to stay quiet. Look now as he rises to stand defiantly over you.

You stayed 'dead' to the invaders and were spared further suffering because of his forethought.

Alba stole a few items half-heartedly to show willing and with a last look over his shoulder, that you couldn't see, he made sure you were safe before he left."

As I spoke, Lilith shuddered and relaxed into Alba's chest. He rubbed her back with words of comfort. Lilith's clothing resumed its homespun grey wool unsullied by the grime of relentless torture. Her clawed hands straightened. Her healed fingers caressed Alba's tortured face. Where her fingers traced Alba's wounds, his bruises and scars dissolved. Time played backwards revealing the velvety down of Alba's first beard. His blue eyes twinkled. Matts of gore encrusted hair that had framed his face, turned into long flaxen locks.

Lilith's healed mouth sought Alba's once more.

The sound of gulls calling from an untroubled sky reminded me of my final task. I motioned to Celeste it was time to bring them their daughter, Grace, blessed with flawless ivory skin. She placed the newborn in her mother's arms. As Lilith and Alba leaned blissfully together forehead to forehead, baby Grace clutched a fistful of her father's hair.

The dark shape of an hysterical crow escaped from Lilith's solar plexus, set off a coughing fit, and after staring transfixed on Dorota, turned into a white dove carrying a poppy as an olive branch.

And as they celebrated, Grace grew into a fair-haired child of nine who hugged Alba farewell, kissed Lilith's cheek, faded into the blue sky, and reappeared at Dorota's side.

Dorota smoothed Grace's hair and looked over at her old best friend in love with a handsome young lad. Grace took Dorota by the hand and led her to Lilith who neglected her demon raging at everyone and no-one. She greeted Dorota with a tearful hug.

They watched Grace grow into a priestess who sat between them.

Celeste returned with Dorota's lost newborn. Me! I recognized my violet eyes and saw Dorota's maternal smile that I'd only imagined. My estranged birth mother was able to hold me and whisper in my ear that she had to leave soon but would always watch over me in one of the goddesses many forms.

Dorota passed me to Evie. "Her name was supposed to be Sinthea," she said. "Her grandparents named her." She watched Evie teach Sam how to hold me properly, and in a twinkling, I sat with Sam in his field of treasures surrounded by the ghosts of lost things.

Dorota aged several years into the lovely nun I recognized in the church graveyard when I was running late for dinner. The hem of her habit had cast a shadow over the weeds of a grave Evie charged me with weeding.

I looked up and waved over at Evie taking down washing as it started to rain. And so, it transpired that Saint 'M' – the future sister Veritas, Dorota, Evie, Sam, and me, shared an afternoon cup of tea while the rains sheeted down in a protective silver curtain. When the curtain parted, a dark cloud approached, struck the church spire, and dispersed into a swarm of blackflies I recognized as flu germs.

Evie stirred them into a vortex that obscured a scene forming of a girl I recognized as Lily Price. I walked her through the morning she lay atop the bedclothes sprawled in a scattering of pills. She smiled peacefully, dreamily massaging her belly swollen with child. Daisy's unborn spirit approached the bed unseen and left her 'beauty book' on Lily's pillow.

For the first time I saw the book's full title. It was *not* 'SLEEPING Beauty'; it was 'BLACK Beauty'!

Daisy collected her mother's pills and threw them away before growing up into a beautiful teenager on a first date where James, a shy charmer, awakened her with a kiss. The rest of the day, Epona used my voice to work her wonders until the sky cleared to light blue and the room shone with redeemed souls.

Yet, somewhere, my day of reckoning waited.

A MILLION HOURS
the book of the Good Fairy

62

LIFTED SPIRITS

"In that book, which is my memory,
On the first page of the first chapter
That is to say, the day I first met you,
Appear the words: here begins a new life"
DANTE ALIGHIERI — THE 'VITA NUOVA'

April 1 – **2023**

- VIOLET -

After the healings, Sam and I were abruptly abandoned, homeless and bodiless, waiting for the penny to drop regarding the horrendous punishment that no doubt I had earned for both of us.

I had inklings from Evie, ever at my side in the form of Sophie the cat. She assured me soul punishments although slow to manifest were swift in deliverance. "Don't worry," she said "I will be accompanying you during what transpires. I am your mother first and foremost. And as a cat, I take motherhood much more seriously. Never doubt a feline's devotion to her kittens.

Your job is to wait and listen to the silence from the perspective of divine release. All will be revealed in due course. You're not to fret about anything. Epona's love is a power beyond reckoning and in the meantime, which is anything but *mean*, I have everything in hand. Transitions take time on a plane where time doesn't exist. What is transpiring has already happened and is, even now, unfolding in ever evolving layers of compassion."

It seemed Sam and I stood on the seashore again, but the truth is one cannot stand anywhere when they're floating in the sky.

Portmatilloch spread beneath us like a tablecloth of green and blue tartan.

Evie materialized below on a green square and proceeded to knead the grass the same way she massaged a wool blanket. Summer, forever young, materialized beside her and chased a fly that wasn't there.

Sam chuckled. "The day at the bus station when we looked older and more dignified, I hadn't understood your remark 'wait until you see Evie', and then there she was, my mother, pawing the attic window of Stonecap House to greet me. Her exuberant welcome, jumping into James's arms at the front door, made quite the impression on Daisy.

"Whatever floated Daisy's boat worked for me too."

We heard Sophie's rapturous purrs from our position in the clouds. Her memories as our mother, Evie, reached us and bid us join her.

We four were immediately transported into a happy reunion in a warm kitchen that no longer existed. And so it was, being home in the shell of an abandoned church warmed by the hearth we reimagined into being. Miss Evie in Sophie's body, Summer, nineteen-year-old Sam, and me the precocious seventeen-year-old wunderkind enclosed in an aura of peace.

I have to say it was disconcerting to find myself an untried teenager of seventeen again. Somehow growing *up* within our elderly hosts had gifted us an advantageous level of stable maturity. It felt as if our punishment had already begun.

"Not so," Evie declared, human again, ladling out chicken and dumplings. "You are now free to choose the form you want to take. Childhood vision is simply a muscle memory. And in case you haven't noticed, I'm a young lady myself."

A beautiful young Evie made a turn about the room to show off her svelte figure. "Furthermore, your punishment won't begin until Lila declares it so. Nothing's sure until the final accounting before the college of souls. And you have me, Summer, Epona, the Lady Flora and the Green Man, and Celeste on your side. Not to mention every fairy, elf, sylph, kelpie, deva, and tree sprite under and the sun and moon, a plethora of loyal bees, and quite possibly, Poseidon."

I balked at the mention of Celeste. Evie heard my mental objection. She pulled a fresh Bannock from the oven and as we broke bread Evie said her version of grace. "Thanks be to Celeste and the fates for lifting our spirits for the storm ahead."

63

S.O.S. – SAVE OUR SELVES

"The man who lies asleep will never waken fame,
and his desire and all his life drift past him like a dream,
and the traces of his memory fade from time
like smoke in air, or ripples in a stream"
DANTE ALIGHIERI — *THE DIVINE COMEDY*

- VIOLET -

I dreamed I leaned into the warm gusts of wind calling my name over Horse Hill. All cares left me as they picked the bones of my memories clean. The outline of the white horse reared up from the grass and galloped as a skeleton until she became Epona, fully fleshed out from absorbing my discarded energy.

She stood, pawing the ground, silhouetted against the moon. "It's time to go," she said curtseying low inviting me to mount.

I grabbed Epona's mane and pulled myself onto her back. Her words *Hold on my angel. I have you* filled my head.

We took the high road to Inverness. I leaned forward sleepily as we gained speed. My arms relaxed into powerful shoulder muscles, my legs melted into forelegs, and my thighs became flanks.

By the time Epona waded into the sparkling waters of the loch my silver hair flowed black and loose into a mane and flared behind me in a glorious tail.

I was a water horse diving beneath the waves. I woke with questions when my hooves touched sand. "Is it far? Will Sam be there?" I asked.

"We're almost home, little goddess," Epona said. "Only a few years more to go. Sam is very close, traveling above us in a sailing ship. You'll be together soon."

I am one with Epona, a horse galloping underwater, churning up the seabed in clouds of sea dust.

Soon, I reached Portmatilloch, both foreign and familiar. Saint 'M' welcomed me with open arms and a beaming smile. She beckoned me into her once cold unfurnished cell where a lavish four poster bed now waited for me with a hot water bottle and the top sheet turned down.

Sister Mary settled me under the covers and kissed my cheek. I caught the edge of her robe, suddenly afraid. "Please…"

She understood perfectly. "No need to fret little one. I promise not to leave until you're asleep. I made a vow to watch over you a long time ago."

- EVIE -

"Sam, my darling boy," I said gently. "You must forget Violet for a while."

I met his blank stare. "Who?" he said.

I smiled happily. The worst was over without wailing and posturing. "You must forget James too."

"Sorry?"

"Two long-lost childhood friends." I patted his shoulder and kissed his cheek. "You've done well," I said. "You've selflessly mentored a kindred spirit through your own troubled times and even when it was impossible, you honored the vow you made…"

"To Violet? Tell me about her."

"She has already forgotten you. In time, you may detect the passing perfume of her namesake flower or feel a warming in your heart quickened by the promise of love. Let them pass without sadness." I placed a Roman coin in his hand. "This is a keepsake you found together on a happy day – an energized touchstone to make you smile."

Sam looked from the coin to me. "And you are?"

"Someone who will always have your back."

"I'm dreadfully tired. It's raining. Rain always makes me tired."

"Yes, I see that. Come with me, child. I want to show you something before you fall asleep. The rain will restore your wits and I promise you will wake refreshed."

We walked arm in arm, Sam holding an umbrella over us, until we reached the beach where he tossed a pebble into the water. Its splash created a succession of ripples radiating from it in slow motion. He stood in deep silence intently listening. "Something important happened here," he said.

I held out my arms towards the waves and invoked Epona. What appeared to be the head of a seal emerged far out to sea. Epona's equine form became obvious as she swam to shore. She'd left a wicker basket, anchored like a lily pad to mark the spot where she first appeared.

"Behold Epona, the soul of Scotland," I whispered as Epona gracefully stepped onto the sand. "The Old One of legend. A water horse."

Sam walked towards her unafraid. "She's magnificent. May I ride her?"

"In the future, perhaps. It will be up to her."

Epona trotted her protection around us three times and slipped back into the water, swimming to the basket. Her wake set the basket moving towards us until it beached at our feet as a white rowboat with no oars. "Epona has gifted you a boat that will carry two," I said, "it's a symbol for the love she bears you."

Sam bowed his head and dropped to his knees, a knight deferring to his queen. "Thank you, My Lady. I am honored," he said, and sent me his first impression. *'It looks like a cradle with blankets and a pillow.'*

Epona's words came over the water. "It's for you and one other, Sam," she replied. "Please give Violet my love."

After I helped Sam into the boat it immediately shuddered into motion. "Look at me, Evie," Sam called out in excitement, already dreaming.

Epona towed the boat swiftly towards her 'door' in the water, where it briefly languished, caught in a vortex.

I watched until the door closed over my son. "Don't worry," Epona called out. "I have him."

I shivered, aware the rain had gathered strength, picked up the umbrella to use as a walking stick, and let the downpour cleanse my soul. By the time I reached Horse Hill the sun had come out. I knelt beside Sam's body delivered safe, lying in the curve of the White Horse's belly and thanked Lila for her leniency.

While my babies slept under spells of forgetfulness, I took them on a lucid out of body journey to save their souls that began with Violet and I visiting the White Horse for a scouring with benefits.

64

PRIME TIME

"We shall not cease from exploration.
And the end of all our exploring.
Will be to arrive where we started.
And know the place for the first time."
T.S. ELIOT

- VIOLET -

Evie and I, now two young women the same age, made a pilgrimage to the White Horse. We took the cliff route and descended to the shore in silence. It was a celebration of a sort because we were together, but the water was a mirror bereft of spirit – a pane of silvered glass trapping our beautiful water horse. "She's down there," Evie said. "Be in no doubt of that."

We left a cairn of red apples at the water's edge for Epona, more as a gratitude prayer than an offering.

Even the murky sun felt good on our skin as we stared up at the White Horse, always a glorious sight seen from afar.

"Back to our pilgrimage," Evie announced. "Ah, there's nothing so magic as letters! Do you detect a hidden message, Violet?"

I did. Evie had made it sound almost cheery, but it was more a future omen than cause for cheer. Two shrill words rang in my head. GRIM AGE. We continued in a silence beyond understanding.

Evie stopped in her tracks. "You *do* remember the word grim means the devil, don't you? But you also know there is no such creature, so don't feel dispirited. Don't mind me. I spoke out of turn."

Horse Hill was two hills overlapping in time. Its glory days hung reflected in the clouds as a misty skyscape. Portmatilloch's present state rested uneasy, shrouded below.

Lady Flora was scouring the horse when we arrived. She'd laid out mallets for each of us along with three goblets filled half full of something that looked like cold milky tea.

"By all means, Mistress Evie, down yours if you will," she said in her sweet loving voice. "But take the other two potions home so Sam and Violet can drink it properly under the stars."

My Lady looked weary, but I was encouraged by her bright voice that hadn't withered like the earth.

Her companion, Pan, on the other hand, continued to hide in the bark of trees. I'd seen him often in the fairy grove as a child, and even left a few tartan ribbons and baubles in the branches as gifts for his fairies.

Lady Flora must have heard my thoughts because she addressed me with a smile. "Pan was always pleased with your thoughtfulness," she said. "You were a generous child. Fairies can be aggressive. Not known for sharing their possessions but your gifts were an exception. The fairies granted several of your wishes as a thank you. Maybe you were too young to notice."

I thanked her prettily, and when the three of us were done scouring, Lady Flora placed a crown of laurel leaves on the White Horse's head and walked into the hill.

Evie and I pressed on to the sylph's shrine to write stars on each others' foreheads. The Summer heat of late afternoon trapped in the thick underbrush of bracken and moss, sent knee-high shimmers of steam rising above the forest floor.

We were in a hurry because the trees closed in at night shuffling closer to the spring. We reached it as the sun dropped into the North Sea. I spent a moment envisioning Epona sensing my presence trotting in a ritual circle on the seabed.

A toothless wind trapped under the dense tree canopy rustled the waist high saplings grown from tiny seedlings I had planted in a fairy circle as a girl. I left the fairies the lucky button I always carried from Sam's shirt. As we left, a pair of curious squirrels approached it chattering over it like old women making a quilt.

I removed the red cord bracelet from my wrist that Sam had braided for me. I'd worn it for ages and sacrificed it now to celebrate the beginning of a new life for Sam and me. I hung it on a low branch of the giant oak overlooking the spring. The last thing I saw was the faint outline of a man's face surrounded by a living halo of leaves, eyes closed, sleeping in the tree's knotty bark. Evie swore she saw him smile.

Evie cornered me on the way home. "What do you remember of Daisy's last hours," she asked. "Was she frightened?"

I looked up and to the right where my most elusive memories reside. "As I recall, Daisy was smiling."

Evie nodded. "And do you know why?"

"No, I was feeling rather unsteady at the time," I answered. "Do *you* know?"

"I do, as it happens," Evie said in a matter-of-fact tone. "I think you should be aware that unbeknownst to you at the time, Daisy beheld a vision of a black horse while you were lying inside the White Horse's belly dreaming of Epona."

"Oh, Evie. I was off in a daydream. Did I kill her!"

"Quite the contrary, your dream heralded in a long overdue

healing. Think on this my child: Epona's appearance sanctified the divine timing of Daisy's death as a tribute to you. The old one is proud of you."

Evie never spilled a drop of the potion as we trudged home. And after a fine repast of warmed up stew, Sam and I sipped it slowly under the moon. It tasted of honey that covered the bitter taste of the herbs and an ingredient I didn't recognize.

"Evie kissed our foreheads with a gleam in her eye. "Sweet dreams my innocent babes," she said and went off to bed.

65

DÉJÀ VU AGAIN

"Tomorrow, and tomorrow, and tomorrow,
Creeps in this petty pace from day to day,
To the last syllable of recorded time;
And all our yesterdays have lighted fools
The way to dusty death.
WILLIAM SHAKESPEARE

- VIOLET -
(pixie - led)

Evie was still smiling when the room stopped spinning.

Sam's form dematerialized and reappeared several times, and from the expression on his face, my form was being equally playful.

We stopped shape-shifting when Evie clapped her hands. "Now then," she said casually, "Time for the grand tour?"

Her glib invitation belied the transformed state of Portmatilloch which had most certainly changed. Lady Flora's enchanted forest had encroached upon the village center, almost completely obscuring the buildings. A garden of flowers blooming larger than life and in brighter colors were suffused with inner light in a population of energetic living lanterns.

Fairies were uncharacteristically in bold attendance compared to their usual camouflage. They were especially adept at blending into petals and leaves to the point of invisibility, so much so, only a rare sensitive child had ever reported seeing one. But now they resembled extraordinarily large butterflies wearing dresses.

A fat honeybee the size of a seagull hovered in my face. "Remember me?" he said. "I'm an old friend of your mother's, but we've met a couple of times. Celeste introduced us. Well, not formally," he buzzed. "She was playing the Daisy movie. You see, I was Daisy's instructor at art school." His chuckle sounded like a fuzzy doorbell. "I looked quite different then," he said. "But I was in human form, you understand."

"I remember you very well. You take seven spoons of sugar in your tea."

Pollen zoomed about in ascending spirals and returned at eye level. "Correct. How did Daisy's movie turn out?"

I reached out and petted Pollen's stripes. "You used to wear a herringbone tweed jacket," I said. "Daisy had a rough go of it for a long time but she's fine now. Happily married to a fine fellow."

Pollen made a joyful loop de loop. "Happy endings are honey to my ears," he declared. "Well, feelers. Bees don't have ears."

Tantalizing glimpses of the church and outbuildings, semi-obscured by vibrant plant life, seemed noticeably greyer, shabbier, and crumbling with age.

Sam was not amused. "It's hardly home sweet home, Mother," he said. "Where the hell are we?"

Evie replied, true to form, somewhat indignant. "There's no such place as hell, *Sam*. I recall instilling that into *both* of you. It was one of my most profound teachings."

Sam returned contrarily. "Heaven then?"

Evie burst into laughter. "Come on you two. It's an adventure. A game. Well, that's what Lila calls it."

"And what do *you* call it?" I asked.

"I call it a trip to a parallel universe. A new *Port* in an old storm. Lady Flora taught me how to traverse time years ago when I was promoted to her personal handmaiden. But only now, due to your unfortunate circumstances, has she given me permission to involve the two of you."

I crossed the garden to Sam and took his arm. "It must be the potion," I said. "A goddess's ticket to dimensions unavailable to human souls. We may as well enjoy being here. Evie wouldn't have brought us here without a good reason." I smiled at Evie, obviously enjoying the moment. "Would you, Mother!"

Evie turned silently and proceeded to wade through waist-high poppies, towards the countryside, delving into an unknown forest where anything might show up.

"Please try to keep up," Evie called over her shoulder. Her accompanying chuckle told us we should enjoy ourselves. But then we heard her subdued remark designed to be overheard "Be lighthearted and open to surprises, my children."

Sam and I exchanged a grimace and kept up the pace. The surprises came quickly.

We reached the cliffs overlooking the North Sea in no time where I eagerly scanned the water for Epona. I ran on ahead, encouraged by a familiar black shape in the water but Evie stayed my arm. "Courage, child. Remember, despite what you see, all is well." After several minutes, she released me with. "Now go and see what you must see." A wave of sickness passed through me when, I heard her bid Sam to hold back for a few minutes.

I reached the shore in record time, growing more disturbed by the lack of movement from the horse's head, black against a pale blue sky.

It was a large, scuttled ship – an ancient design with a carved wooden figurehead looking for all the world like the chess piece of a knight.

Sam caught up to me and wrapped me in his arms. "This isn't our home," he reminded me. "Epona was not a dream. She will be safe, waiting for you at home, as Evie promised."

A private look I'd seen many times passed between Sam and

Evie. Sam had a question. Evie shushed him with a finger over mouth and an overly cheerful "Everything is in hand. No need to rock the boat."

I whimpered into his Sam's shoulder. "I thought it was her."

"I'll explain *later*, Violet," Evie said, emphasizing the word later, and giving Sam another silencing glare. "But now it's time to move on to another slightly disturbing place that we'll quickly pass by and proceed to a site neither of you have seen, although a version of it *does* exist under the skin of *our* Portmatilloch.

Horse Hill was gone and the glyph of the White Horse with it. In its place was a long barrow covered in grass. Sam squeezed my hand, and I forced myself not to ask questions. I trusted Evie. It was enough that she'd promised to explain later. But it bothered me that Evie and Sam had a secret.

The flat lands beyond the hills abounded with wild horses that showcased a tall structure on the horizon. We approached it on a long-worn path – a straight shallow ditch carved into the grass, the width of a cart, between banks a foot high.

Sam recognized what it was, first. "A stone circle," he called out. But then amended it. "No. I'm mistaken. It's a wooden henge. This is a sacred place, and this pathway is a sanctified corridor called a cursus."

A circle of stripped trees with their crowning foliage intact were posted six feet apart like sentinels on a raised embankment that protected an inner raised circle separated by a wide ditch.

A break the width of a dozen posts bid us enter.

Evie broke the silence, her voice lowered in reverence. "For all intents and purposes, it's a paddock," she whispered. "But Sam is correct. It *is* a holy site."

"I draw your attention to the single stone pillar laid horizontal at the far end, called a…" She looked at Sam for the answer.

"A recumbent megalith," Sam replied. "May we take a closer look?"

"Not yet, Evie said mysteriously. "But we will tonight when the moon is in eclipse. I have my reasons. You will have to wait."

I mused silently but Sam's archaeological interests were piqued. His eyes widened, impatient with a breathless question. "You say there's an invisible henge like this in OUR Portmatilloch!"

"The same design built with megalith standing stones," Evie replied. "Also, I don't need to tell either of you it's Lady Flora's holy of holies. A shrine dedicated to Epona. You'll see it soon enough. It's the arena scheduled for your... *she coughed...* 'review', that I refuse to call a trial. But it would be best, Violet, if you composed a statement to be read before the assembled college."

"I'm famished," Sam whined. "Does Portmatilloch Two have the restaurants we saw during James's and Daisy's honeymoon?"

Evie seemed distracted. "Not a one, but there's no need. Lady Flora will provide us with food."

Sam rolled his eyes. "As long as there won't be any more potions!"

Evie held up her hand. "I promise to serve only pure spring water. It's all quite safe."

Back in the village, Evie pulled aside a confusion of plants. We joined her as she stepped through to where the ruins of buildings in various stages of wanton neglect, stood fully disclosed. "I'm showing you a quick look before we dine. There are too many secrets to reveal at once. We will digest our meal before..."

Sam spoke for both of us when he interrupted. "I'm afraid to ask. But before what?"

Evie answered immediately. "Before the main course, of course, silly."

"No desert?" Sam asked a tad hopefully.

"Your just deserts will be served soon enough," Evie said.

Neither Evie, Sam, nor I laughed.

66

HAPPY HEMLOCK

"I am forgetful of everything
but seeing you again –
my life seems to stop there –
I see no further. You have absorb'd me.
I have a sensation at the present moment
as though I were dissolving."
JOHN KEATS

- SAM -

By happy coincidence, Lady Flora's feel-good elixir had distracted Violet and I from our trial of just deserts to come.

But now, in an unexpectedly playful mood, Evie arranged us around a ridiculous dining table shaped like a toadstool. I made light of her choice. "A bit over-the-top wouldn't you say," I joked. "What's next? Are you going to sprout wings?"

"I will tell you a story while you eat," Evie said, ignoring my attempt at levity without involuntarily crinkling one of her laugh lines. Something I hadn't thought possible.

"It's a story that could have happened to you. And by that, I mean it *did* happen to you which is why you're watching it now from a safe distance. Twice removed from the viewpoint of an unstable mind.

After you're released from your nightmare of cosmic service that may be long or short, you will remember this lapse from real time as a lucid dream with lasting beneficial effects."

Violet suddenly had no appetite, but I dug into the fairy stew without a second thought. I looked over at Violet after several mouthfuls. "You *will* let me know if I turn into anything untoward, won't you?" I said accompanied by a grin, to lighten the tension. Violet looked near breaking point. It was time I strongly suggested to Evie we should go home. I would have to pick the right moment with diplomacy and cunning.

Evie's story was so engrossing neither Violet nor I asked a single question until it was over.

In the meantime, we participated as best we could in the unnerving nonlocal location of a world turned topsy turvy.

"No questions with your mouths full, please," Mother Evie began. "It's like this."

The stern look on Evie's face made me put down my spoon.

Evie nodded her approval. "It is *exactly* like this: Both Portmatillochs were attacked on the same date by the same Vikings, but since all parallels are not created completely equal, there was a significant difference." She rapped the mushroom with my spoon. "The Vikings arrived here in TWO dragon ships." She paused, busily polishing my spoon as if life depended on it. "Of course, the local menfolk were routinely killed, *blah blah blah*, and eventually, the curmudgeonly chieftain sailed away with his gore encrusted comrades loaded with whatever booty they could carry."

She straightened the rest of the cutlery. "But something more momentous occurred that changed the course of history here.

After Alba-FirstBlood, the chieftain's named successor, mated with Lilith he decided to stay!

There's no need to relate the ensuing melodrama. Suffice it to say, a heated discussion took place resulting in Alba claiming Portmatilloch for himself as his father's heir. Amazingly contracted without bloodshed.

Orders were hastily given to the younger warriors of a certain age, to stay behind and settle the newly conquered land, to be named Alba, in obeyance to Viking law. The horrors inflicted on anyone who failed to obey would be quick and total. One dragon ship, now the property of Alba, signified the new colony would be monitored. A sign the chieftain would return.

Twenty or so teenagers of the Viking persuasion complied and within a few years, Portmatilloch 2 harboured a violent generation of Viking brats with an eye to subduing the nearby villages. But as a positive consequence, one savage hate crime was averted. Lilith and Alba lived a long time, and their daughter Grace survived. However, sadly, many violent wrongs were still committed against the neighboring settlements."

Without warning, Evie leaped to her feet, clearly overwrought, waving her arms as if fending off an invisible attacker. She heard my thoughts and apologized.

"My attacker is a memory I'd rather forget. It's not one I'm proud of but it happened and that's that. All of us live with our mistakes, don't we. The main thing is to atone for them."

Violet, suddenly revived, spoke up. "What are you suggesting? Do you mean me?"

Evie smashed her fist on the table so hard the cutlery required arranging again. "You see, Lady Flora had to retire to the forest after Pan merged with the Viking god, Thor, and she recruited me to help her. Naturally, I followed her. Consequently, I became acquainted with the ways of dark magic. I had the knack of it which is why I'm able to travel between universes at will.

The thing is, I may have inadvertently altered time." Evie stood abruptly. "Perhaps we should take a break. This visit is meant to be therapeutic for you, not a confessional for me."

Violet closed her eyes, swayed in her chair, and grabbed my hand.

"Does Lady Flora know how to make regular milky tea with no added funny business?" I asked. "Violet could use a cup of tea."

Evie smiled. "I was thinking the same thing. Look, we'll be home within the hour. It's safer to wait. Fairy tea can be tricky."

I chose that moment to press my urgent request to leave. "I'll hold you to that, Mother. I'm worried about Violet. It's my duty to protect her. I don't mean to be critical, but I've come to regard this little side 'trip' as rather a MISadventure."

Evie shuddered. I'd never seen her so contrite. She smoothed the hair from Violet's eyes. "Forgive me, Violet. I may have misread your state of mind. I've always thought of you as indestructible."

Timeout was a brisk stretch of our legs during which Evie turned our toadstool into an elegant patio set.

Once comfortably seated in upholstered chairs, Evie's storyteller voice took on the familiar tone of a mother reading her child a bedtime story.

"Well, one day, a star-crossed cargo ship floundered offshore, the exact spot yours sank, Petal. It listed in a wild storm and to save it, the captain dumped over a hundred horses into the water.

I'm happy to report, the horses made it to shore and thrived as the wild horses you saw dotting the hills. As a result, a generation of new Vikings learned to ride, and a horse culture emerged that eclipsed the hardships of sailing. Portmatilloch became infamous as a community of inhumane warriors ravaging villages on horseback.

In time, the aging dragon-ship proved unseaworthy, and Alba buried it with the honors due a chieftain in the barrow you saw.

Not long afterwards, Christians arrived to occupy an ancient church built over the sacred shrines of the old Green Gods. To everyone's surprise the intruders weren't killed outright. I think Lilith had a lot to do with that. She was forever schooling the savages in the goddess's laws of loving kindness. In fact, it was what saved her.

Lilith was never formally accused of witchcraft. Her crime according to Christian doctrine was cohabiting with a pagan. Even so, the religious community didn't last long after a priest propositioned her. Alba had him tortured and killed along with his accomplice, a witch hunter who routinely persecuted any woman who dared speak familiarly with animals or birds.

The church decreed medicinal herbal elixirs and healing ointments were the work of demons. And when it became obvious the wisewomen of Portmatilloch had magical sway over life and death, the remaining priests fled from them as much as their ruthless husbands.

Ironically, they passed a boatload of nuns from France on their way to Portmatilloch to join the church. Alone and helpless, the nuns were absorbed into the population, thereby increasing the number of children by eleven in one year.

Dorota, possessed by Lady Flora, mated with Pan. She sailed away and gave birth to a healthy daughter during the voyage. She named her Sin-thea. Her eyes were violet.

Sister Mary Lee, the new prioress, isolated one of the sisters exhibiting symptoms of plague in an acolyte's cell attached to the church, but it was too late. Plague broke out with murderous outbreaks recurring every ten years until it finally wiped out the entire population of Portmatilloch.

It has been, as you see, a village of ghosts for generations. But Viking ghosts learn to live side-by-side with those they killed, and fairies delight in teasing superstitious ghosts. Playing tricks on human souls is, and always will be, one of their favorite pastimes.

Thor disappeared soon after, mightily vexed; Pan reinstated Lady Flora who scuttled the remaining Horse-ship. Her revived goddess culture thrived as you see, unencumbered by priests or warriors. Lady Flora left the ship as a monument to serve notice to any newcomers who dared to defile her shrines."

Evie clapped her hands like an efficient schoolmarm again. "Righty-o, that's that then!" Violet and I responded like trained animals. "Right then, before we go, we must inspect the buildings," she said. "I promise it won't take but a minute."

The old cell we remembered as belonging to Saint 'M' was so dilapidated, the walls had disintegrated into an open alcove where a statue of Violet posing as a saint with precious inlaid amethysts for eyes, stood within an aura of golden light.

When evening fell, we trudged back to the henge.

Violet noted the constellations hadn't altered. I was relieved, impressed the universe knew when to protect a perfect design.

Fairy magic had carved a figure of me posed as a knight, into the recumbent altar stone. It resembled a sarcophagus, with an intricate border of Celtic knots.

When the moon dropped low and skimmed the top of the altar stone, I saw the stone knight blink. "Mother, please don't tell me Violet and I have doppelgangers," I said. "Or worse, automatons."

"You absolutely do *not* but that isn't to say you can't be in two places at the same time if the Lady Flora wishes it so. She is a great alchemist with every plant at her beck and call. You will now fully wake in your true home. The goddess's magic elixir is no longer in effect. You will remember this parallel universe as a dream."

"Then we are copies? Brought here without our consent. Drugged!"

Evie suddenly loomed larger in keeping with the scale of giant vegetation. "WERE copies!" she corrected. "Temporarily cloned for safety under the protection of a feel-good potion. Universe hopping is not safe for humans."

"Then why do *you* do it?" Violet asked, put out.

My response was angrier. "Protection! Have we been in danger this whole time? Our souls have been used most cruelly in one compassionate universe. Are we to trust this one is equally without guile? How could you have possibly protected us?"

"My dear children," Evie said softly. "There's a perfect explanation why I can universe hop… I'm NOT human."

67

ROW HARDER...
Violet's alternate reality

*"The owl and the pussycat went to sea
in a beautiful pea green boat
O let us be married! too long we have tarried:
But what shall we do for a ring?"*
EDWARD LEAR

- VIOLET -

A small rowboat covered in blistered green paint drifted out to sea on an expanse of glassy water.

Sam cupped his hands over his mouth and shouted to the figure of a small girl huddled in the boat *"Row harder, my angel. Don't keep me waiting."*

The oars remained slack. Perhaps she hadn't heard.

Sam's soul stirred the wind into a gale that whipped the sea into whitecaps.

The boat, caught in an undercurrent, sent it spinning anti-clockwise.

Sam shouted louder against the tempest. "Sweet girl, I can't wait much longer. It's me, Sam!"

The gulls circling the boat echoed back *'longer... longer... longer.'* The girl shaded her eyes and shivered. "Do I know you?"

'you... you... you' the gulls called back. The sweet girl lowered her arm and hugged her shawl close. "Whoever you are, I haven't the strength to row. I need to rest awhile," she muttered to herself.

Sam's whisper, close in her ear, startled her. "You're the strongest person I know. Sleep comes to those who complete a difficult task. Please, Violet, I have orders to wait for a short while. If we're to be together again you must come to me, Now!"

The girl raised her head, puzzled. "Why?"

Sam sighed. "Because I'm bound by the rules of this place."

"This place?"

"The Punishment Time."

A strong current pushed the boat in the direction of the shore. "I've been here before, haven't I?"

"You died, Violet."

"When?"

"Daisy is gone. You're free. We're both free. I'm your Sam."

"I'm free," the girl said. "You're my Sam. We're free?"

"Yes," Sam replied gently. "We're free."

The girl recoiled. A look of terror crossed her face. "Lost at sea again. Abandoned!"

Desperate not to alarm her, Sam used his normal speaking voice as the boat grated the shore. "You were found twice. Remember?"

"I remember you calling me. Didn't I find *you*!"

Sam chuckled. "Clever girl. Yes, you did. You did!"

"Where's my ship? There was a ship."

"It sank, precious girl." Sam held out a closed fist. "But look what I've found. It has plenty to say but it will only speak with you."

The girl's voice shook in alarm as the boat beached firmly on a field of pebbles. "Are *you* my soul?"

Sam forced himself not to grab the girl's hand. "All you have to do is climb out of the boat and take my hand. I promised the guardians of this place I'd wait. Please, Violet, I can't stay much longer. It isn't allowed."

"That's a silly rule."

"Agreed."

"Sam, I'm frightened. Are you real?"

"Dearest girl. Trust me. I'm *really* here. We *both* are."

"I want my mother."

"Evie will be along soon. No worries."

"Open your hand," the girl said at last. "Please. I want to see."

Sam's open palm revealed a scarab made of gold. "It's our best find yet."

The girl clutched the side of the boat and eagerly clambered out in tears. "Don't leave me, Sam. I don't like it here."

Sam beckoned the girl by wiggling his fingers as if she was a cat. "Good lass. You're almost here. Come on sweet one, a few more inches."

The shore disappeared when their hands touched. The girl and Sam sat holding hands on a green hill beside daisies arranged in the outline of a tribal horse. The golden scarab listened on the grass before them. Its wings trembled. The girl tightened her grip. "Show me the light exactly where you found it."

Sam squeezed the girl's clenched fist and kissed the back of her hand. "We haven't found it yet. It's in our future."

"Egypt?"

"Of course."

The girl held her breath. "When can we go?"

A river of sand flowed from a fissure in the horse's mouth into a cone-shaped mound. The great pyramid of Giza rose from it to its full height. Desert supplanted the daisies.

"We're already there," Sam said softly.

I brushed the hair from Sam's eyes and searched his face. "Where on earth have you been?"

"WE'VE been dreaming," Sam said. "It's time to wake up, Sleeping Beauty. If anyone can avert a curse, it's Evie."

68

THE WATER IS FINE…
Sam's alternate reality

"Here is the deepest secret nobody knows
here is the root of the root and the bud of the bud
and the sky of the sky of a tree called life; which grows
higher than a soul can hope or mind can hide
and this is the wonder that's keeping the stars apart"
e.e. CUMMINGS

- SAM -

Violet dangled her toes in the sea, lost in thought as her rowboat drifted further away.

I called out. "Come on in, the water's fine."

Violet studied the dark water. "It's a shame I can't swim, then."

"Tis'. You needn't sound so disparaging. By the way, while I have you captive, I have a question to ask you."

Violet sent me a long meaningful stare. "I suggest you proceed with caution. Some things are best left as a surprise."

My eyebrows lifted. "Okay. Noted. How did you know the full reach of Daisy's past to choose her as the one who could complete your mission?"

The rowboat stopped drifting. "I knew," Violet said "because I recognized one of my own. Not one of a kind but one of a sacred multitude of immortal wisewomen prepared to die for love. Which makes this the perfect time to tell you the rest."

"I trust you not to shock me senseless."

Violet dried her toes and proceeded to deliver precisely that.

I caught a whiff of sadness in Violet's voice and cautiously massaged her foot in slow motion.

Violet hesitated, choosing her words carefully. "In the long run, reincarnation may have our backs but…" she averted her gaze to stare into the water.

"But?"

She lifted her head to meet my eyes. "But, precious boy, in no way does it diminish the sacrifices that postpone our own souls mating for hundreds of years or more."

"What if the earth is no more by then?" I asked.

"There are other earths. Look deeply into the firmament and tell me there aren't. Did you think the universe wouldn't clone its finest hour!?"

"I'm already forgetting what we had."

"Sam, listen carefully. I charge you to forget. Precious boy, we can always meet in dreams when our souls yearn for union."

I clung to Violet's hands as she pulled them away. "Not yet. Please. Wait!"

"I have it on good authority that the universe always unfolds according to plan," Violet said. "Strangely, there are no mistakes. And you of all people know the guardians of this place won't let me wait."

THE HIGH COURT SUPREME
the book of Divine Law

69

THE CIRCLE OF FATES

"Do not be afraid;
fate cannot be taken
from us; it is a gift."
DANTE ALIGHIERI

June 20 – **2024**

- CELESTE -

Lady Flora deliberated with Evie, and between them they set Violet's trial date for dawn on the summer solstice as the most auspicious date for a favorable outcome.

The faint outline of the Bronze-Age complex silhouetted against the rising sun gave the stone circle the appearance of a glass amphitheatre, then a moss-covered coliseum before settling into a proper henge of stone.

As the morning mist burned away, an ancient circle of standing stones emerged like nine ancestral ghosts shimmering without substance, materializing, and dematerializing until they too, stabilized as the fates – beacons of eternal presence.

The two invisible pillars of Hypnos – Sleep, and Momus – blame, were also in attendance as being especially relevant to Violet's case.

As ever-present energetic forces given no stone to empower them beyond the abstract, they vibrated steadily, ever vigilant. Hypnos promised the positive duality of sweet dreams and nightmares; Momus threatened to undermine the great strides humanity had reached and was still reaching for.

One by one, nine unearthly sarsens arranged themselves in a circle within a circle surrounded by a ditch and a steep bank. Beyond the henge lay a vast moor where the College of Souls had been gathering for three successive days and nights. By dawn the assembly covered the landscape to the point where the natural curve of the earth dropped away.

Nine Bluestone megaliths tipped with the first rays of the sun hummed like tuning forks on the periphery of the holy of holies. Their high-pitched tone rebounded from one to the other escalating into the buzzing of a million bees.

Soon a canopy of uplifting music rose above the proceedings in a choir of souls chanting for justice.

As the hour approached for Epona to arrive, Lady Flora bid me scatter a swathe of lavender and laurel branches, ripe with extra healing properties in accord with the solstice's power, leading directly from the entrance to the epicenter.

Evie had me arrange a pyramid of sweet apples there for Epona's pleasure, on a low plinth of polished flint. And to honor the presence of Lila, an empty throne carved from a single stone block had been placed at the far end of the circle under a square arch – formed from a lintel connecting a pair of shorter uprights.

Moments later, the birdsong that had serenaded the emergence of the Welsh sarsens descending from the sky, silenced abruptly. A barely audible thudding of hooves was heard in the distance like beating wings.

Epona appeared like a black star on the horizon. A telepathic message quickened the gathering who joined hands to watch her approach through closed eyes.

Evie, the younger, rode Epona bareback, dressed in the robes of a druid priestess, her unbound red hair cascading over her shoulders like licking flames. Horse and rider, newly emerged from the sea, streamed with water, leaving a phosphorescent trail of microscopic sea life behind them. Epona's coat gleamed like black satin. Her flowing tail braided with seaweed sparkled with diamondlike grains of fine sand and barnacles, and asingle starfish caught in her mane.

The ground shook like an earthquake as Epona thundered up the cursus sending clods of turf flying. She presented herself at the entrance, bowed her magnificent head and suddenly wheeled to the right and began circling the outermost parameter anti-clockwise at a slow gate.

After acknowledging the multitude of souls, she broke into a canter and made a dignified lap around the innermost boundary of the gathering.

Back at the entrance, Epona picked her way over the laurel carpet. Her hooves clip-clopped onto the platform made from three slabs of burnished flint.

Evie looked like a child empress, carrying a large trident to honor Poseidon. She wore a crown of laurel in the shape of a crescent moon and the hem of her homespun robe had been finely worked with seashells and pearls. Silver armbands encrusted with moonstones adorned both her arms.

Her forest green eyes searched the crowd, daring any soul who might speak out of turn and disturb her children who were able to see and hear all that was said.

Epona bowed to the empty throne and Evie inclined her head reverently towards it to acknowledge the presence of Lila.

Violet and Sam were seated side-by-side, stone effigies with lips sealed, ears to hear and eyes to see, hands folded in their laps.

Evie dismounted, bowed her head, and waited for the sign. When Epona whinnied and tossed her mane, Poseidon's trident emitted blinding flashes of aquamarine light.

Before she took her place beside her children, Evie used the trident to score a blazing circle of protection around the circumference of the arena.

Epona pawed the grass, nudged the topmost capstone apple and gazed at me solemnly.

She'd already tutored me on what she wanted said, so I was prepared. Her testimony would come last. Within the hour, one of the fates would cast the first vote. The others would follow. The final tally of affirmative and negative votes would be announced.

Nyx as the goddess of regeneration and mother of the fates, was ready to intervene as a tiebreaker if necessary. The enthusiastic response of the crowd was taken into consideration, and the trident would announce the verdict had been reached in an explosive eruption of color.

Nyx's children: Moros - Doom, The Keres - Destruction, Thanatos – Death, The Oneiroi – bad dreams, Oizys – Pain and distress, Nemesis – Retribution, Apate – Deceit, Philotes – Friendship, and Geras – Old Age, closed their eyes the better to hear the truth.

Evie delivered her plea, seated on horseback like a queen.

70

PARDON ME?!

*"And whether or not it is clear to you,
no doubt the universe
is unfolding as it should."*
MAX EHRMANN

- EVIE, the elder -

I allowed my divine presence to fill me before I spoke, and even though I felt Violet's and Sam's eyes upon me, I refused to engage them.

I began in my strongest commanding voice: "The maxim that *'time in and of its true nature does not exist'* is not the meekest way to open a spiritual conversation such as this. It's an ironic statement to make when a time-sensitive trial is in session during a time that doesn't exist.

No matter. Needs must. My children's souls are at stake!

That said, arbitrary calendar dates and signatures are markers invented to satisfy the human need to be located and labeled. And so, in the nick of time or despite the lack of it, I will begin my testimony where Violet's mission appeared to end, in the year 2023, as far as earthly dates may be reckoned.

As an immortal goddess, briefly serving as Violet's earthmother, as well as my eternal service through Lady Flora's unbroken line of power as Violet's *goddess-mother,* it is incumbent upon me to set Violet's chronicle to rights. And so, I place it firmly where it originated, in the non-terrestrial, aptly named, *firm*-ament. The soul domain of the unmanifested.

Be assured, Violet's fabled rocky birth was nothing compared to the rocky road she had to travel to get here to plead for her lifeforce and that of her companion, Sam.

My first duty is to neutralize the present circumstances in which Violet and Sam face annihilation for crimes inadvertently committed, through no fault of their own, albeit directly triggered by Violet's altered egoic state, set in motion by Lila as a test.

Violet couldn't help but miss the pertinent details in her chronicle of unfinished souls, mired as she was and still is, under the universal caveat of secrecy during missions of extreme karmic sensitivity. Sam as her twin soul, is guilty by association, subject to the same punishment.

The automatic recycling of souls is a sentence akin to death. It will stand until I can overturn it. Please listen carefully.

Violet was seemingly a human born to expressly voice the divine love of truth on earth. But this was not so. Her prime mission remains a secret. Her secondary mission was to resolve a severe disruption of karmic energy within a group incarnation duly entrusted to her (volunteered as she was, under the terms of The Forgetfulness Act) by me, her overruling deity.

Essentially, Violet was programmed (in other words automatically compelled) to seek a connection to her host body, Daisy Sinclair, for a higher purpose than curiosity, but not one she was allowed to remember (which to her credit, she achieved nobly in the end).

It is good to remind ourselves often that souls are created, not born. And as such, they cannot die as humans know death.

Even so, it is sometimes necessary for a few rare souls to be granted the occasional lifetime as humans for training purposes. And in those cases, death companions them.

But before I delve into the flaws of Violet's hijacked memories, for indeed they had to be set aside without her knowledge, I need to clarify a distinction regarding identities. Whereas humans are given proper names; souls belong to group designations best translated as impersonal titles earned over eons of time – an elected elite sadly and incorrectly referenced all too often as 'the choir invisible'.

As unlikely as it sounds, it appears to me that Lila may have been blindsided by Universal Law. Together, here, you and I shall play out this possibility and judge what comes. We cause no harm. We simply remain neutral until otherwise determined.

As such, new evidence will be introduced of an astonishing nature. Please, hear it in silence and think on it well as a sacred duty lest one of you find yourself in the unenviable position to not only defy the powers that be but to consciously alter them for the highest universal good.

A smattering of applause and a few grunts of approval ran through the assembly.

Clumsy accounts of a fictional nature, serve, as do all fairy tales, to bridge the gap between fantasy and *'understanding'* which, in divine terms, was never meant to be understood by humans at all.

And as many of you will have experienced in your dealings with the fairy world, nothing is quite as it seems. Extenuating conditions apply within the elemental realm. With that in mind, today's testimony begins and ends on a slippery slope.

The indisputable facts are these:

In 901 A.D. Lilith, a dedicated follower of the Goddess Flora, was barely sixteen when blue-eyed marauders charged over Horse Hill to cut her husband's throat. Their arrival had been predicted but not expected.

For years it was rumored a storm was brewing but it manifested calmly which was why it came as a surprise. Evolution moves at constellation speed – an imperceptible repositioning of star pictures in the night sky. As such, a disinterested Orion watched benignly from on high as one of the last gasps of Viking aggression hit the east coast of Scotland in a lustful surge of masculine hostility. Portmatilloch lay directly in its path.

An innocent morning descended into bloodshed, and as the smoke cleared a new clan of women survivors emerged, slow to recover, yet all the stronger for the Lady Flora's unwaning support.

The goddess's counterpart of male energy destined to supplant her had come to pass – one of evolution's more clumsy attempts to balance the polarities of feminine and masculine.

Word spread quickly, passed through the elementals of air, fire, water, and the earth devas of animated plant life.

The forest was in an uproar and the sea frothed, but Epona the 'old one' waited patiently in silence, knowing the world could only be restored through rebirth because motherhood always holds the sacred reigns of creative power.

While the menfolk formed armies vowing to destroy the invading hoards or expire trying, wisewomen gathered under the moon to reform their circles of power. There was work to do.

I cleared my throat in preparation for delivering the shocking truth. "Lilith Ross was never raped," I began. "A young Viking warrior in his teens made love to her in the true spirit of chemical attraction and as such, transmuted lust into the scared act of marriage.

But sadly, Lilith came to the attention of a lustful holy man who, when spurned for his crude advances, sought revenge from a witch hunter he hired to exact punishment under the unscrupulous umbrella of witchcraft, torture, and execution.

And Lilith, after being tortured senseless by prolonged brutality went mad. I challenge you to beg the question how you would fare under like circumstances. Lilith as a new mother sacrificed herself so her daughter, Grace might survive.

Sadly, it was not to be but Lilith died trying – a brave act when suffering the affliction of madness. She responded to barbaric rituals with dignity as befitting a follower of the goddess.

Lilith's soul was an apprentice, too young to invoke the power of forgiveness after her execution. Tragically, it succumbed to Lilith's incensed ego, determined to survive through the negative vibrations of hate and revenge. Lilith's ego resurfaced in a half-life to become what humans and souls alike, know as a demon.

Violet's daunting challenge was healing the episodic consequences of a trapped family of humans in karmic suspension in danger of being permanently lost to time. She was given no choice to agree or disagree. She did not volunteer. Violet was chosen due to a unique situation begging a singular solution, both complex and dangerous that required powers she would have to gain along the way.

Esteemed college. I ask you to please bear with me repeating what you and I already know. It helps me to hear it said aloud from my own lips, and so may it help you. So, I must first correct the separation of human bodies from soul entities. When the priest left Lilith's daughter Grace to die, the child became the ward of Epona who took pity on her by returning her to her ancestral group soul as Daisy Sinclair.

Consequently, Dorota martyred herself so her daughter, Sin-thea, would live. I overstepped my authority by renaming the infant Violet, for her hypnotizing eyes.

Lila's masculine counterpart and by that we may as well consider male in deference to the unmanifested force, Sol. Neither takes physical form. Lila is the personification of human events unfolding as a succession of games known as life lessons.

Similarly, as Evie Watts, I am the personification of earthmother fame.

I take human form from time-to-time but remain formless in nature. I am the essence of maternal energy – the first woman and therefore the first mother.

The female child of Lilith and Alba-FirstBlood was given her father's name, Alba, in accord with Norse tradition but Lilith renamed her Grace. Grace perished swaddled in fear under the wind and rain, and later incarnated as the infant Daisy.

Dorota in turn, gave birth to a daughter whose name was intended to be Sin-thea for divine protection, but as a newly appointed godmother, I was inspired to rename her from my intuitive need to protect her.

Consequently, I received a new name as well. Lady Flora's fairies being overly sarcastic, addressed me as Mother Superior.

All was well until a virus of demonic origin cut Violet's life short as well as that of my son, Sam. I had to be seen to perish at that time to comply with village life.

When Sam and Violet were released from their bodies by the Spanish demon, their names ceased to exist.

As you can see by now, it is not only my children who are on trial. In a way, I am also, which is why I believe Lila may have felt it best to cover my mistake. I am grateful to her loyalty but unwilling to let Violet pay for decisions I came to make under duress.

Sam and Violet reverted, as do all rare humans, to apprentice souls. In essence, doppelgangers – incomplete life forces missing the essential divine spark of consciousness necessary for soul duty. As such, they were 'unfinished', Violet, especially so, because she was no longer protected under the divine name Sin-thea.

Epona counted Violet as her own child bestowing extraordinary powers upon her.

Violet did her best as a 'placemark soul' to heal the violations against the land and sea between a primitive race of unconscious human hunters and gentle conscious gatherers in a physical clash of blood and pain.

As a matter of divine transmutation, after serving their physical hosts, human memories reincarnate in new bodies who must grapple with the leftover residues of inherited experiences. Crossover incarnations invariably clash, during traumatic episodes of spiritual whiplash.

Any ethereal entities that remain after death are ghosts with unfinished business. But as an exception to the rule, Sam and Violet were allowed to retain their names in order to rescue a hapless band of ghosts clinging together in karmic limbo for eternity. A truly unconscionable situation.

Sam and Violet were released after their hosts' physical deaths, unjustly caught between heaven and earth to be tried here as dispirited sparks – dubbed self-created mutineers.

This is in large part due to the ongoing re-emergence of the Green Goddess, who never deserted her immortal forms of animal vegetable and mineral.

Sam and Violet symbolize the human counterparts of the mythical 'Adam and Eve' now more appropriately named from 'Epona's anima and animus. As twin souls they represent the perfect embodiment of cause and effect.

It behooves me to backtrack for all our sakes. Let me retrace the necessary elusions to gender and molecular structure to address the chronicle of the human pairs named Violet/Daisy and Sam/James.

Given that souls are purely energetic in nature, divinely created as ethereal entities aligned to universal categories, James and Daisy could never have had souls named Sam and Violet. Nor could Sam and Violet, as organic human beings, ever commandeered their nameless souls at their deaths or indeed, any other time.

And yet, time travel stands still without legs to travel. Violet believes she arrived in Portmatilloch in 1901 and so she did. What she hadn't remembered until recently was that her ship floundered in 901 A.D.

She had a dim recollection of Epona towing her to shore beyond the confines of the fossil record when life was a massive vapor cloud looking for a place to land.

Violet was delivered to me to reach her appointed destiny with Epona who awakened her from her first sleep of death.

I pointed to the witness box. "Violet and Sam wait here suspended in a cryogenic stasis in an arena intended to resolve the deepest issues of a cosmic nature.

I stand here, before Lila to plead for renaissance. I hereby call on my Lady Epona's wisdom to clarify the shaky laws of free will.

And now, if my testimony fails to alter the unalterable, my children may be lost forever. May the goddess forgive me."

71

HORSE SENSE
Epona's testimony delivered by Celeste

*"I should have been a pair of ragged claws
Scuttling across the floors of silent seas."*
T.S. ELIOT

- EPONA -

It was a terrible burden to live during the vicious eon when the unconscious sons of man had the audacity to kill for land under the guise of pleasure, but sadly, it was expected. The world played out in dizzying cycles, and the darkness of fear came full circle to prepare the ground to eclipse peace and light.

But tides turned on a terrible crime against the goddess, and as it was her divine nature to destroy as much as heal, a rift in universal protocol turned the world in on itself. The straightforward handover of power evaporated in a cosmic hiss where gods and goddesses vied for victory on the battlefield of natural selection.

The momentum for joy had never been greater. Sky omens heralded an end to petty bitterness but in a singular act of cruelty, the path of humankind was set back.

I'd hoped Lila/Sol would intervene at the eleventh hour. No matter, Evie has everything in hand. In the end, this hearing must stand as a deposition for the hall of records.

Reincarnation as conceived by the timeless universe imposed the dual horrors of curses and blessings, past and future, on weak populations.

The human devolution that Violet and Sam were sent to equalize was reduced to the crucial balancing point where a single human woman, primed to receive her true feminine powers, gave birth to a daughter during a time when the world held goddess energy sacred.

Warring factions of crazed men, pockets of wise women, and the Green Goddess played against each other on a planet desperately trying to evolve. The stakes were high. Hatred had had its day. Change was at hand. Love was finally due. And then it wasn't.

It remains for me to thank Sam for helping Violet achieve a state for which she remains unaware.

72

FREE SPIRITS

*"A kiss makes the heart young again
and wipes out the years."*
RUPERT BROOKE

retro time-slip, March 21 – **2024**

- SAM -

"Welcome home," Evie said. "All is as it should be. Take your time. Your legs may be a tad wobbly after a hundred years."

To the best of our groggy knowledge, Violet and I were still on a mini break in Portmatilloch with our mother, Evie in the guise of Sophie the cat.

Evie was talking in riddles. My mind received them as fluffy sound bytes that disintegrated on contact with the air.

"I expect you're hungry," she said.

"Disoriented, overtired, and thirsty," I replied.

"I feel as if I'm sleep walking," Violet added. "The sensation feels oddly normal. What happened?"

"A fairy tale happened," Evie said. "I told you a bedtime story and voila! You passed out and slept for a hundred years.

You needed a therapeutic retreat, but Findhorn was fully booked so, I sent you on a classic enchanted retreat with the fairies. Which was a smart move because your initial sentence was banishment for a million hours of separation in exile.

Luckily, the universe not being overly fond of decimal points, and since reckonings by fairies under my jurisdiction are calculated on a slightly skewed abacus, your sentence was rounded down to one hundred years.

Creative mathematics rule the universe. Everyone knows that.

Your hundred-years sentence passed while we ate a fine meal at Lady Flora's table. Remember the toadstool table? It was a fairy table meant to distract and trigger trouble-free innocent dreams and bypass the nightmare of separation. I felt you had both suffered enough."

I was incredulous. "Let me get this straight. Violet's kangaroo trial is over, we were convicted, sentenced to 100 years in exile, and served our time while eating a magic lunch we hardly remember!"

"*Fairy* lunch," Evie corrected.

"So," Violet interrupted. "Just to be clear. For petty violations beyond the pale of understanding, a soul may receive a declaration: you are hereby sentenced to go directly to the void of no return and report in for recycling? Would it have been as easy as that? In a universe founded on love and compassion, could it be as heartless as that?"

Evie's answer was instant. "Yes, sometimes it must. Lila is real. Games within games were not created for the world's indulgence or entertainment but to raise human standards of fair play. Tough love teaches the unconscious diehards to shape up or be shipped out.

But the void of no return is actually a misnomer. It recycles without prejudice. Is it so terrible a punishment if a human being past all reclamation is reborn as a tree!

Life can be like a game of Monopoly. Sometimes a player swans around the board collecting money while others are snowed under by debt.

Chances are, if you're lucky you receive a *'get out of jail free'* card or a *'slip through the cracks'* card, or *'forgive me I made a stupid mistake'* card. But more often than not, it's the *'bread and water in solitary confinement'* card. No need to thank me, it's my job as your mother."

"Do you mean our *fairy* godmother?"

"Only on Wednesdays. But I have a few tricks up my sleeves the rest of the week."

"Well, that's a given," Violet said.

I was dubious. "So, are you saying if Violet and I play our cards right and if the dice aren't weighted, and if Lady Luck isn't hiding dark side of the moon or in a snit, we're in line for rebirth?"

"Yes. Absolutely."

Violet shook her head. "I'll keep my fingers crossed, then."

Evie's voice sounded miffed. "You are Epona's chosen daughter, Violet, which is why she chose you above all others for your Daisy mission. Epona actually swayed the tenth fate by disclosing her own covert actions that waylaid your rebirth. An amazing feat even for her."

A MILLION GAMES
the book of Lila

73

FINIT HIC PESTUS
here plague ends

"Variety
is the spice of death."
LILA

April 1 – **2024**

- EVIE -

My travels grow ever more mindful with time. I'm not always sure which Portmatilloch calls me the loudest. No matter, I join Lila in play and together we make the best of our considerable creative powers.

In one world I'm a druid princess leading a procession of wisewomen to an ancient woodland shrine. In another I'm a tired servant scouring a white horse on a hillside with Lady Flora. In yet another I'm a bee named Pollen bringing Sam and Violet up to speed after an unsettling session with hallucinatory plant nectar.

But it is through loyalty to Epona that I continue to honor this particular promontory of the Scottish Highlands as my earthly home.

I have a promise to keep and a mission to fulfil, so it is with mixed feelings that I say goodbye to Sam and Violet for a time yet remain true to form regarding a solemn oath.

The newest parallel universe forming today is where I leave Sam and Violet to their next Egyptian lifetime while remaining constant to the dream Epona has been dreaming for a thousand years in the Portmatilloch of her birth.

I have gone ahead to make everything just so for Sam and Violet. My children will have no memories of their recent trials both legal and personal. Suffice to say, they both acquitted themselves well and as a result, this next promised life awaits them as Portmatilloch duplicates itself once more and takes up a new position in a different star system.

But even as I am fully there, I am always back in the village where Sam and I await the arrival of a darling infant girl named Sin-thea with violet eyes, in accord with the desires of My Lady Flora and the goddess Epona.

Sam's soul stares across the empty sea where the rowboat and Violet disappear. In its place, a whirlpool spins in concentric circles glowing like red fire under the surface of the water.

As Sam flies over for a closer look, a powerful force sucks him under, and Violet Seaborn awakes, a squalling infant. The year is 2024.

The attending doctor, slightly more dumbfounded than the others, modifies his voice to reassure the new mother and steps forward to offer his congratulations. "It's twins," he declares calmly, "a healthy boy and girl".

He hides his astonishment, moving towards the door, slowly backing out of the room unnoticed, lowering his voice as he passes the attending midwife, Sister Vera. "It's not every day one sees a seventy-four-year-old give birth."

Nurse Vera, already putting the room to rights, whispers back under her breath, *the times they are a changin'* Dr. Tilloch.

Dorothea Samuels lays back contentedly on a fresh pillow cuddling her newborn twins with the violet eyes. She smiles radiantly at her husband's awestruck face and speaks with the gentle authority befitting a woman of magical powers. "Evan," she says, "our daughter shall be named Cynthia and our son, Albert."

And so, Cynthia (the former baby Sin-thea – the late Violet Seaborn), and Albert (the former Alba-FirstBlood – the late James Eriksen), are twins free to marry the loves they lost.

Across the hall, Emma Watson, the former Lilith Ross, nurses her newborn twins, Margarita (the former baby Grace – the late Daisy Sinclair) and Simon (the late Sam Watts).

Later, in the dark, Emma hears Dorothea, the former Dorota, singing to her red-haired twins:

> *"We two have paddled in the stream,*
> *from morning sun till dine;*
> *But seas between us broad have roared*
> *since auld lang syne."*

74

THE BOAT FLOAT
Evie's gift

"Has this been thus before?
And shall not thus time's eddying flight
Still with our lives our love restores."
DANTE GABRIEL ROSSETTI

2045

- SOPHIE -

I speak from a pedestal perched high atop the capstone of the great pyramid of Giza with the supreme sentience of a sleek Abyssinian cat.

Not for the first time nor will it be my last, to influence humans in the guise of a feline. As Daisy's cat, Sophie, I was named for the goddess of wisdom. And I take full advantage as all cats will, as divine incarnations of unequivocal entitlement, sensitivity, and extrasensory perception.

But old lessons and power trips die hard. And I still dream what cannot be and must not be and what may come.

I still play out the dreams that Lila incubates at will.

Cynthia and Simon's marriage in 2045 was tricky. A hundred years in exile had intensified Violet and Sam's love but the deeply ingrained ghosts of hard-won lessons, sour memories, and the latent fear of karmic punishments remained real. As such, Cynthia and Simon deport themselves with cautious optimism by testing the victorious waters of their new incarnation, one toe at a time.

And so, I act as their personal fairy godmother again, finally enabling their Egyptian wish to play out. I bide my time in accord with my royal status – a goddess in my own right, a privileged feline of the eighteenth dynasty.

I watch over Cynthia and Simon out the corner of my eye as I pretend to sleep.

As a sacred feline, I enjoy the privilege of being pampered. I am kept, indeed revered, in the ancient Egyptian tradition as a member of the royal house of Bast – a daughter of the goddess herself. I am deferred to with respect. Always!

Violet and Sam indulge me with the choicest delicacies and the softest pillows in accord with the splendor due an oracle in the holy of holies.

And being a feline equipped with highly emotional claws, I engage or withdraw them according to my impeccable sense of entitlement. I never scratch humans deep enough to hurt. My cunning, as ever, is subject to whatever takes my fancy. Always!

I am, in no way, the soul of discretion. As Sam and Violet's old guardian I help Simon and Cynthia forget the past that no longer serves them.

Cynthia has Violet's fear of water this time around and there are lingering traces of James's shyness under Simon's skin. Likewise, Daisy bequeathed Violet her tendency to hide in the shadows, so unlike my feisty daughter. Like Violet, I prefer to keep dry, but much to my horror, I am sometimes taken on boat trips against my will as a ghastly special treat.

Ancient death lacks its sting now, and during the first few days of a new season, I am amused the way Simon invariably revisits the Egyptian concept of the afterlife with disdain. This is James's influence.

Simon is embarrassed for an otherwise flawless race of intelligent mathematicians and engineers. But it never fails, that early on, some small artifact of undiluted power charges his emotional landscape with spiritual energy, and once engaged, Simon's senses soar again with my country's obsessive romance with the underworld.

Simon and Cynthia pack suitcases like Christmas presents. Things wrapped… crinkling in new packaging, small secrets rolled to fit in the corners and special things they couldn't beg in Egypt at any price: good pens, dark chocolate, hard American toothbrushes, wine gums, barley sugar, oatmeal soap, the latest bestseller, bee pollen capsules, tea bags, and a dozen other items they would forget and rediscover with childish delight on arrival… *I thought you would like this.*

As a cat, I am not designed to endure boats and floating.

Cynthia invariably clings to the side of boats white-knuckled as a reluctant flyer and I cringe under a tarpaulin dreaming of land. Only solid ground gives us a sense of correct placement, an attitude due to Cynthia assimilating my strong feline aversion to water.

At twenty-two, Cynthia is a petite dynamo, valiantly trying to come off as a seasoned sailor by cutting a casual Peter Pan figure. She visualizes herself standing confidently, feet apart, hands on hips against the dazzle of sunlight, while her purple shadow taps its foot impatiently… *Simon, let's go HOME please!*

She intently searches the water for Simon, but he always returns quickly knowing how she frets when he's out of sight underwater.

Cynthia balances perpendicular to the deck, and bravely grabs a tough triangle of sail to steady herself as the boat shifts. She smiles casually but still holds her breath.

Simon's beloved pixie-woman, with salty windblown hair never could nor will learn to swim.

Cynthia once again astounds Simon with Violet's natural fieldwork, as she works her special magic over the mysteries of shrouded dry and bleached things that the miserly desert offers up with reluctant irregularity. She handles each buried treasure casually and fleshes out spent lives with intuitive certainty.

Cynthia is not an amateur psychometrist feigning a 'read'. Violet's intuition remains within her as sharp as ever.

I watch proudly as Cynthia defies fear by leaning into the wind. She wears no jewelry in Egypt except a modest wedding band of heavy red gold.

Unlike Violet, Cynthia's a bit of a fashion icon. At home she prefers her signature avantgarde rings bold and out of scale on her delicate hands. Even so, I see Daisy's influence in evidence.

Cynthia's rings dazzle everyone in close attendance. But she enjoys how they take attention away from herself, so she can retreat behind them in anonymity, as if the jewels are wearing *her*.

Old souls balancing old habits demands surrender and courage. It's only a matter of time before James and Daisy will fade into a forgotten dream. I am here to banish them. Somewhere Daisy is struggling to overcome Violet's need for the spotlight and James marvels at the ease he helps his wife to believe in herself.

2155

In another time and place, four children – two sets of twins, Cynthia and Albert Samuels, and Margarita and Simon Watson celebrate a double anniversary – their thirty-third birthday and tenth wedding anniversary.

It's been ten years since Cynthia Samuels married Simon Watson in a double ceremony where Cynthia's brother, Albert, married Simon's sister, Margarita.

Once more they cherish the extraordinary coincidence of their mothers giving birth to twins on the same day. Together with their parents, Dorothea and Evan Samuels, and Emma and Erik Watson, Cynthia makes a toast to the powers that be, marveling how destiny happens when one least expects it.

Violet's chronicle was completed the day her soul graduated with honors. Sam continues to be my steadfast immortal assistant, and I am as young as I ever was or will ever be. The rewards and accolades continue.

Dorota deserved another chance to mother Violet, and as twin souls it was only right that Violet and Sam be born twins. But they couldn't marry if they had the same mother, and so I conspired a scheme to make the impossible happen.

Lilith and Dorota were about to reincarnate, so pairing them as best friends again healed their negative karma and provided a channel ideally suited, not only to compensate for Violet's and Sam's missed appointment with consummated love, but to offset James's and Daisy's loss of the forty years they were meant to be together.

One perfect arrangement atoned for a multitude of mistakes.

Seven souls were vindicated, set free to live again: Dorota, Lilith and Alba-first blood, Sam and Violet, and James and Daisy, were redeemed in seamless alignment with universal law.

Epona was restored to power, the Green Gods worked their healing magic on the land, and Sam fulfilled his mission to mentor Violet until she inherited, as will soon become apparent, the great secret destiny for which she'd been born.

Life and death move on, and love prevails. Lila made up for lost time and continues to play in mysterious ways.

75

HORSEPLAY
Violet's Last Testament

"O' ye'll tak' the high road,
And I'll tak' the low road,
And I'll be in Scotland a'fore ye."

- VIOLET -

The magnificence of Horse-Kind was spiritually aligned in deference to Lila's philosophy that the world was created to experience the forces of life as a divine game, so much so, that its natural exuberance for unbridled freedom inspired the playful state of 'horsing around' known as HORSEPLAY.

A water horse frequents the land at night to feel the wind, and the earth beneath their hooves, to delight once more in the scent of grasses and trees, and occasionally brave the daylight to experience the glorious warmth of sunshine on its back.

The genus Equus Caballus despite being captured, broken, saddled, and resigned to the whip, enslaved as ill-used WORKHORSES including but not limited to: the indignities of being harnessed to the plow and industrial treadmills, forced to brave the horrors of the cavalry charge and the wholesale carnage as canon fodder on the battlefields of endless war, to bear the tortures down the mines as pit ponies, exploited for man's greedy pleasures gambling on the racecourses for entertainment and profit under the romantic guise as the Sport of Kings, and not forgetting the gentle donkeys and burrows that suffered backbreaking loads as beasts of burden, enduring entire lives under blistering suns.

And as if that wasn't enough, at the end of their exhaustive working life, horse-kind is treated most unkindly, unceremoniously dumped, dispirited, worn out, and ill into heartless knackers' yards to be slaughtered for dog food and glue.

Even so, the horse continues to serve humans by displaying the essential life affirming freedom of uninhibited horseplay.

The blight that immediately preceded the wasting sickness that felled me, destroyed the land. But it was more than the ensuing imbalance of seasons that exiled Epona to the back of beyond, destined to waste away for eternity. I know now, until her determined vow to save her sacrificed clanswomen from the underworld was realized, she intended to endure a half-life at the bottom of the sea. I was the one she summoned to save them, her powers, and ultimately myself.

The warring savagery of the Vikings ushered in the chaotic death knell of masculine energy that desecrated the shrines of the goddess. In a single heartbeat, barbaric marauders changed the world by killing the essential spirit of loving compassion that had been the mainstay of the goddess culture.

But earlier still, in the beginnings of prehistory, goddesses mothered the earth and its inhabitants with dignity and wisdom.

In ancient Egypt the royal lines of accession ascended through a divine matriarchal hierarchy, presided over by the goddess Isis, the great mother. The cat goddess Bast (motherhood and nurturing) and Sekhmet the lioness (healer and destroyer of cruelty) were worshipped as the ultimate expressions of natural divine power.

Epona's hill carving grew pale in the shadow of Thor's thunderous appetite for murder and Zeus's deadly lighting bolts of power-hungry lust to subjugate the daughters of man.

And later still, the indignities Epona still endures being labelled a monster, hounded for photographs to perpetuate an industry of tourism that disrespected and despoiled the land, and polluted the water.

Epona is still relentlessly trophy-hunted for sport by brutes who will, whenever they can, kill the last of a species to extinction to reclaim the reptilian warrior nature that never entirely leaves them.

Once released from the hellish afterlife of inflicted hate crimes, my reincarnated ancestors continue to serve the goddess. Epona, protected by the extraordinary powers of her wisewomen clan, has waited a thousand years to mother a new generation of her ancient bloodline.

Let the games continue.

There are compelling enchantments and mysteries in Scotland which is why I never left for long.

My scariest times were there. My happiest times were there. My true love, Sam, lived there, and once, not long ago, we died there. My fairy godmother visits frequently.

Epona and I live there, still.

I was a stubborn child. Evie called me feisty. And so, true to form, I completed my education the hard way.

I once felt the suffering doled out to humankind to be a poor substitute for compassion – the *breadcrumbs* of love.

But I was wrong. The greatest acts of compassion dish out the *challenges* of love. And in terms of compassion, the act of *doling* has nothing to recommend it. *Dishing*, however, is the art of serving with style.

I eventually forgave my hastiness to judge the divine consciousness that caused the world into being. By doubting the motives of supreme intelligence, I foolishly 'threw the baby out with the bathwater' which was reckless because infants and water loomed large in my life.

Sam never had to forgive me nor I him. We were one mind with a thousand hearts specifically chosen to course-correct the true north of every human's spiritual journey… especially our own. As twin souls we were the perfect embodiment of cause and effect.

On the other hand, Evie, our ageless mother was the embodiment of forgiveness, the eternal good fairy, and Fairy Godmother to Sam and me.

I realize now that Evie was preparing me for my destiny by her bedtime story of choice, 'Sleeping Beauty'. Although I always felt it somewhat sinister to leave a sensitive child like me with the image of a girl cursed into sleeping a hundred years before saying sweet dreams, a kiss goodnight, and turning off the light.

I tell you this: Your soul chose you, which is to say, you chose yourself. Be grateful for your challenges. When possible, learn everything the hard way.

In the end, finishing school awards human graduates the tribute 'SUMMA CUM LAUDE' – *with highest honors.*

And now Lila takes up my chronicle and you may share with me the wonders of the true essence of eternal love.

THE DEEP END
the book of Epona

– The Celtic goddess
of horses, ponies
and donkeys

76

HORSE LATITUDES

Our love shines clearly against the storm,
Turns darkest night to brightest day,
Turns turbulent waters to perfect calm,
A blazing lamp to light our way.
THE WATER IS WIDE

- EVIE -

Weathering a storm is more than a cliché for emotional ups and downs. Actual weather coupled with the heartless cruelty of men created the water horses that inhabit the waters of the earth.

Doldrums with erratic weather patterns, clashing trade winds near the equator, clear skies, light winds, dry winds, or no wind at all, became the conditions that produced the unique patches of Atlantic dead zones – the infamous Horse Latitudes that turned calm waters into arenas of equine death.

As for mariners, their lack of forethought by carrying too many horses and not enough water led to a nightmare where horses dying of thirst competed with sailors who saved themselves by sacrificing their equestrian cargo to the deep.

If it wasn't for the intervention of a powerful sea god, the highlands would be bereft of soul.

In the spirit of hands-across-the-sea, I tell you this. In every country there be dragons retold as legendary sea monsters and none of them are true.

People who believe they've seen a water horse are usually mistaken. Seals, dead tree branches, and wakes from boats are optical illusions that mimic the real thing. And on the rare authentic sighting, cameras are rendered inoperable. No water horse has ever been captured on film.

An enchanted spirit horse is overly sensitive, elusive by nature, and capable of out cunning the slipperiest fairy. They're too shy to be seen in the daylight and too transparent for humans to sense in the dark, but once befriended by a true believer they're visible and trustworthy to a fault.

Epona spirits herself throughout the length and breadth of the highlands, but Portmatilloch holds a special place in her heart.

To date, Epona has left her graceful mark on Horse Hill for several thousand years since the first ice-age.

Many a moonlit night finds a terrified sleepwalking woman on her knees asking for deliverance from their dreams of supernatural horses… nightmares!

At first, I warned them to keep kept their nightly visitations to themselves, citing visions of the 'Night Mare' carrying off their newborn children. But later, Lady Flora found a way to cancel all memories of magic horses as baby snatchers with a simple infusion made from deadly nightshade and apple peels steeped in saltwater under the moon.

Legends must be seeded with truth to weave a solid cloak of fear. It was common knowledge Violet Seaborn was a curse from the sea. Violet's appearance hinted she was a kidnapped infant, and as such she was tainted with fearful magic returned from the watery depths towed to shore in a basket from a ship that sank in a thousand years of turbulent water.

I let it be known that an equestrian visitation at midnight was preventable by refraining from 'seeking out' otherwise known as 'calling down' untoward requests in prayer by mentioning an incident where a girlchild had been taken from her cradle and whisked away to the watery deep never to be seen again.

But it was the prim convent sisters of Portmatilloch who were the worst offenders, kissing their crucifixes before citing false eye-witness reports of seeing the witch's child, Violet Seaborn, riding the Night Mare, a blue-black horse, galloping over the hills, water streaming from its mane flowing over its back with Violet's unmistakable silver locks cascading over her shoulders looking for all the world like a waterfall.

Saint 'M' delivered her predictions in a theatrical style that I taught her, calculated to unhinge the most determined holdouts against hocus pocus. Her performances struck fear into mothers, grandmothers, and mothers-to-be with old wives' legends of slighted fairies who stilled the breath of sleeping babes, kidnapped their souls, and soured the milk by morning.

When the moon was full, the confessional rustled with paper absolutions and the clinking of pennies exchanging hands. "No good comes from moonbeams on the pillow," Saint 'M' warned in her trance-like state. And soon, infected moon pillows found their way to donation boxes for the poor and local bonfires.

The sin of guilt was glibly slipped into casual conversations for causing equal amounts of awe and dread predicting a day when the sea would deliver another demon child. It kept superstitious mothers and grandmothers averting their eyes and crossing their fingers whenever an innocent carthorse trotted through the streets after dark. Old wives' tales were standard fare in the highlands where genuinely supernatural occurrences mingled freely with horrifying threats of brimstone and hellfire.

The local church followers were primed to expect all manner of lurking demons ready to pounce on even the least stimulating carnal pleasure. Guilty comeuppances were often considered badges of honor, worn proudly in private, but that said, 'just-in-case' was a wise precaution to take in public.

The regular occurrence of hooves thudding in the distance required a common explanation. Thunder came in handy as did the high winds strong enough to make the trees creak. But instead of consolation, the creaking of trees swaying in the moonlight constituted a new threat of angry tree sprites or fairies in a pique over empty trees when folks were lax with offerings.

77

FAIRIES UNMASKED

"I have heard the mermaids singing, each to each.
I do not think that they will sing to me.
I have seen them riding seaward on the waves
Combing the white hair of the waves blown back
When the wind blows the water white and black.
We have lingered in the chambers of the sea.
By sea-girls wreathed with seaweed red and brown
Till human voices wake us, and we drown."

T.S. ELIOT

- EPONA -

Evie taught Violet all manner of guises and that a myth that rings true is due to its fairy ancestry. Truth be told, fairies are good at spinning yarns in hidden code precisely so humans can best assimilate their own higher reality. Suffice to say, only a rare few reach this level.

Great times are afoot. And although it's my instinct to step back from the problems of man, I am the 'animal' nature conceived in myth by the first humans as the ruling force of land and water – the Deva of Devas, ruling the queendoms of Flora & Fauna and the deep blue sea.

Folklore stems from the *'folk-flora'* of plants and the spirit devas who animate them.

Sparks of energetic chlorophyll conceived as fiery truths, or the 'first ones' namely 'the fieries', settled deep in the human mindset as benevolent fairies, renamed the 'fair ones' whose tales encompass the duality of bitterness to counterbalance the honey of white magic.

Anyone who assumes Fairy folk are masters of camouflage are correct, but fairy *creatures* are much trickier. The art of concealment is a badge of honor for me.

That said, unsweetened pixies with teeth maintain a strict order of discipline in the plant kingdom. Many a lost human has been pixie-led into a morass of undergrowth to be lost forever.

Lila, the great gamer, moves on so I may re-establish the love that anchors my heart and soul to the earth. But while destroying and starting over springs to mind it would put me in the same league as the sons of man. Immortality requires the wisdom of gentler stuff.

Humans ongoing flirtation with the supernatural continue to wreak havoc. Overly sensitive women with spontaneous dreams of witches on broomsticks were called 'hag ridden' and were soundly regarded as lost on a slippery slope to hell unless a certain potion was taken that Evie Watts distilled from an herbal recipe passed down to her from Saint 'M'.

Mindful spinnings of Winter daydreams and midsummer tales never cease to quicken equinox memories, installing them deep into the human psyche never to be forgotten.

Contrary to ignorance and malignant gossip, the 'old one' refers to the benevolent immortal protector of water as related to the preservation of landscape: the springs, streams, lakes, lochs, fiords, waterfalls, the rivers of forest glades, and the open sea as much as the hills, valleys and fields present in the legendry greenwoods since time immemorial.

But my myth begins with Poseidon, who fairies tell is, the Master of Water sylphs and kelpies.

"Long ago," as Evie always began the tale, *"ships carrying silks and spices following ancient routes passed down in memory, often floundered in areas of low pressure called doldrums."*

"Albeit," Evie used to add, *"more a place of lassitude in my opinion where laziness and apathy eclipsed the tricky art of sailing."* She'd nod slyly and give Violet a wink. *"Twas where your ship was headed, Petal, or so they say."*

"And how do you know that?" Violet always asked.

Why, your mother told me, Evie always replied, shaking her head as if Violet was a numpty.

The story unfolded of regular transports of wild horses from distant countries where horses were numerous and therefore relatively worthless compared to exotic spices, were thrown overboard to lighten a ship's cargo to make swifter progress on listless sails.

On a particular day, when no doubt Poseidon was passing, a herd of horses was sacrificed to the sea for the sake of pepper and silkworms, a truly unconscionable decision that mightily enraged the god.

Poseidon sunk the ship and rescued the horses, thinking them to be a stolen herd of his Hippokampoi specially created with fishy scales and tails, to win the heart of the goddess Demeter, his intended paramour.

But noticing the horses' long wispy tails, Poseidon realized his mistake and taking pity on the horses of the land, awarded them immortality, and subsequently sent them to the far corners of his watery realm to reclaim the native land they'd lost to the heartless greed of humans.

And so it was that the English word 'mare' a female horse, grew from the Latin word 'mer', the sea, and the areas of the sea where doldrums prevailed became immortalized as the Horse Latitudes for an inconceivable act of cruelty. I know this because I was there.

As the 'old one' I had reigned in Scotland since time immemorial until my benign legend grew into a grotesque fantasy as men's pea-brained imaginings are wont to do. In no time at all, sightings of me were reported as the demonic presence of a fierce male monster – an enemy for Godfearing men to subdue and send back to hell with a crucifix.

It was the beginning of the end for my noble image. A massive fraud perpetrated crimes against a shy enchanted sylph of the sea that not only forgave the heartless cruelty of the men who tried to kill her, but was a gentle creature born to never harm a soul.

Money was to be made from fake sightings ramped up for a thriving tourist trade. And so, by playing Lila's game of financial gain, unconscious men shamelessly exploited a benevolent nature goddess. Hoaxes lured the paparazzi in search of a story at any price. The Loch Ness Monster sold newspapers.

The Loch Ness industry sold dreams and toys, but Loch Ness lies drove me into hiding.

Lady Flora decreed her followers would serve me – the soul of Scotland, by celebrating my compassion and honoring my need for undisturbed solitude in a tranquil sanctuary.

78

HORSEPOWER

We two have run about the hills,
and picked the daisies fine;
But we've wandered many a weary foot,
since auld lang syne.
ROBERT BURNS

- EPONA -

Karma, the universe's ego, acts in accord with delicate balances of past present and future for the highest good. These operate under the timeless nature of the universe. Oddly it works because Karma makes up its rules as it goes along.

It can be brushed under carpets, drowned, buried up to its neck in sand or otherwise delayed but never for long.

Without a doubt, love requires equal skills of hanging back and diving in. The truth is that truth alone never sets a human free. Extenuating circumstances of lies and deception must ever play a part if a question requires resolving. In fact, psychic cunning is the basis for a harmonic existence. As is mathematics.

Alchemy chuffs along in the shadows as Grandfather Science, fit to burst from its pride of place as head of the family.

It remains for me to declare that although I occasionally swim in Loch Ness, I do not lurk there to frighten the local fishermen, who incidentally, conjure my shape and image from their nightmares; nor to lure dollars from the pockets of gullible tourists who crave monsters and terror for their entertainments.

For years, the unwritten words of Violet's chronicle hovered over her like a flock of hungry gulls. She couldn't be told the full story of her beginnings and endings because the fullness of some stories can never be known until they're said aloud for the first time, so, her childhood purposely remained a mystery. Until now.

Violet died too soon. But all was not lost. She had several goddesses, including me, who believed in her as well as a birthright of natural earth magic. She eventually gained humility not from overcoming her strange beginnings but by celebrating them.

Humans are only able to chronicle what they remember after being persuaded to forget a great deal. After coming of age, and to be fully initiated into the Clan of the Horse, Violet had to be purged of ego. Evie tried not to spoil her, but Violet was born of enchanted stock. Entitled, self indulgent, haughty when roused, and proud as a peacock. I cherish her for all these things.

Evie kept her on the path of unconditional love in all its complex simplicity while giving her the freedom to explore the power she was born to serve.

Evie was a born storyteller; Violet and Sam were keen listeners, but young Violet created stories that blew ships out of the water.

There was a time, so the nursery rhyme goes, according to Evie, that a girl with strange eyes went to sea in a beautiful pea green ship. She was spirited away to a land where an owl and a pussycat were married by a turkey who lived on a hill. Violet took it to mean Horse Hill. There was no such thing as a plain old hill in her mindset.

But Evie made it perfectly clear that when one challenges Gaia and her league of Green Gods or Nyx's daughters of fate, there were consequences.

Evie told me Violet spent hours musing to any cat that would listen or sleep through her blather: *Once upon a time, I was in a wee boat woven from straw and met a friend who swam like a fish and married cats and birds as well as me and Sam and if you want to attend my wedding, you will have to mind your claws and not play with the balloons that Evie will float everywhere. Because the noise of even one burst balloon will frighten you into the middle of next week.*

Lady Flora instructed her followers to perform their service to me in secret undercover of darkness. A sacred promise had to remain unbroken so an ancient Scottish secret could be kept.

It was the duty of my clanswomen to refute sightings of me with a wee drop of Lady Flora's *holy water* easily slipped into a cup of tea or a pint or an accidental spritz that substituted a vision of a seal or a deer in place of me.

Evie called me the embodiment of incarnate glory and the possessor of unfathomable wisdom. She was always one to spin words into poetry. But this came from her life as a Greek philosopher poet when she was still human.

Evie put it about that anyone cursed with meeting a fairy horse would succumb to insanity.

As such, warnings were posted with further precautionary measures of protection before and after a bad equestrian dream by bathing themselves in seawater under a full moon.

Elaborate instructions made a visitation holier than holy. But holy came at a price in Portmatilloch.

After Sister Mary Lee became the oracle of the Highlands, the road to Portmatilloch was widened and paved. Small booths along its length sold souvenirs. People crossed themselves whenever approaching Saint 'M's shrine on the north wall of the church. My own hill shrine was invisible in those days. Lady Flora would brook no interference with my memory.

St. 'M's anchorage was thoroughly doused with the church's

useless holy water and abandoned without its door, open to the weather.

Before her later claim to fame, and when it pleased her to be left alone, Evie's ongoing pretense of simple-mindedness meant she was eventually overlooked as a person who might, if pressed, know a few juicy tidbits to take away as gossip over special tea and perchance, cakes baked with a generous sprinkle of holy-terror water in the batter.

The ability to see the future had its benefits as well as drawbacks. Violet's arrival by sea was foretold. Evie expected her for nine months as if she were with child.

My chosen one had been a circle on a calendar for several of those months. St. 'M' anticipated, more than predicted, a plague year was due. But Evie knew when people would die which meant Violet had to be initiated into the clan before her training was finished.

It was deliberately overstated that sightings of me turned sensible beholders into possessed lunatics.

But then, those were the uncomfortable years when the ignorant often painted madwomen and wisewomen with the same brush.

79

THE NIGHT MARE BEGINS

Should auld acquaintance be forgot,
and never brought to mind?
Should auld acquaintance be forgot,
and auld lang syne?
ROBERT BURNS

- EPONA -

The sky was orange without a hint of wind on my last day on board ship.

The water trough was bone dry. I was dying of thirst, so I kicked out at the sides of my stall in protest. I'd been restless the whole night, and now my ears were pricked back sensing danger.

I saw Jack, the lad who fed and watered me, approaching emptyhanded but for a coil of rope over his shoulder.

That's when the ship suddenly bucked and tilted, nearly capsizing.

Jack slipped sideways on the wet deck and had to make the rest of his way to me hand-over-hand holding onto whatever he could.

He untied me and led me to the deck where a skittish group of horses skated towards the downed gangplank that disappeared beneath the water.

The ship had listed to such a steep angle that the surface of the ocean reached high enough to slop over the deck.

Jack's eyes were red from crying. He rested his forehead on mine and scratched my ears. Finally, he pulled away and looked into my eyes. "I'm so sorry," he said. "Forgive me." He was sobbing as he slapped my rump and eased me forward.

I didn't have to leap. I walked down the gangplank as if disembarking onto a dry dock and slipped into the ocean without a ripple. At first, the water was pleasantly refreshing under a scorching sun, but I soon swam into a frenzy of terrified horses.

A force sucked me under, and I nearly collided with a chariot racing across the ocean floor pulled by horses with tails like a fish. Its driver carried a pitchfork, but I saw the man wore a crown and his trident was a scepter. He was a king.

A bolt of lightning shot from his trident and finished off the ship. I spared a moment to mourn Jack but was too excited breathing underwater. The other horses had gathered into a herd, prancing happily kicking up the sand like yearlings on a spring day.

Poseidon treated us like his long-lost children and granted each of us a territory to rule of our own. From that day to this, I have reigned as The Soul of the Scottish Highlands' lochs and rivers and its surrounding seas.

LONG LIVE AQUA EQUOS! LONG LIVE THE WATER HORSES!

80

CONSUMMATUM EST
She is finished

For auld lang syne, my jo,
for auld lang syne,
we'll tak' a cup o' kindness yet,
for auld lang syne.
ROBERT BURNS

- LILA -

Violet feels strangely lightheaded when she stares across the water. "I'm not really here anymore," she says to Sam. "I'm disappearing. I want to sleep all the time. What's happening to me? Please. No more secrets."

Sam is wise. He takes both her hands in his, kneels and chooses his words carefully. "Majesty, that strange day when we visited the parallel universe, Evie revealed to me that you and I were charged with a secret mission more sacred than we could have imagined.

This is our lifetime to transcend humanity, sweeting. As Evie's newly appointed apprentice, it was prearranged that I would assist your training by participating from a distance throughout your vital testing period.

The lightness you feel is immortality," he says. "Your soul is ready. Your training is *finished*. It's time to be the goddess you were meant to be. You were chosen a thousand years ago, and now Lady Flora has summoned you."

Violet gazes wistfully at a patch of sunlight on the water. Suddenly she grabs Sam's arm. "Sam, you will come with me, won't you?"

"Haven't I always promised to never leave you," he replied. "This was always our destiny. It's time to come into your true power. You will see me again very soon."

Violet's expression is puzzled. "I don't know what to do. I don't know who I am. I feel faint."

"Just breathe," he said. "You were born for this."

"How can I be free after what I did to Daisy?"

"My darling Violet. You're free *because* of what you did."

Sam kisses the tip of her nose like the old days when she was out of sorts. "You are just beginning. I'm so proud of you.

And by the way, Epona is pregnant."

Sam Watts the elder, Master of the Horse, stands alone on Portmatilloch Beach at sunrise, looking out to sea. He flexes his bare toes in the water, digs them into the sand, and salutes the sun as Evie taught him a hundred years ago when he was but a lad of nineteen – to call the water horse by name and feed her an apple or two. It was still his happy task to help Evie remove barnacles from Epona's silver hooves and comb the seaweed from her mane with his fingers.

For a while now, Epona has allowed his three-year-old son, Sampan, to ride her as she trots gently over the sand. But today is different. Sam is alone. He's brought blankets, a soft grooming brush, and a basket of sweet baby carrots from his wife's garden.

A circular patch in the glassy water turns gold heralding Epona's approach. When Sam feels the warmth of the sun on his face, he calls out "Do you have her, My Lady?" Epona's answer fills his heart. "I have her, Sam. You have done well. I thought she'd never come."

Epona's blue-black head breaks the surface. A moment later she emerges from the sea with her newborn foal – a daughter.

A bonny white horse with a silver mane and violet eyes.

AQUA EQUA PRINCEPS
water horse princess

My soul is gentle, my soul is fine
The sweetest flower when first t'was new.
My soul turns gold and waxes bold
and never wanes, forever true.

VERONICA KNOX

a tribute to

The **WHITE HORSE** of **UFFINGTON**

Violet Seaborn's story
is set in the highlands of Scotland,
and so, I combined the mythical and historical
of two profoundly inspiring horse cultures
into one that venerates the legendary spirit of
the water horse that inhabits the lochs of Scotland,
and the mysterious culture that created the ancient
White Horse on a hilltop near Uffington, England.
This historical site is maintained by English Heritage.

I am indebted to Daniel Eidsmoe for this stunning
aerial photograph of the Uffington Horse.

The prehistoric tribal glyph cut into the English countryside
over 3,000 years ago is a manmade (and no doubt women-made)
beacon that continues to honor the spirit of ancestors who
revered the horse enough to mark out and carve a 360-foot sky map.

I am envious of those living near the White Horse.
Thanks must go to the local inhabitants of Uffington
who preserve their cultural inheritance by
scouring the chalk horse in a celebratory festival,
I hope to join one day

ACKNOWLEDGEMENTS

I have incorporated the wisdom teachings I favor best of: *Paramahansa Yoganada, Alan Watts, Eckhart Tolle, Michael Singer, Rupert Sheldrake, and the classic stoics: Zeno of Citium, Marcus Aurelius, and Seneca.*

I have happily attended several master classes of *Donald Maass* at The Surrey International Writers Conference and continue to receive his brilliant advice through the 'Writer Unboxed' website where he is a regular contributor.

I am fortunate to live in a supportive community of friends in The Sooke Writers Collective of Vancouver Island, and especially the critical feedback from The Sooke Long Prose Group: *Doni Eve, David Reichheld, Dee Lambert, Terry Groves, Linda M Green Abraham, Anne O'Neil, and Tony Blenman.*

My dear friend, *Richard Ashton*, has been a selfless sounding board. And it's not every day an author can claim *Lana Turner* as both friend and beta reader.

And as always, I'm grateful to my children *Sarah & David.*

Thank you, *Daniel Eidsmoe* for your spectacular aerial shot of the Uffington Horse.

At the end of the day, it takes a dedicated creative technician to bring a manuscript home. Thank you, *Charity Chimni.*

VIOLET SEABORN'S CHRONICLE was inspired by:
The White Horse of Uffington, England, The Findhorn Community of Scotland, James Taylor's haunting rendition of 'The Water is Wide', The UK television show 'Ancient Lives' hosted by John Romer, and my art teacher, Mr. P.V. Moon.

OTHER BOOKS by V KNOX

The Fine Art of Haunting – Ghosts in the Gallery series…
Paranormal Romance… & Middle-grade Time-Travel Adventures

'LISABETTA'– *a fanciful biographical trilogy of Leonardo da Vinci's historical half-sister, Lisabetta.* To reclaim her true identity, the embittered spirit of the 'Mona Lisa' trapped in her portrait for 500 years must join forces with an autistic boy and his troubled mother. A picture isn't 'worth a thousand words'… it hides a thousand secrets.

THE 'MONA LISA' MAY BE PRICELESS… NOW SHE MUST BECOME A WOMAN WORTH SAVING

'DISAPP'EARRING TWICE' – Aurelia Marcus, an aging eccentric shadowed by the spirit of a girl from a famous painting, rents a castle by the sea to write a novel before she forgets the story she feels compelled to write based on her recurring dreams of a past life.

AURELIA MARCUS DISAPPEARED LONG BEFORE SHE RAN AWAY FROM HOME

'ADORATION – Loving Botticelli' – The romance between a retired art history professor and a five-hundred-year-old portrait leads from obsession to seduction.

LIFE CAN BE AN IMMORTAL COMEDY

'WOO WOO – the posthumous love story of Miss Emily Carr' – the artist Emily Carr, an eccentric spinster, comes to her senses sixty-seven years after her death and calls down the energy of her animal totem, Woo the monkey, to rekindle the love of a rejected suitor – *a fanciful homage to Emily Carr inspired by her memoirs.* MONKEY BUSINESS UNPLUGGED

'THE UNTHINKABLE SHOES' – *a story of reincarnation and extraordinary sacrifice inspired by a museum exhibit of child's shoes from the Titanic.* When death separates two children on the Titanic who were destined to marry, the barefoot ghost of the boy chooses to remain earthbound as the surviving girl's invisible childhood companion. Finding a pair of lost shoes is their one chance to stay together. A 'LOST BOY' FROM TITANIC LOSES HIS SHOES BETWEEN HEAVEN AND THE DEEP BLUE SEA

'THE INDIGO PEARL' – *a story of YOUNG LOVE & OLD SOULS - book one of two:* When the consciousness of Delphi Sharpe, an autistic woman with the extrasensory ability to converse with paintings and birds, is transplanted into the circuits of an android programmed to retrieve famous works of art lost in the distant past, intelligence is no longer artificial. Delphi must fight her way back to love, one pearl at a time.

AI = AUTISTIC INTELLIGENCE – 'STATE OF THE ART' TIME TRAVEL JUST BECAME TRANSCENDENTAL

'PEARL BY PEARL' – *a story of YOUNG LOVE & OLD SOULS - book two of two:* Two rivalling 'art whisperers' become single-mindedly obsessed to consummate the love of Delphi's life – a teenage boy in a 500-year-old portrait. But while the spirit of Delphi wants to rest in peace with her beloved, her counterpart intends to exact revenge on the art syndicate that exploited them. SOMETIMES IT TAKES TWO LIVES TO MAKE ONE WOMAN

'I WAS THERE' – the art of time travel in a 15th century poetry dreamscape

THE BEDE SERIES: – GHOSTS WHO INVITE READERS TO COME ALIVE

'TWINTER – the first portal' – a magical realism time-slip adventure *book one of four in 'The Bede Series':* Bede Hall, an abandoned and disgruntled stately home, is desperate. It must rally its dispersed family before it's sold to developers. Its new residents, a pair of thirteen-year-old twins, seek out a girl lost in time whose apparition has haunted the estate for generations, but meeting her opens a time portal that reveals a terrible secret. In order to rescue her and protect the future, the teens form a team of otherworldly allies called the 'Twinters'. GHOSTS ARE NOTHING COMPARED TO THE CHALLENGES HAUNTING A CURMUDGEONLY BUILDING WITH A DESIRE FOR ETERNAL LIFE… BEDE HALL IS ALIVE, BUT ALL IS NOT WELL!

'TIME FALLS LIKE SNOW' – a magical realism time-slip adventure *book two of four in 'The Bede Series':* The secrets of Bede Hall's timely past continue with the sixteen-year-old twins working in league with a team of ghosts and 'twice-borns' who have been monitoring Bede's secrets for hundreds of years. It falls to the rules of twindom, the Great Sphinx of Egypt, and a colony of mystical cats to save the future. THE 'TWINTERS' ARE RUNNING OUT OF TIME IN A LANDSCAPE WHERE HISTORY IS POSITIVELY ANCESTRAL

'TOMORROW AGAIN' – a magical realism time-slip adventure *book three of four in 'The Bede Series':* To save Bede Hall, a disgruntled stately home nestled against Hadrian's Wall in England, a pair of telepathic twins, at odds over logic and metaphysics, must fulfill an ancient prophecy, and rescue its resident ghost. But sending them to ancient Egypt, Pangea, and Mars turns out to be the shortest route to saving the planet from a nuclear winter. MAN SAYS TIME PASSES; THE PYRAMIDS SAY MAN PASSES.

'SNOW BEHIND THE DOOR' – *book four of four in 'The Bede Series'* documents the *time-slipped* memories of the abandoned ghost-child of Bede Hall, named Snow, in search of the family she glimpses in dreams and the dusty mirrors of a stately home that has sheltered earth's time portals, guarded by an ancient line of royal Egyptian cats for thousands of years.

THE MEMOIR OF A CHILD GHOST WITH AMNESIA

*Finalist in the Chanticleer Gertrude Warner award for the best middle-grade book of 2023

'DOGGED STAR' – A star-crossed woman haunted by a lucid dream is aided by the ghost of a dog whose unwavering loyalty to her master, Leonardo da Vinci, transcends death and hounds her to life.

AN INVISIBLE 'SEEING-EYE-DOG' GUIDES A WOMAN GOING BLIND TO SEE THE TRUTH IN HER STARS

AUTHOR'S BIO

V Knox writes 'metaphysical' novels for imaginative bookworms who savor exploring the realms of creative history and Paranormal Romance. Her invented genres of choice are 'Cozy Outer Limits', 'The Fine Art of Haunting' (her 'Ghosts in the Gallery' series), and Time-slip Adventures for Middle-grade readers of all ages.

Veronica obtained a Fine Arts degree from the University of Alberta where she developed an imaginative take on art history that led to an untapped source for stories. She discovered that inanimate objects were rarely bereft of life and that paintings have juicy secrets to tell.

She explores the creative inner worlds of autistic savants and master artists, and in one case, the unknown child in the Titanic cemetery. She explores the discrepancies between reality and lucid dreams, fishes the depths of the subconscious, the afterlife, reincarnation, the anomalies of parallel lives and dimensions, the classic psyche of 'the ghostly lover', reconciles historical facts with surreal fiction, and has written seventeen 'outer limits' novels.

Veronica remains intent on listening to the ethereal echoes from objects in museums and the voices of the Italian Renaissance – the artists as well as their anonymous subjects and companions. She grants them second chances to air their grievances, tell their stories, and together they set the dreariest history books on fire.

AMAZON
https://www.amazon.com/V-Knox/e/B0094K0Q7Y
WEBSITE & CURIOUS ART HISTORY BLOG
https://veronicaknox.com

If you enjoyed
'Violet Seaborn's Unfinished Soul'
please help me spread the word.
Thank you

Veronica Knox – April 15, 2024

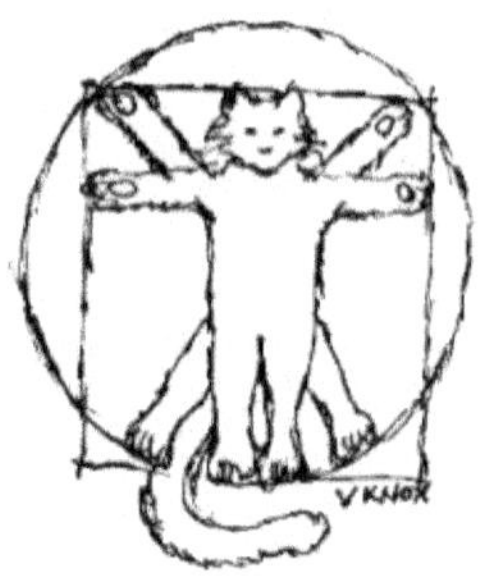

SILENT K PUBLISHING — Vancouver Island, Canada
https://veronicaknox.com